SCOT

GORDON JARVIE began his career as an English teacher, later working as a textbook publisher and writer. His recent books include the *Bloomsbury Grammar Guide* (2nd edn, 2007) and *100 Favourite Scottish Poems to Read Out Loud* (2007); and with his wife he has written several *Scottie Books* for children. His recent poetry appears in *Poems Mainly from the East Neuk, Fife* (2007) and *Another Working Monday* (2005). He lives near St Andrews, in the East Neuk of Fife.

Scottish Folk
and Fairy Tales
From Burns to Buchan

Selected and edited by
GORDON JARVIE

PENGUIN BOOKS

PENGUIN CLASSICS

Published by the Penguin Group
Penguin Books Ltd, 80 Strand, London WC2R ORL, England
Penguin Group (USA) Inc., 375 Hudson Street, New York, New York 10014, USA
Penguin Group (Canada), 90 Eglinton Avenue East, Suite 700, Toronto, Ontario, Canada M4P 2Y3
(a division of Pearson Penguin Canada Inc.)
Penguin Ireland, 25 St Stephen's Green, Dublin 2, Ireland
(a division of Penguin Books Ltd)
Penguin Group (Australia), 250 Camberwell Road, Camberwell, Victoria 3124, Australia
(a division of Pearson Australia Group Pty Ltd)
Penguin Books India Pvt Ltd, 11 Community Centre, Panchsheel Park, New Delhi – 110 017, India
Penguin Group (NZ), 67 Apollo Drive, Rosedale, North Shore 0632, New Zealand
(a division of Pearson New Zealand Ltd)
Penguin Books (South Africa) (Pty) Ltd, 24 Sturdee Avenue, Rosebank, Johannesburg 2196, South Africa

Penguin Books Ltd, Registered Offices: 80 Strand, London WC2R ORL, England

www.penguin.com

First published as *Scottish Folk and Fairy Tales* in Puffin Classics 1992
This revised and expanded edition published in Penguin Classics 2008

012

Selection and editorial material copyright © Gordon Jarvie, 1992, 2008
All rights reserved

The moral right of the editor has been asserted

The Acknowledgements on p. ix constitute an extension of this copyright page.

Set in 10.25/12.25pt PostScript Adobe Sabon
Typeset by Rowland Phototypesetting Ltd, Bury St Edmunds, Suffolk

Printed and bound in Great Britain by Clays Ltd, Elcograf S.p.A.

Except in the United States of America, this book is sold subject
to the condition that it shall not, by way of trade or otherwise, be lent,
re-sold, hired out, or otherwise circulated without the publisher's
prior consent in any form of binding or cover other than that in
which it is published and without a similar condition including this
condition being imposed on the subsequent purchaser

ISBN: 978-0-141-44226-6

www.greenpenguin.co.uk

MIX
Paper from
responsible sources
FSC® C018179

Penguin Books is committed to a sustainable
future for our business, our readers and our planet.
This book is made from Forest Stewardship
Council™ certified paper.

Contents

Part Two: Tall Tales, Giants, Monsters

Part Three: Wanchancy Apparitions, Second Sight, Witches

Part Four: A Classic Victorian Fairy Tale

Part Five: Letting Go?

Part Six: Envoy

Acknowledgements

Grateful acknowledgement is made to the following sources for permission to reproduce copyright material: A. P. Watt Ltd for the story 'The Magic Walking-Stick', by John Buchan; the late John Lorne Campbell of Canna for 'Why Everyone Should Be Able To Tell a Story', from his *Stories from South Uist* (1961); two poems, 'The Kelpie' and 'The Rowan', by Violet Jacob, from *Voices from Their Ain Countrie: The Poems of Marion Angus and Violet Jacob* (2006, ed. K. Gordon), reprinted by permission of Malcolm Hutton; David Higham Associates for the story 'The Lonely Giant', by Alasdair MacLean, from *The Noel Streatfeild Summer Holiday Book* (1973); Birlinn Ltd for the story 'Thomas the Rhymer, Son of the Dead Woman', by Margaret Fay Shaw, from her *Folksongs and Folklore of South Uist* (1955); the School of Scottish Studies at the University of Edinburgh for the story 'The Man in the Boat', by Betsy Whyte, reprinted by permission. Every effort has been made to trace copyright holders of works published in this book. If any material has been included without appropriate acknowledgement, the publishers will be glad to make amendment in future editions.

I should like to thank Judy Moir for practical help in kick-starting the revision of this project; Jane Robertson for a meticulous editorial eye; and staff at the National Library of Scotland for providing all the professional support with sources that one could possibly expect, help that was as resolute and apposite for the 2008 edition as for the 1992 original.

Introduction

Do you believe in fairies? . . . If you believe, clap your hands.

J. M. Barrie, *Peter Pan*

In Scotland as elsewhere, fairy tales are part of a rich and wide-ranging folk tapestry. And as the countryman Barnaby said long ago (in James Hogg's story 'The Wool-Gatherer'), 'Ye had need to tak care how ye dispute the existence of fairies, brownies and apparitions! Ye may as well dispute the Gospel of St Matthew.' The Scottish folk tapestry covers a multitude: fairy lore sits alongside stories of the 'Otherworld' and the Celtic *sidhe*, of seers and second sight, of witchcraft, black and white, of cures, omens and taboos, of clan lore, myths and legends from Scottish history. Even geography provides Scots with a wide scatter of fairy names such as the Fairy Bridge in Skye (by Dunvegan, with its Fairy Flag), Schiehallion ('the fairy hill of the Caledonians'), Ben Hee and Ben Tee ('fairy hill', from *Beinn Shìth* and *Beinn an t-Sithein*), Mullach Sithidh ('fairy summit') and Stob an Fhir-bhogha (peak of the Fir-Bolgs, one of the mythical races of Irish fairies).

This anthology tries to reflect some of this background, and includes stories – and poems – based on the work of those indefatigable collectors of folk tales: Sir Walter Scott, James Hogg and Robert Chambers in Edinburgh and the Borders, Robert Burns in the west, and J. F. Campbell in the Gaelic-speaking part of the West Highlands and the Hebrides. Also included are stories by some great Victorian and twentieth-century writers, such as Robert Louis Stevenson, Andrew Lang and Sir Arthur Conan Doyle.

We have to remember that as late as the seventeenth century in Scotland the Brahan Seer (Kenneth MacKenzie) was prophesying the building of the Caledonian Canal and the coming of the railways, and foretelling how the hill of Tomnahurich (also called Tom-na-Sitheichean, or the Fairies' Hill) would end up under lock and key with the spirits of the fairies chained within: in 1859 it was duly laid out as the town cemetery of Inverness. And right up to that period, long after the heyday of the Scottish Enlightenment, instances of ghosts, 'visions' and second sight were widespread in Scotland, often involving deaths, marriages, boats and journeys, battles, drownings and other calamities.

It is also useful to remember that the burning of the last 'witch' in Scotland took place at Dornoch as late as 1722, less than seventy years before Robert Burns wrote his poem about Tam o' Shanter. Epilepsy, miscarriages, suicides and all sorts of misfortunes were widely attributed to witchcraft. The notion that a witch couldn't pass across a running stream was widespread; Tam o' Shanter was familiar with this folklore, which was why he rode pell-mell for the comparative safety of the Brig o' Doon. Once over the river, he knew he'd be safe from the witches . . .

We need to recall, too, examples of cures, omens, auguries and taboos. Violet Jacob's twentieth-century poem 'The Rowan' highlights the still-common view that a rowan tree had certain protective powers in warding off misfortune and evil spirits, while other plants possessed different properties. There was also a widely held belief in the healing powers of certain wells, whether in the matter of overcoming infertility in women, or curing consumption, or overcoming deafness. A spring near Ayr was said to have cured Robert Bruce of his leprosy. There were firm views about the auspiciousness (or otherwise) of undertaking important projects on certain days of the week. Quarter Days were particularly lucky, for example.

All these notions remain a part of the *dualchas* (culture), especially in rural areas, even if less pervasively than in the past. The following anecdote illustrates this. A friend, who had moved to Skye in the 1980s and was in the process of making his cottage habitable, proposed to cut down a rowan tree that threatened to block the light beside the front door. He happened to mention the matter in conversation with the late Sorley Maclean (1911–96), a distinguished poet and one-time headmaster of Plockton High School, a man who had seen active war service in North Africa and Europe. Sorley strongly advised against the removal of the rowan. When my friend professed scepticism on the matter, Sorley (who hadn't visited the house) asked on which side of the house the door was located. My friend thought for a minute, and then replied, 'The north side.' Sorley then shook his head and said, 'Especially do not remove a rowan tree on the *north* side of the house.' The tree still stands, a sain (or form of protection) against ill: a symbol of the culture and wisdom of the North-West Highlands that has not been eroded by modern life.

Part Five of this collection is called 'Letting Go?' and comprises three more recent texts that are not fairy tales in the traditional sense, but which successfully continue to feed off the spirit and atmosphere of such tales. Violet Jacob has already been referred to. Many of her poems, including the two printed in this collection ('The Kelpie' and 'The Rowan'), famously achieve a spooky atmosphere of part-Christian, part-supernatural fear of the unseen that once kept youngsters running scared of the dark shadowlands and the world 'beyond'. Assisted by references to kelpies and rowan trees, the story called 'The Man in the Lochan' achieves a similar frisson. These texts remind us that, living as we all now do – theoretically – in an age of reason and rationality, we remain susceptible to the world 'beyond', and are still engrossed enough to write and read recent stories and poems about it. Many other good writers have continued to mine this seam: Helen Cruickshank, Marion Angus, Betsy Whyte, Robert Rendall, Peter Ratter and Stanley Robertson among them.

Joseph Jacobs once estimated that there were more than 2,000 Scottish folk tales – a substantial corpus. And of course they also had countless local variants, so this anthology barely reveals the tip of a large iceberg. But it tries to convey within a single collection a hint of the literature's variety and vitality.

STORY ATTRIBUTIONS

The stories listed in this book by 'J. F. Campbell', by 'Elizabeth Grierson' or by 'Joseph Jacobs' are not original to those writers. It is in the nature of folk tales and the oral tradition that many versions of a story exist. So, for example, Miss Grierson's version

of 'The Milk-white Doo' is based on that recorded by Robert
Chambers (in his *The Popular Rhymes of Scotland*, 1826, with
numerous reprints). Her 'Assipattle and the Mester Stoorworm'
is probably based on a similar story recorded by W. Traill
Dennison in *Scottish Antiquary*, vol. V (1891). Her source
for 'The Well o' the World's End' is J. F. Campbell's *Popular
Tales of the West Highlands* (1860–62), with other sources
including poems by John Leyden (1771–1811) and James Hogg
(1770–1835), as well as Victorian and Edwardian texts from
The Folklore Journal. The ancestry of James Hogg's poem 'The
Mermaid' may well be related to J. F. Campbell's 'The Sea
Maiden', orally collected by the latter in the course of his
fieldwork.

Similarly, the text that here appears under the name of Margaret Fay Shaw ('Thomas the Rhymer, Son of the Dead Woman')
is, as she tells us, her English translation of a Gaelic tale taken
down by her husband John Lorne Campbell in November 1935,
and published by him in a booklet called *Sia Sgialachdan* (*Six
Stories*) in 1938. His oral source was the story-teller Seonaidh
Campbell, of Glendale in South Uist, who in turn probably had
the story from another oral source. And bearing in mind that it
was a story about Thomas the Rhymer, it might well have gone
back a very long way. Many if not most oral stories have come
down to us in this manner.

Part of the aim of writers like Jacobs or Grierson was to
popularize the writings of earlier collectors like J. F. Campbell.
Sometimes, in the interests of authenticity, the original collectors'
texts tended to be long and turgid and over-repetitive, and in the
print medium this was a factor that limited their popularity: the
defence of the collectors was that they were writing down stories
or poems as told to them or as they heard them. By shortening,
simplifying and occasionally 'anglifying', later editors like Jacobs
and Grierson were able to widen the popularity of the oral folk
literature once it had become available in print. And it has to be
added that, ever since Scott's *Minstrelsy* and probably earlier,
efforts were made to anglicize stories in order to render them
accessible to readers furth of, or beyond, Scotland.

As well as this tradition of oral folk tales in Gaelic and English,

Scotland also had a long-standing anonymous ballad tradition dealing with aspects of the supernatural: 'Tam Lin' and 'Thomas the Rhymer' are among the oldest of these works, dating back to the fourteenth or fifteenth centuries. They are included here in versions collected respectively by Robert Burns (1796) and Sir Walter Scott (1802–3).

Literary, written texts represent the other end of the spectrum or tapestry of Scottish fairy tales, some of them in verse and some in prose. Many readers would identify Robert Burns's memorable poem 'Tam o' Shanter' as the keystone of that bridge into the corpus. Based on but transforming a local Ayrshire folk tale, this poem is one of many original texts, and Scottish literature is fortunate that so many of its great writers have contributed new material to the genre: as well as Burns, original texts by Robert Louis Stevenson, James Hogg, Arthur Conan Doyle, John Buchan, Andrew Lang and others are included here.

In this context it is a real pleasure to reprint Andrew Lang's story 'The Gold of Fairnilee', which has been described – rightly, as it seems to me – as one of the finest of all the Victorian fairy tales. It is interesting to note the entirely realistic historical background to this story – the horrors of a war on your own doorstep – whose action was triggered off by the battle of Flodden in 1513. Watch out in this magic narrative for the ingenious explanation of Tam Hislop's seven-year disappearance on the eve of the battle, not to Fairyland at all (as Hislop told his neighbours) but a simple deserter hiding out at Perth, well away from the perils of front-line Border warfare. Similarly, note how the action in James Hogg's story 'Adam Bell' commences with the disappearance of the main character 'on the very day that Prince Charles Edward Stewart defeated General Hawley on Falkirk Muir' in that other momentous year of 1745. Tales of the supernatural may well flourish best in periods of civil strife, of which Scotland once had its fair share. But I'm sure that if I had lived at the time of Flodden, I too might have been tempted to do a seven-year disappearing trick rather than get dragged into some suicidal war.

Further Reading

BACKGROUND

Bennett, M., *Scottish Customs from the Cradle to the Grave* (Edinburgh: Polygon, 1992).

Frazer, J. G., *The Golden Bough*, 12 vols (London: Macmillan, 1890–1915).

Kirk, R., *The Secret Common-Wealth of Elves, Fauns and Fairies* (1691, reprinted London: David Nutt, 1893).

Mackenzie, A., *The Prophecies of the Brahan Seer* (Stirling: Eneas Mackay, 1899).

Mackillop, J., *Dictionary of Celtic Mythology* (Oxford: Oxford University Press, 1998).

Martin, M., *A Description of the Western Islands of Scotland* (London, 1703, reprinted Stirling: Mackay, 1934).

McNeill, F. M., *The Silver Bough*, 4 vols (Glasgow: MacLellan, 1956–68).

Ross, A., *The Folklore of the Scottish Highlands* (London: Batsford, 1976).

Shaw, M. F., *Folksongs and Folklore of South Uist* (London: Oxford University Press, 1955).

COLLECTIONS

Bruford, A. J. and D. A. MacDonald, *Scottish Traditional Tales* (Edinburgh: Polygon, 1994).

Campbell, J. F., *Popular Tales of the West Highlands*, vols I and II (Edinburgh: R. & R. Clark, 1860); vols III and IV (Edinburgh: R. & R. Clark, 1862).

Campbell, J. L., and A. MacLellan, *Stories from South Uist* (London: Routledge & Kegan Paul, 1961).

Chambers, Robert, *The Popular Rhymes of Scotland* (Edinburgh: Chambers, 1826; 2nd edn, 1870).

Douglas, G., *Scottish Fairy and Folk Tales* (London: W. Scott, 1894).

Grierson, E. W., *The Scottish Fairy Book* (London: Philip Allan, 1906).

Jacobs, J., *Celtic Fairy Tales* (London: David Nutt, 1892).

Jacobs, J., *More Celtic Fairy Tales* (London: David Nutt, 1894).

Montgomerie, W. and N., *The Well at the World's End* (London: Bodley Head, 1956).

Note on the Texts

This book is an expanded version of the 1992 first edition, *Scottish Folk and Fairy Tales* issued first as a Puffin Classic and then from 1997 reprinted as a Penguin Popular Classic. Because the original collection had a young readership in view, it excluded texts in Scots on grounds of readability and difficulty of access. That meant making do with prose retellings of 'Tam Lin' and 'Thomas the Rhymer' and avoiding 'Tam o' Shanter', a poem with good claim to be the greatest and best known of all Scottish folk tales.

This new edition contains twenty-nine texts. It includes all twenty-one of the texts that appeared in the 1992 edition, except that the 1992 retellings of 'Tam Lin' and 'Thomas the Rhymer' are here replaced by their late eighteenth-century Scots verse versions. Additionally, eight other texts in Scots prose and verse have been added in an attempt to provide readers with a wider, more authentic and more comprehensive selection. Thus approximately one third of the texts in this new edition use the Scots language in varying degrees of density. All these Scots texts are provided with glossaries. In the case of the poetry, Scots words are glossed alongside the lines where they occur. In the case of the prose, they are glossed in footnotes at the foot of the relevant page. Words that are merely spelt differently in Old Scots are not glossed (e.g. 'boozing' for 'bousing'). Perhaps the easiest way to make sense of the Scots words here is to read the text aloud. Otherwise, readers requiring further assistance with Scots vocabulary are referred to the *Concise Scots Dictionary* (1985, ed. Mairi Robinson) or to www.dsl.ac.uk/ for online information.

PART ONE

MAGIC LORE

THE MILK-WHITE DOO

Elizabeth Grierson

There was once a man who got his living by working in the fields. He had one little son, called Curly-locks, and one little daughter, called Golden-tresses; but his wife was dead, and, as he had to be out all day, these children were often left alone. So, as he was afraid that some evil might befall them when there was no one to look after them, he, in an ill day, married again.

I say 'in an ill day', for his second wife was a most deceitful woman, who really hated children, although she pretended, before her marriage, to love them. And she was so unkind to them, and made the house so uncomfortable with her bad temper, that her poor husband often sighed to himself, and wished that he had let well alone, and remained a widower.

But it was no use crying over spilt milk; the deed was done, and he had just to try to make the best of it. So things went on for several years, until the children were beginning to run about out of doors and play by themselves.

Then one day the Goodman chanced to catch a hare, and he brought it home and gave it to his wife to cook for the dinner.

Now his wife was a very good cook, and she made the hare into a pot of delicious soup; but she was also very greedy, and while the soup was boiling she tasted it, and tasted it, till at last she discovered that it was almost gone. Then she was in a fine state of mind, for she knew that her husband would soon be coming home for his dinner, and that she would have nothing to set before him.

So what do you think the wicked woman did? She went out to the door, where her little stepson, Curly-locks, was playing in the sun, and told him to come in and get his face washed. And while she was washing his face, she struck him on the head with a hammer and stunned him, and popped him into the pot to make soup for his father's dinner.

By and by the Goodman came in from his work, and the soup was dished up; and he, and his wife, and his little daughter, Golden-tresses, sat down to sup it.

'Where's Curly-locks?' asked the Goodman. 'It's a pity he is not here while the soup is hot.'

'How should I ken where he is?' answered his wife crossly. 'I have other work to do than to run about after a mischievous laddie all the morning.'

The Goodman went on supping his soup in silence for some minutes; then he lifted up a little foot in his spoon.

'This is Curly-locks' foot,' he cried in horror. 'There's been ill work here.'

'Hoots, havers,' answered his wife, laughing, pretending to be very much amused. 'What should Curly-locks' foot be doing in the soup? 'Tis the hare's forefoot, which is very like that of a bairn.'

But presently the Goodman took something else up in his spoon.

'This is Curly-locks' hand,' he said shrilly. 'I ken it by the crook in its little finger.'

'The man's demented,' retorted his wife, 'not to ken the hind foot of a hare when he sees it!'

So the poor father did not say any more, but went away back to his work, sorely perplexed in his mind; while his little daughter, Golden-tresses, who had a shrewd suspicion of what had happened, gathered all the bones from the empty plates, and, carrying them away in her apron, buried them beneath a flat stone, close by a white rose tree that grew by the cottage door.

And, lo and behold! those poor bones, which she buried with such care –

> 'Grew and grew,
> To a milk-white Doo,
> That took its wings,
> And away it flew.'

And at last it lighted on a tuft of grass by a burnside, where two women were washing clothes. It sat there cooing to itself for some time; then it sang this song softly to them:

> 'Pew, pew,
> My mimmie me slew,
> My daddy me chew,
> My sister gathered my banes,
> And put them between two milk-white stanes.
> And I grew and grew
> To a milk-white Doo,
> And I took to my wings and away I flew.'

The women stopped washing and looked at one another in astonishment. It was not every day that they came across a bird that could sing a song like that, and they felt that there was something not canny about it.

'Sing that song again, my bonnie bird,' said one of them at last, 'and we'll give you all these clothes!'

So the bird sang its song over again, and the washerwomen gave it all the clothes, and it tucked them under its right wing, and flew on.

Presently it came to a house where all the windows were open, and it perched on one of the window-sills, and inside it saw a man counting out a great heap of silver.

And, sitting on the window-sill, it sang its song to him:

> 'Pew, pew,
> My mimmie me slew,
> My daddy me chew,
> My sister gathered my banes,
> And put them between two milk-white stanes.
> And I grew and grew
> To a milk-white Doo,
> And I took to my wings and away I flew.'

The man stopped counting his silver, and listened. He felt, like the washerwomen, that there was something not canny about this Doo. When it had finished its song, he said:

'Sing that song again, my bonnie bird, and I'll give you a' this siller in a bag.'

So the Doo sang its song over again, and got the bag of silver, which it tucked under its left wing. Then it flew on.

It had not flown very far, however, before it came to a mill where two millers were grinding corn. And it settled down on a sack of meal and sang its song to them.

> 'Pew, pew,
> My mimmie me slew,
> My daddy me chew,
> My sister gathered my banes,
> And put them between two milk-white stanes.
> And I grew and grew
> To a milk-white Doo,
> And I took to my wings and away I flew.'

The millers stopped their work, and looked at one another, scratching their heads in amazement.

'Sing that song over again, my bonnie bird!' exclaimed both of them together when the Doo had finished, 'and we will give you this millstone.'

So the Doo repeated its song, and got the millstone, which it asked one of the millers to lift on to its back; then it flew out of the mill, and up the valley, leaving the two men staring after it dumb with astonishment.

As you may think, the milk-white Doo had a heavy load to carry, but it went bravely on till it came within sight of its father's cottage, and lighted down at last on the thatched roof.

Then it laid its burdens on the thatch, and, flying down to the courtyard, picked up a number of little chuckie stones. With them in its beak it flew back to the roof, and began to throw them down the chimney.

By this time it was evening, and the Goodman and his wife, and his little daughter, Golden-tresses, were sitting around the table eating their supper. And you may be sure that they were all very much startled when the stones came rattling down the chimney, bringing such a cloud of soot with them that they were almost smothered. They all jumped up from their chairs, and ran outside to see what the matter was.

And Golden-tresses, being the littlest, ran the fastest, and when she came out at the door the milk-white Doo flung the bundle of clothes down at her feet.

And the father came out next, and the milk-white Doo flung the bag of silver down at his feet.

But the wicked stepmother, being somewhat stout, came out last, and the milk-white Doo threw the millstone right down on her head and killed her.

Then it spread its wings and flew away, and has never been seen again; but it had made the Goodman and his daughter rich for life, and it had rid them of the cruel stepmother, so that they lived in peace and plenty for the remainder of their days.

THE WELL O' THE WORLD'S END

Elizabeth Grierson

There was once an old widow woman, who lived in a little cottage with her only daughter, who was such a bonnie lassie that everyone liked to look at her.

One day the old woman took a notion into her head to bake a girdleful of cakes. So she took down her baking-board, and went to the meal-chest and fetched a basinful of meal; but when she went to seek a jug of water to mix the meal with, she found that there was none in the house.

So she called to her daughter, who was in the garden; and when the girl came she held out the empty jug to her, saying, 'Run, like a good lassie, to the Well o' the World's End and bring me a jug of water, for I have long found that water from the Well o' the World's End makes the best cakes.'

So the lassie took the jug and set out on her errand.

Now, as its name shows, it is a long road to that well, and many a weary mile had the poor maid to go ere she reached it.

But she arrived there at last; and what was her disappointment to find it dry.

She was so tired and so vexed that she sat down beside it and began to cry; for she did not know where to get any more water, and she felt that she could not go back to her mother with an empty jug.

While she was crying, a nice yellow puddock, with very bright eyes, came jump-jump-jumping over the stones of the well, and squatted down at her feet, looking up into her face.

puddock, frog.

'And why are ye crying, my bonnie maid?' he asked. 'Is there anything I can do to help you?'

'I am crying because the well is empty,' she answered, 'and I cannot get any water to carry home to my mother.'

'Listen,' said the puddock softly. 'I can get you water in plenty, if you'll promise to be my wife.'

Now the lassie had but one thought in her head, and that was to get the water for her mother's oatcakes, and she never for a moment thought that the puddock was serious, so she promised gladly enough to be his wife, if he would just get her a jug of water.

No sooner had the words passed her lips than the beastie jumped down the mouth of the well, and in another moment it was full to the brim with water.

The lassie filled her jug and carried it home, without troubling any more about the matter. But late that night, just as her mother and she were going to bed, something came with a faint 'thud, thud' against the cottage door, and then they heard a tiny little wee voice singing:

> 'Oh, open the door, my hinnie, my heart,
> Oh, open the door, my ain true love;
> Remember the promise that you and I made
> Down i' the meadow, where we two met.'

'Wheesht,' said the old woman, raising her head. 'What noise is that at the door?'

'Oh,' said her daughter, who was feeling rather frightened, 'it's only a yellow puddock.'

'Poor bit beastie,' said the kind-hearted old mother. 'Open the door and let him in. It's cold work sitting on the doorstep.'

So the lassie, very unwillingly, opened the door, and the puddock came jump-jump-jumping across the kitchen, and sat down at the fireside.

And while he sat there he began to sing this song:

> 'Oh, gie me my supper, my hinnie, my heart,
> Oh, gie me my supper, my ain true love;

> *Remember the promise that you and I made*
> *Down i' the meadow, where we two met.'*

'Gie the poor beast his supper,' said the old woman. 'He's an uncommon puddock that can sing like that.'

'Tut,' replied her daughter crossly, for she was growing more and more frightened as she saw the creature's bright black eyes fixed on her face. 'I'm not going to be so silly as to feed a wet, sticky puddock.'

'Don't be ill-natured and cruel,' said her mother. 'Who knows how far the little beastie has travelled? And I warrant that it would like a saucerful of milk.'

Now, the lassie could have told her that the puddock had travelled from the Well o' the World's End; but she held her tongue, and went into the pantry, and brought back a saucerful of milk, which she set down before the strange little visitor.

> *'Now chap off my head, my hinnie, my heart,*
> *Now chap off my head, my ain true love,*
> *Remember the promise that you and I made*
> *Down i' the meadow, where we two met.'*

'Hout, havers, pay no heed, the creature's daft,' exclaimed the old woman, running forward to stop her daughter, who was raising the axe to chop off the puddock's head. But she was too late; down came the axe, off went the head; and, lo and behold! on the spot where the little creature had sat, stood the handsomest young Prince that had ever been seen.

He wore such a noble air, and was so richly dressed, that the astonished girl and her mother would have fallen on their knees before him had he not prevented them by a movement of his hand.

'It is I that should kneel to you, Sweetheart,' he said, turning to the blushing girl, 'for you have delivered me from a fearful spell, which was cast over me in my infancy by a wicked fairy, who at the same time slew my father. For long years I have lived in that well, the Well o' the World's End, waiting for a maiden to appear, who should take pity on me, even in my loathsome disguise, and promise to be my wife – a maiden who would also have the kindness to let me into her house, and the courage, at my bidding, to cut off my head.

'Now I can return and claim my father's kingdom, and you, most gracious maiden, will go with me, and be my bride, if you will have me.'

And this was how the lassie who went to fetch water from the Well o' the World's End became a princess.

THE SEAL CATCHER AND
THE MERMAN

Elizabeth Grierson

Once upon a time there was a man who lived not very far from John-o'-Groat's House, which, as everyone knows, is in the far north of Scotland. He lived in a little cottage by the sea-shore, and made his living by catching seals and selling their fur, which in those days was very valuable.

He earned a good deal of money in this way, for these creatures used to come out of the sea in large numbers, and lie on the rocks near his house basking in the sunshine, so that it was not difficult to creep up behind them and kill them.

Some of those seals were larger than others, and the country people used to call them 'Roane', and whisper that they were not seals at all, but mermen and merwomen, who came from a country of their own, far down under the ocean, who assumed this strange disguise in order that they might pass through the water, and come up to breathe the air of this earth of ours.

But the seal catcher only laughed at them, and said that those seals were most worth killing, for their skins were so big that he got an extra price for them.

Now it chanced one day, when he was pursuing his calling, that he stabbed a seal with his hunting-knife, and whether the stroke had not been sure enough or not, I cannot say, but with a loud cry of pain the creature slipped off the rock into the sea, and disappeared under the water, carrying the knife along with it.

The seal catcher, much annoyed at his clumsiness, and also at the loss of his knife, went home to dinner in a very downcast frame of mind. On his way he met a horseman, who was so tall and so strange-looking, and who rode on such a gigantic horse, that he stopped and looked at him in astonishment, wondering who he was, and from what country he came.

The stranger stopped also, and asked him his trade, and on hearing that he was a seal catcher, he immediately ordered a great number of seal skins. The seal catcher was delighted, for such an order meant a large sum of money to him. But his face fell when the horseman added that it was absolutely necessary that the skins should be delivered that evening.

'I cannot do it,' he said, in a disappointed voice, 'for the seals will not come back to the rocks again until tomorrow morning.'

'I can take you to a place where there are any number of seals,' answered the stranger, 'if you will mount behind me on my horse and come with me.'

The seal catcher agreed to this, and climbed up behind the rider, who shook his bridle rein, and off the great horse galloped at such a pace that he had much ado to keep his seat.

On and on they went, flying like the wind, until at last they came to the edge of a huge precipice, the face of which went sheer down to the sea. Here the mysterious horseman pulled up his steed with a jerk.

'Get off now,' he said shortly.

The seal catcher did as he was bid, and when he found himself safe on the ground, he peeped cautiously over the edge of the cliff, to see if there were any seals lying on the rocks below.

To his astonishment he saw below him no rocks, only the blue sea, which came right up to the foot of the cliff.

'Where are the seals that you spoke of?' he asked anxiously, wishing that he had never set out on such a rash adventure.

'You will see presently,' answered the stranger, who was attending to his horse's bridle.

The seal catcher was now thoroughly frightened, for he felt sure that some evil was about to befall him, and in such a lonely place he knew that it would be useless to cry out for help.

And it seemed as if his fears would prove only too true, for the next moment the stranger's hand was laid upon his shoulder, and he felt himself being hurled bodily over the cliff, and then he fell with a splash into the sea.

He thought that his last hour had come, and he wondered how

anyone could commit such a wrong deed upon an innocent man.

But, to his astonishment, he found that some change must have come over him, for instead of being choked by the water, he could breathe quite easily, and he and his companion, who was still close at his side, seemed to be sinking as quickly down through the sea as they had flown through the air.

Down and down they went, nobody knows how far, till at last they came to a huge arched door, which appeared to be made of pink coral, studded over with cockle-shells. It opened, of its own accord, and when they entered they found themselves in a huge hall, the walls of which were formed of mother-of-pearl, and the floor of which was of sea-sand, smooth, and firm, and yellow.

The hall was crowded with occupants, but they were seals, not men, and when the seal catcher turned to his companion to ask him what it all meant, he was aghast to find that he, too, had assumed the form of a seal. He was still more aghast when he caught sight of himself in a large mirror that hung on the wall, and saw that he also no longer bore the likeness of a man, but was transformed into a nice, hairy, brown seal.

'Ah, woe is me,' he said to himself, 'through no fault of mine this artful stranger has laid some baneful charm upon me, and in this awful guise will I remain for the rest of my natural life.'

At first none of the huge creatures spoke to him. For some reason or other they seemed to be very sad, and moved gently about the hall, talking quietly and mournfully to one another, or lay sadly upon the sandy floor, wiping big tears from their eyes with their soft furry fins.

But presently they began to notice him, and to whisper to one another, and presently his guide moved away from him, and disappeared through a door at the end of the hall. When he returned he held a huge knife in his hand.

'Did you ever see this before?' he asked, holding it out to the unfortunate seal catcher, who, to his horror, recognized his own hunting-knife with which he had struck the seal in the morning, and which had been carried off by the wounded animal.

At the sight of it he fell upon his face and begged for mercy, for he at once came to the conclusion that the inhabitants of the cavern, enraged at the harm which had been wrought upon their comrade, had, in some magic way, contrived to capture him, and to bring him down to their subterranean abode, in order to work their vengeance upon him by killing him.

But, instead of doing so, they crowded around him, rubbing their soft noses against his fur to show their sympathy, and implored him not to be afraid, for no harm would befall him, and they would love him all their lives long if he would only do what they asked him.

'Tell me what you ask,' said the seal catcher, 'and I will do it, if it lies within my power.'

'Follow me,' answered his guide, and he led the way to the door through which he had disappeared when he went to seek the knife.

The seal catcher followed him. And there, in a smaller room, he found a great brown seal lying on a bed of pale pink seaweed, with a gaping wound in his side.

'That is my father,' said his guide, 'whom you wounded this morning, thinking that he was one of the common seals who live in the sea, instead of a merman who has speech, and understanding, as you mortals have. I brought you here to bind up his wounds, for no other hand than yours can heal him.'

'I have no skill in the art of healing,' said the seal catcher, astonished at the forbearance of these strange creatures, whom he had so unwittingly wronged; 'but I will bind up the wound to the best of my power, and I am only sorry that it was my hands that caused it.'

He went over to the bed, and, stooping over the wounded merman, washed and dressed the hurt as well as he could; and the touch of his hands appeared to work like magic, for no sooner had he finished than the wound seemed to deaden and die, leaving only a scar, and the old seal sprang up, as well as ever.

Then there was great rejoicing throughout the whole Palace of the Seals. They laughed, and they talked, and they embraced each other in their own strange way, crowding around their comrade, and rubbing their noses against his, as if to show him how delighted they were at his recovery.

But all this while the seal catcher stood alone in a corner, with his mind filled with dark thoughts, for although he saw now that they had no intention of killing him, he did not relish the prospect of spending the rest of his life in the guise of a seal, fathoms deep under the ocean.

But presently, to his great joy, his guide approached him, and said, 'Now you are at liberty to return home to your wife and children. I will take you to them, but only on one condition.'

'And what is that?' asked the seal catcher eagerly, overjoyed at the prospect of being restored safely to the upper world, and to his family.

'That you will take a solemn oath never to wound a seal again.'

'That will I do right gladly,' the seal catcher replied, for although the promise meant giving up his means of livelihood, he felt that if only he regained his proper shape he could always turn his hand to something else.

So he took the required oath with all due solemnity, holding up his fin as he swore, and all the other seals crowded around him as witnesses. And a sigh of relief went through the halls when the words were spoken, for he was the most famous seal catcher in the North.

Then he bade the strange company farewell, and, accompanied by his guide, passed once more through the outer doors of coral, and up, and up, and up, through the shadowy green water, until it began to grow lighter and lighter, and at last they emerged into the sunshine of earth.

Then, with one spring, they reached the top of the cliff, where the great black horse was waiting for them, quietly nibbling the green turf.

When they left the water their strange disguise dropped from them, and they were now as they had been before, a plain seal catcher and a tall, well-dressed gentleman in riding clothes.

'Get up behind me,' said the latter, as he swung himself into his saddle. The seal catcher did as he was bid, taking tight hold of his companion's coat, for he remembered how nearly he had fallen off on his previous journey.

Then it all happened as it happened before. The bridle was shaken, and the horse galloped off, and it was not long before the seal catcher found himself standing in safety before his own garden gate.

He held out his hand to say 'goodbye', but as he did so the stranger pulled out a huge bag of gold and placed it in it.

'You've done your part of the bargain – we must do ours,' he said. 'Men shall never say that we took away an honest man's work without giving him some compensation for it, and here is what will keep you in comfort to your life's end.'

Then he vanished, and when the astonished seal catcher carried the bag into his cottage, and turned the gold out on the table, he found that what the stranger had said was true, and that he would be a rich man for the remainder of his days.

THE MERMAID

James Hogg

'Oh where won ye, my bonnie lass,   *won*, dwell
Wi' look sae wild an' cheery?
There's something in that witching face
That I lo'e wondrous dearly.'

'I live where the harebell never grew,
Where the streamlet never ran,
Where the winds o heaven never blew.
Now find me gin you can.'   *gin*, if

' 'Tis but your wild an' wily way,
The gloaming maks you eerie,   *gloaming*, evening light
For ye are the lass o the Bracken Brae
An' nae lad maun come near ye: *maun*, may

'But I am sick, an' very sick
Wi' a passion strange an' new,
For ae kiss o thy rosy cheek   *ae*, one
An' lips o the coral hue.'

'O laith, laith wad a wanderer be   *laith*, loath
To do your youth sic wrang,   *sic*, such
Were you to reive a kiss from me   *reive*, steal
Your life would not be lang.

'Go hie you from this lonely brake,   *hie*, speed
Nor dare your walk renew;   *brake*, hollow
For I'm the Maid of the Mountain Lake,
And I come wi' the falling dew.'

'Be you the Maid of the Crystal Wave
Or she of the Bracken Brae,
One tender kiss I mean to have;
You shall not say me nay.

'For beauty's like the daisy's vest
That shrinks from the early dew,
But soon it opes its bonnie breast,   *opes*, opens
And sae may it fare wi' you.'   *sae*, thus, so

'Kiss but this hand, I humbly sue   *sue*, beg
Even there I'll rue the stain;
Or the breath of man will dim its hue,   *Or*, Ere
It will ne'er be pure again.

'For passion's like the burning beal   *beal*, fever
Upon the mountain's brow,
That wastes itself to ashes pale;
And sae will it fare wi' you.'

'O mother, mother make my bed,
An' make it soft and easy;
An' with the cold dew bathe my head,
For pains of anguish seize me.

'Or stretch me in the chill blue lake
To quench this bosom's burning,
An' lay me by yon lonely brake,
For hope there's none returning.

'I've been where man should not have been,
Oft in my lonely roaming;
And seen what man should not have seen,
By greenwood in the gloaming.

'Oh, passion's deadlier than the grave,
All human things undoing!
The Maiden of the Mountain Wave
Has lured me to my ruin!'

THE LAIRD OF MORPHIE AND THE WATER KELPIE

Elizabeth Grierson

There was once a Scottish laird whose name was Graham of Morphie, and, as he was rich and great, he determined to build himself a grand castle. But, besides being rich, he was somewhat miserly, and he did not like the thought of having to pay a great deal of money for the building of it. So he hit on a plan by which he thought he could get labour cheaply. And this was the plan.

Down in the valley, close to where he lived, there was a large deep loch, and in the loch, so the country folk said, there dwelt a water kelpie.

Now water kelpies, as all the world knows, are cruel and malicious spirits, who love nothing better than to lure mortals to destruction. And this is how they set about it:

They take the form of a beautiful chestnut horse, and come out of the water, all saddled and bridled, as if ready to be mounted; then they graze quietly by the side of the road, until some luckless creature is tempted to get on their back. Then they plunge with him into the water, and he is no more seen. (At least, so the old folk say, for I have never met one of these creatures myself.)

To go on with the story, however. The Laird of Morphie knew that the water kelpie who haunted the loch on his property was in the habit of coming out of the water in the gloaming in the way I have described, and grazing quietly by the roadside.

And as he knew also that these uncanny horses were very strong, he determined to gain the mastery over this one, and force it to do his work. And the only way to do this was to take off the magic bridle which it wore and put it on again – no very easy task.

The Laird of Morphie, however, was a man who did not know what fear meant, and he was quite certain that he would be able to conquer the kelpie.

So one evening he took down his sword from the wall, and, calling to his wife, told her that he was in need of a servant, and that he thought the water horse would make a very good one, so he was going out to master him.

'Only,' he added, 'I cannot do it without your help, so listen to what I tell you. You must go out into the garden, and pluck two twigs from the rowan tree that grows by the gate, and fashion them into a Cross, and put it up over the outside of the door, which you must bar and bolt.

'That will keep the creature from entering the house; for no evil spirit can endure the rowan wood, let alone the Holy Sign.

'Then you must open the kitchen window; for although I want to keep the kelpie out, I myself need to get in. Do you understand?'

But if the Laird was not afraid of water horses, his wife was, and, instead of answering him, she threw her arms around his neck and wept bitterly, and begged and besought him not to meddle with spirits, but to bide quietly at home.

Which, of course, he would not agree to do, and he pushed the poor woman away from him roughly, and told her not to be a fool, but to attend to his words and do his bidding. Then he went out and left her, and she was so terrified that she went at once and picked the rowan twigs and made a Cross of them, and put it up outside the door. Then she shut herself into the house, and opened the kitchen window, exactly as her husband had told her to do. After which she crept away to her bed, and hid her head below the blankets.

Meanwhile, the Laird walked boldly down the road, until he came to a place where it ran between two hills, and was out of sight of any house; and in this lonely spot he saw, as he had expected, a fine chestnut horse, nibbling the sweet short grass by the roadside.

It carried a saddle and bridle of the finest leather, and it looked so quiet and docile that it might have been a lady's palfrey.

The Laird was not misled by its looks, however. As he

approached it he drew his sword, and when he came up to it he suddenly struck it a sharp rap on the side of the head, completely severing the strap which held its bridle in position.

The creature, taken by surprise, reared high in the air, and, seeing that there was no chance of tempting this cautious mortal to climb on its back, was turning to gallop down to the loch, when its bridle fell from its neck to the ground.

In a moment the Laird had picked it up, and put it into his pocket; for he knew that when a water horse lost its bridle its power was gone, and that it could not go back to its watery abode until it found it again.

No sooner had he done so, than, to his astonishment, the creature began to talk like any mortal, and to beg him to give it back its bridle, reminding him that it had never in its life done him any harm.

'I cannot thank you for that,' said the Laird drily, 'for, methinks, had I once been fool enough to mount on your back we would soon have seen whether you would have done me harm or no. Ha, ha, my bonnie nag, I have your bridle safe in my pocket, and I think I had better keep it there.'

Then the water horse grew angry, and showed his teeth in a way that would have frightened most men.

'You will never set foot in your own house,' he said, 'till you have given me back my bridle; for I can travel quicker than you can, and I will go and take possession of it.'

With these words he galloped off in the direction of the Laird's house.

But the Laird only laughed, and followed at his leisure, for he knew that no spirit, be it witch, or warlock, or demon, could enter a dwelling that was guarded by a Cross of rowan.

And he was right, for when he reached home he found the water horse standing stock still in front of the door, apparently determined that, since it could get no further, it would at least prevent the owner of the house entering.

But, as we know, the kitchen window was open, and the Laird went round the back of the house and jumped in at that.

Then he went upstairs, and put his head out of one of the upper windows, and began to bargain with the kelpie.

'See here,' he said. 'You're very anxious to get your bridle back, for without it you are helpless, and must remain for the remainder of your life on land. I, on my side, have a castle to build, and I need a good strong horse to cart the stones. So if you'll promise to do that for me, I will promise, when you are finished, to give you back your bridle.'

And as there seemed no other way, the water horse agreed to the bargain.

Now, if the kelpie were naturally cruel, I am afraid the Laird was cruel also, for he loaded the poor beast with such heavy loads that its shoulders were often chafed and bleeding, and it grew thin and miserable-looking.

Indeed, he worked it so hard that it was almost dead by the time the castle was completed.

Then, as he had no further use for it, he gave it back its bridle, and told it that it could go back to where it had come from.

Alas! he did not know what he had laid up in store for himself and his family. For the water kelpie, enraged at the sufferings which it had been made to endure, looked over its shoulder as it was about to plunge into the loch, and solemnly uttered these words:

> 'Sair back, and sair banes,
> Drivin' the Laird o' Morphie's stanes!
> The Laird o' Morphie'll never thrive
> As lang as Kelpie is alive.'

And his words came only too true; for one misfortune after another fell on the Laird and his descendants, until at last his name died out altogether.

So by this token let all those who read this story learn that it is never wise to persecute anybody, not even a water kelpie.

THE LAIRD O' CO

Elizabeth Grierson

It was a fine summer morning, and the Laird o' Co was having a
dander on the green turf outside his castle walls. His real name
was the Laird o' Colzean, and his descendants today bear the
proud title of Marquises of Ailsa, but all up and down Ayrshire
nobody called him anything else than the Laird o' Co: because
of the Co's, or sea caves, which were to be found in the rock on
which his castle was built.

He was a kind man, and courteous, always ready to be interested in the affairs of his poorer neighbours, and willing to listen
to any tale of woe.

So when a little boy came across the green, carrying a small
can in his hand, and, pulling his forelock, asked him if he might
go to the castle and get a little ale for his sick mother, the Laird
gave his consent at once, and, patting the lad on the head, told
him to go to the kitchen and ask for the butler, and tell him that
he, the Laird, had given orders that his can was to be filled with
the best ale that was in the cellar.

Away the boy went, and found the old butler, who, after
listening to his message, took him down into the cellar, and
proceeded to carry out his master's orders.

There was one cask of particularly fine ale, which was kept
entirely for the Laird's own use, which had been opened some
time before, and which was now about half full.

'I will fill the bairn's can out o' this,' thought the old man to
himself. ''Tis both nourishing and light – the very thing for sick

dander, stroll.

folk.' So, taking the can from the child's hand, he proceeded to draw the ale.

But what was his astonishment to find that, although the ale flowed freely enough from the barrel, the little can, which could not have held more than a quarter of a gallon, remained always just half full.

The ale poured into it in a clear amber stream, until the big cask was quite empty, and still the quantity that was in the little can did not seem to increase.

The butler could not understand it. He looked at the cask, and then he looked at the can; then he looked down at the floor at his feet to see if he had not spilt any.

No, the ale had not disappeared in that way, for the cellar floor was as white, and dry, and clean, as possible.

Plague on the can; it must be bewitched, thought the old man, and his short, stubby hair stood up like porcupine quills around his bald head, for if there was anything on earth of which he had a mortal dread, it was warlocks, and witches, and suchlike bogles.

'I'm not going to open up another barrel,' he said, gruffly, handing back the half-filled can to the lad. 'So ye may just go home with what is there; the Laird's ale is too good to waste on a whipper-snapper like you.'

But the boy stood his ground. A promise was a promise, and the Laird had both promised, and sent orders to the butler that the can was to be filled, so the boy would not go home till it was filled.

It was in vain that the old man first argued, and then grew angry – the boy would not stir a step.

The Laird had said that he was to get the ale, and the ale he must have.

At last the perturbed butler left him standing there, and hurried off to his master to tell him he was convinced that the can was bewitched, for it had swallowed up a whole half cask of ale, and after doing so it was only half full; and to ask if he would come down himself, and order the lad off the premises.

'Not I,' said the genial Laird, 'for the lad is quite right. I promised that he should have his can full of ale to take home to his sick mother, and he shall have it if it takes all the barrels in my cellar to fill it. So go back to the cellar again, and open up another cask.'

The butler dared not disobey; so he reluctantly retraced his steps, but, as he went, he shook his head sadly, for it seemed to him that not only the boy with the can, but his master also, was bewitched.

When he reached the cellar he found the bairn waiting patiently where he had left him, and, without wasting further words, he took the can from his hand and broached another barrel.

If he had been astonished before, he was more astonished now. Scarce had a couple of drops fallen from the tap, than the boy's can was full to the brim.

'Take it, laddie, and begone, with all speed,' he said, glad to get the can out of his fingers; and the boy did not wait for a second bidding. Thanking the butler most earnestly for his trouble, and paying no attention to the fact that the old man had not been so civil to him as he might have been, he departed. Nor, though the butler took pains to ask all around the countryside, was anything heard of him again, nor of anyone who knew anything about him, or anything about his sick mother.

Years passed by, and sore trouble fell upon the House o' Co. For the Laird went to fight in the wars in Flanders, and, chancing to be taken prisoner, he was shut up in prison, and condemned to death. Alone, in a foreign country, he had no friends to speak for him, and escape seemed hopeless.

It was the night before his execution, and he was sitting in his lonely cell, thinking sadly of his wife and children, whom he never expected to see again. At the thought of them the picture of his home rose clearly in his mind – the grand old castle standing on its rock above the Firth of Clyde, and the bonnie daisy-spangled stretch of links which lay before its gates, where he had been wont to take a dander in the sweet summer mornings. Then, all unbidden, a vision of the little lad carrying the can, who had come to beg ale for his sick mother, and whom he had long ago forgotten, rose up before him.

The vision was so clear and distinct that he felt almost as if he were acting the scene over again, and he rubbed his eyes to get

rid of it, feeling that, if he had to die tomorrow, it was time that
he turned his thoughts to higher things.

But as he did so the door of his cell flew noiselessly open, and
there, on the threshold, stood the self-same little lad, looking not
a day older, with his finger on his lip, and a mysterious smile
upon his face.

> *'Laird o' Co,*
> *Rise and go!'*

he whispered, beckoning to him to follow him. Needless to say,
the Laird did so, too much amazed to think of asking questions.

Through the long passages of the prison the little lad went, the
Laird close at his heels; and whenever he came to a locked door,
he had but to touch it, and it opened before them, so that in no
long time they were safe outside the walls.

The overjoyed Laird would have overwhelmed his little deliv-
erer with words of thanks had not the boy held up his hand to
stop him. 'Get on my back,' he said shortly, 'for you are not safe
till you are right out of this country.'

The Laird did as he was bid, and, marvellous as it seems, the
boy was quite able to bear his weight. As soon as the Laird was
comfortably seated the pair set off, over sea and land, and never
stopped till, in almost less time than it takes to tell it, the boy set
him down, in the early dawn, on the daisy-spangled green in
front of his castle, just where he had spoken first to him so many
years before.

Then he turned, and laid his little hand on the Laird's big one:

> *'Ae gude turn deserves anither,*
> *Tak' ye that for being sae kind to my auld mither,'*

he said, and vanished.

And from that day to this he has never been seen again.

THE BROWNIE O' FERNE-DEN

Elizabeth Grierson

There have been many brownies known in Scotland; and stories have been written about the Brownie o' Bodsbeck and the Brownie o' Blednock, but about neither of them has a prettier story been told than that which I am going to tell you about the Brownie o' Ferne-Den.

Now, Ferne-Den was a farmhouse, which got its name from the glen, or 'den', on the edge of which it stood, and through which anyone who wished to reach the dwelling had to pass.

And this glen was believed to be the abode of a brownie, who never appeared to anyone in the daytime, but who, it was said, was sometimes seen at night, stealing about, like an ungainly shadow, from tree to tree, trying to keep out of sight, and never, by any chance, harming anybody.

Indeed, like all brownies that are properly treated and let alone, so far was he from harming anyone, that he was always on the look-out to do a good turn to those who needed his assistance. The farmer often said that he did not know what he would do without him; for if there was any work to be finished in a hurry at the farm – corn to thresh, or winnow, or tie up into bags, turnips to cut, clothes to wash, corn-sheaves to be kirned, a garden to be weeded – all that the farmer and his wife had to do

brownies, spirits who were on the whole friendly and domesticated. They were associated with farms and steadings, and in some areas the householder would leave some food or milk – or even clothes – for them in order to gain their protection.
kirned, prepared for the celebration marking the end of the harvest; this was called the *kirning*. The last sheaves of corn were sometimes ornamented (as kirn babies or kirn dollies) for display purposes.

was to leave the door of the barn, or the turnip shed, or the milk house open when they went to bed, and put down a bowl of new milk on the doorstep for the Brownie's supper, and when they woke the next morning the bowl would be empty, and the job finished better than if it had been done by mortal hands.

In spite of all this, however, which might have proved to them how gentle and kindly the creature really was, everyone about the place was afraid of him, and would rather go a couple of miles round about in the dark, when they were coming home from kirk or market, than pass through the glen, and run the risk of catching a glimpse of him.

I said that they were all afraid of him, but that was not true, for the farmer's wife was so good and gentle that she was not afraid of anything on God's earth, and when the Brownie's supper had to be left outside, she always filled his bowl with the richest milk, and added a good spoonful of cream to it, for, said she, 'He works so hard for us, and asks no wages, he well deserves the very best meal that we can give him.'

One night this gentle lady was taken very ill, and everyone was afraid that she was going to die. Of course, her husband was greatly distressed, and so were her servants, for she had been such a good mistress to them that they loved her as if she had been their mother. But they were all young, and none of them knew very much about illness, and everyone agreed that it would be better to send off for an old woman who lived about seven miles away on the other side of the river, who was known to be a very skilful nurse.

But who was to go? That was the question. For it was black midnight, and the way to the old woman's house lay straight through the glen. And whoever travelled that road ran the risk of meeting the dreaded Brownie.

The farmer would have gone only too willingly, but he dare not leave his wife alone; and the servants stood in groups about the kitchen, each one telling the other that he ought to go, yet no one offering to go themselves.

Little did they think that the cause of all their terror, a queer, wee, misshapen little man, all covered with hair, with a long beard, red-rimmed eyes, broad, flat feet like a frog's, and enormous long arms that touched the ground, even when he stood upright, was within a yard or two of them, listening to their talk, with an anxious face, behind the kitchen door.

For he had come up as usual, from his hiding-place in the glen, to see if there was any work for him to do, and to look for his bowl of milk. And he had seen, from the open door and lit-up windows, that there was something wrong inside the farm-house, which at that hour was usually dark, and still, and silent; and he had crept into the entry to try and find out what the matter was.

When he gathered from the servants' talk that the mistress, whom he too loved so dearly, and who had been so kind to him, was ill, his heart sank within him; and when he heard that the silly servants were so taken up with their own fears that they dared not set out to fetch a nurse for her, his contempt and anger knew no bounds.

'Fools, idiots, dolts!' he muttered to himself, stamping his queer, misshapen feet on the floor. 'They speak as if a body were ready to take a bite off them as soon as ever he met them. If they only knew the bother it gives me to keep out of their road they wouldna be so silly. But, by my troth, if they go on like this, the bonnie lady will die amongst their fingers. So it strikes me that Brownie must just gang himself.'

So saying, he reached up his hand, and took down a dark cloak which belonged to the farmer, and was hanging on a peg on the wall. Throwing it over his head and shoulders in an effort to hide his ungainly form, he hurried away to the stable, and saddled and bridled the fleetest-footed horse that stood there.

When the last buckle was fastened, he led the horse to the door, and scrambled on its back. 'Now, if you ever travelled fast, travel fast now,' he said; and it was as if the creature understood him, for it gave a little whinny and pricked up its ears; then it darted out into the darkness like an arrow from the bow.

In less time than the distance had ever been ridden in before, the Brownie drew rein at the old woman's cottage.

She was in bed, fast asleep; but he rapped sharply on the window, and when she rose and put her old face, framed in its

white mutch, close to the pane to ask who was there, he bent
forward and told her his errand.

'You must come with me, Goodwife, and that quickly,' he
commanded, in his deep, harsh voice, 'if the lady of Ferne-Den's
life is to be saved; for there is no one to nurse her up-bye at the
farm there, save a lot of empty-headed servant wenches.'

'But how am I to get there? Have they sent a cart for me?'
asked the old woman anxiously; for, as far as she could see, there
was nothing at the door save a horse and its rider.

'No, they have sent no cart,' replied the Brownie, shortly. 'So
you must just climb up behind me on the saddle, and hang on
tight to my waist, and I'll promise to land ye at Ferne-Den safe
and sound.'

His voice was so masterful that the old woman dare not re-
fuse to do as she was bid; besides, she had often ridden pillion-
wise when she was a lassie, so she made haste to dress herself,
and when she was ready she unlocked her door, and, mounting
the louping-on stane that stood beside it, she was soon seated
behind the dark-cloaked stranger, with her arms clasped tightly
around him.

Not a word was spoken till they approached the dreaded glen,
then the old woman felt her courage giving way. 'Do ye think
that there will be any chance of meeting the Brownie?' she asked
timidly. 'I would fain not run the risk, for folk say that he is an
ill-omened creature.'

Her companion gave a curious laugh. 'Keep up your heart,
and dinna talk havers,' he said, 'for I promise ye ye'll see naught
uglier this night than the man whom ye ride behind.'

'Oh, then, I'm fine and safe,' replied the old woman, with a
sigh of relief; 'for although I havena' seen your face, I warrant
that ye are a true man, for the care you have taken of a poor old
woman.'

She relapsed into silence again till the glen was passed and the
good horse had turned into the farmyard. Then the horseman
slid to the ground, and, turning round, lifted her carefully down

   mutch, a close-fitting white linen hat or hood worn by older ladies.
   louping-on stane, for mounting or dismounting from a horse.
   havers, nonsense, rubbish.

in his long, strong arms. As he did so the cloak slipped off him, revealing his short, broad body and his misshapen limbs.

'In a' the world, what kind o' man are ye?' she asked, peering into his face in the grey morning light, which was just dawning. 'What makes your eyes so big? And what have ye done to your feet? They are more like a frog's webs than anything else.'

The queer little man laughed again. 'I've wandered many a mile in my time without a horse to help me, and I've heard it said that ower-much walking makes the feet unshapely,' he replied. 'But waste no time in talking, good Dame. Go your way into the house; and, hark'ee, if anyone asks you who brought you hither so quickly, tell them that there was a lack of men, so you just had to be content to ride behind the Brownie o' Ferne-Den.'

KATHERINE CRACKERNUTS

Elizabeth Grierson

There was once a King whose wife died, leaving him with an only daughter, whom he dearly loved. The little Princess's name was Velvet-Cheek, and she was so good, and bonnie, and kind-hearted that all her father's subjects loved her. But as the King was generally engaged in transacting the business of the State, the poor little maiden had rather a lonely life, and often wished that she had a sister with whom she could play, and who would be a companion to her.

The King, hearing this, made up his mind to marry a middle-aged countess, whom he had met at a neighbouring court, who had one daughter, named Katherine, who was just a little younger than the Princess Velvet-Cheek, and who, he thought, would make a nice playfellow for her.

He did so, and in one way the arrangement turned out very well, for the two girls loved one another dearly, and had everything in common, just as if they had really been sisters.

But in another way it turned out very badly, for the new Queen was a cruel and ambitious woman, and she wanted her own daughter to do as she had done, and make a grand marriage, and perhaps even become a queen. And when she saw that Princess Velvet-Cheek was growing into a very beautiful young woman – more beautiful by far than her own daughter – she began to hate her, and to wish that in some way she would lose her good looks.

'For,' thought she, 'what suitor will heed my daughter as long as her stepsister is by her side?'

Now, among the servants and retainers at her husband's castle there was an old henwife, who, men said, was in league with the evil spirits of the air, and who was skilled in the knowledge of charms, and philtres, and love potions.

'Perhaps she could help me to do what I seek to do,' said the wicked Queen; and one night, when it was growing dusk, she wrapped a cloak around her, and set out to this old henwife's cottage.

'Send the lassie to me tomorrow morning before she has broken her fast,' replied the old dame when she heard what her visitor had to say. 'I will find out a way to mar her beauty.' And the wicked Queen went home content.

Next morning she went to the Princess's room while she was dressing, and told her to go out before breakfast and get the eggs that the henwife had gathered. 'And see,' added she, 'that you don't eat anything before you go, for there is nothing that makes the roses bloom on a young maiden's cheeks like going out fasting in the fresh morning air.'

Princess Velvet-Cheek promised to do as she was bid, and go and fetch the eggs; but as she was not fond of going out of doors before she had had something to eat, and as, moreover, she suspected that her stepmother had some hidden reason for giving her such an unusual order, and she did not trust her stepmother's hidden reasons, she slipped into the pantry as she went downstairs and helped herself to a large slice of cake. Then, after she had eaten it, she went straight to the henwife's cottage and asked for the eggs.

'Lift the lid of that pot there, your Highness, and you will see them,' said the old woman, pointing to the big pot standing in the corner in which she boiled her hens' meat.

The Princess did so, and found a heap of eggs lying inside, which she lifted into her basket, while the old woman watched her with a curious smile.

'Go home to your lady mother, hinny,' she said at last, 'and tell her from me to keep the press door better snibbit.'

The Princess went home, and gave this extraordinary message to her stepmother, wondering to herself meanwhile what it meant.

press, pantry, walk-in cupboard.   *snibbit*, bolted.

But if she did not understand the henwife's words, the Queen understood them only too well. For from them she gathered that the Princess had in some way prevented the old witch's spell doing what she intended it to do.

So next morning, when she sent her stepdaughter once more on the same errand, she accompanied her to the door of the castle herself, so that the poor girl had no chance of paying a visit to the pantry. But as she went along the road that led to the cottage, she felt so hungry that, when she passed a party of country-folk picking peas by the roadside, she asked them to give her a handful.

They did so, and she ate the peas; and so it came about that the same thing happened that had happened yesterday.

The henwife sent her to look for the eggs; but she could work no spell upon her, because she had broken her fast. So the old woman bade her go home again and give the same message to the Queen.

The Queen was very angry when she heard it, for she felt that she was being outwitted by this slip of a girl, and she determined that, although she was not fond of getting up early, she would accompany her next day herself, and make sure that she had nothing to eat as she went.

So next morning she walked with the Princess to the henwife's cottage, and, as had happened twice before, the old woman sent the royal maiden to lift the lid off the pot in the corner in order to get the eggs.

And the moment that the Princess did so off jumped her own pretty head, and on jumped that of a sheep.

Then the wicked Queen thanked the cruel old witch for the service that she had rendered to her, and went home quite delighted with the success of her scheme; while the poor Princess picked up her own head and put it into her basket along with the eggs, and went home crying, keeping behind the hedge all the way, for she felt so ashamed of her sheep's head that she was afraid that anyone saw her.

Now, as I told you, the Princess's stepsister Katherine loved her dearly, and when she saw what a cruel deed had been wrought on her she was so angry that she declared that she would not remain another hour in the castle. 'For,' said she, 'if my mother can order one such deed to be done, who can hinder her ordering another? I think it's better for us both to be where she cannot reach us.'

So she wrapped a fine silk shawl round her poor stepsister's head, so that none could tell what it was like, and, putting the real head in the basket, she took her by the hand, and the two set out to seek their fortunes.

They walked and they walked, till they reached a splendid palace, and when they came to it Katherine made as though she would go boldly up and knock at the door.

'I may perchance find work here,' she explained, 'and earn enough money to keep us both in comfort.'

But the poor Princess would fain have pulled her back. 'They will have nothing to do with you,' she whispered, 'when they see that you have a sister with a sheep's head.'

'And who is to know that you have a sheep's head?' asked Katherine. 'Just hold your tongue, and keep the shawl well around your face, and leave the rest to me.'

So up she went and knocked at the kitchen door, and when the housekeeper came to answer it she asked her if there was any work that she could give her to do. 'For,' said she, 'I have a sick sister, who is sore troubled with the migraine in her head, and I would fain find a quiet lodging for her where she could rest for the night.'

'Do you know how to nurse a sickness?' asked the house-keeper, who was greatly struck by Katherine's soft voice and gentle ways.

'Ay, I do,' replied Katherine, 'for when one's sister is troubled with the migraine, one has to learn to look after her, and to go about softly and not to make a noise.'

Now it chanced that the King's eldest son, the Crown Prince, was lying ill in the palace with a strange disease, which seemed to have touched his brain. For he was so restless, especially at nights, that someone had always to be with him to watch that he did himself no harm; and this state of things had gone on so long that everyone was quite worn out.

And the old housekeeper thought that it would be a good

chance to get a quiet night's sleep if this capable-looking stranger could be trusted to sit up with the Prince.

So she left her at the door, and went and consulted the King; and the King came out and spoke to Katherine, and he, too, was so pleased with her voice and her appearance that he gave orders that a room should be set apart in the castle for her sick sister and herself, and he promised that, if she would sit up that night with the Prince, and see that he came to no harm, she would have, as her reward, a bag of silver pennies in the morning.

Katherine agreed to the bargain readily. *For*, thought she, *'twill always be a night's lodging for the Princess; and, forbye that, a bag of silver pennies is not to be got every day.*

So the Princess went to bed in the comfortable chamber that was set apart for her, and Katherine went to watch by the sick Prince.

He was a handsome, comely young man, who seemed to be in some sort of fever, for his brain was not quite clear, and he tossed and tumbled from side to side, gazing anxiously in front of him, and stretching out his hands as if he were in search of something.

And at twelve o'clock at night, just when Katherine thought that he was going to fall into a refreshing sleep, what was her horror to see him rise from his bed, dress himself hastily, open the door, and slip downstairs, as if he were going to look for somebody.

'There's something strange in this,' said the girl to herself. 'I'd better follow him and see what happens.'

So she stole out of the room after the Prince and followed him safely downstairs; and what was her astonishment to find that apparently he was going some distance, for he put on his hat and riding-coat, and, unlocking the door, crossed the courtyard to the stable, and began to saddle his horse.

When he had done so, he led it out, and mounted, and, whistling softly to a hound which lay asleep in a corner, he prepared to ride away.

'I must go too, and see the end of this,' said Katherine bravely; 'I'm sure he's bewitched. These are not the actions of a sick man.'

So, just as the horse was about to start, she jumped lightly on its back, and settled herself comfortably behind its rider, all unnoticed by him.

Then this strange pair rode away through the woods, and, as they went, Katherine pulled the hazel-nuts that nodded in great clusters in her face. 'For,' said she to herself, 'dear only knows where next I may get anything to eat.'

On and on they rode, till they left the greenwood far behind them and came out on an open moor. Soon they reached a hillock, and here the Prince drew rein, and, stooping down, cried in a strange, uncanny whisper, 'Open, open, green hill, and let the Prince, and his horse, and his hound enter.'

'And,' whispered Katherine quickly, 'let his lady enter behind him.'

Instantly, to her great astonishment, the top of the knowe seemed to tip up, leaving an aperture large enough for the little company to enter; then it closed gently behind them again.

They found themselves in a magnificent hall, brilliantly lighted by hundreds of candles stuck in sconces around the walls. In the centre of this apartment was a group of the most beautiful maidens that Katherine had ever seen, all dressed in shimmering ball-gowns, with wreaths of roses and violets in their hair. And there were sprightly youths also, who had been treading a measure with these beauteous damsels to the strains of fairy music.

When the maidens saw the Prince, they ran to him, and led him away to join their revels. And at the touch of their hands all his languor seemed to disappear, and he became the brightest of all the throng, and laughed, and danced, and sang as if he had never known what it was to be ill.

As no one took any notice of Katherine, she sat down quietly on a bit of rock to watch what would befall. And as she watched, she became aware of a little wee bairnie, playing with a tiny wand, quite close to her feet.

He was a bonnie bit bairn, and she was just thinking of trying to make friends with him when one of the beautiful maidens passed, and, looking at the wand, said to her partner, in a

knowe, hilltop.

meaning tone, 'Three strokes of that wand would give Katherine's sister back her pretty face.'

Here was news indeed! Katherine's breath came thick and fast; and with trembling fingers she drew some of the nuts out of her pocket, and began rolling them carelessly towards the child. Apparently he did not get nuts very often, for he dropped his little wand at once, and stretched out his tiny hands to pick them up.

This was just what she wanted; and she slipped down from her seat to the ground, and drew a little nearer to him. Then she threw one or two more nuts in his way, and, when he was picking these up, she managed to lift the wand unobserved, and to hide it under her apron. After this, she crept cautiously back to her seat again; and not a moment too soon, for just then a cock crew, and at the sound the whole troop of dancers vanished – all but the Prince, who ran to mount his horse, and was in such a hurry to be gone that Katherine had much ado to get up behind him before the hillock opened, and he rode swiftly into the outer world once more.

But she managed it, and, as they rode homewards in the grey morning light, she sat and cracked her nuts and ate them as fast as she could, for her adventures had made her marvellously hungry.

When she and her strange patient had once more reached the castle, she just waited to see him go back to bed, and begin to toss and tumble as he had done before; then she ran to her stepsister's room, and, finding her asleep, with her poor misshapen head lying peacefully on the pillow, she gave it three sharp little strokes with the fairy wand, and, lo and behold! the sheep's head vanished, and the Princess's own pretty one took its place.

In the morning the King and the old housekeeper came to enquire what kind of night the Prince had had. Katherine answered that he had had a very good night; for she was very anxious to stay with him longer, and now that she had found out that the elfin maidens who dwelt in the green knowe had thrown a spell over him, she was resolved to find out also how that spell could be broken.

And fortune favoured her; for the King was so pleased to think that such a suitable nurse had been found for the Prince, and he was also so charmed with the looks of her stepsister, who came out of her chamber as bright and bonnie as in the old days, declaring that her migraine was all gone, and that she was now able to do any work that the housekeeper might find for her, that he begged Katherine to stay with his son a little longer, adding that, if she would do so, he would give her a bag of gold sovereigns.

So Katherine agreed readily; and that night she watched by the Prince as she had done the night before. And at twelve o'clock he rose and dressed himself, and rode to the fairy knowe, just as she had expected him to do, for she was now quite certain that the poor young man was bewitched, and not suffering from a fever, as everyone thought he was.

And you may be sure that she accompanied him, riding behind him all unnoticed, and filling her pockets with nuts as she rode.

When they reached the fairy knowe, he spoke the same words that he had spoken the night before. 'Open, open, green hill, and let the young Prince, and his horse, and his hound enter.' And when the green hill opened, Katherine added softly, 'And his lady behind him.' So they all passed in together.

Once again, Katherine seated herself on a stone, and looked around her. The same revels were going on as yesternight, and the Prince was soon in the thick of them, dancing and laughing madly. The girl watched him narrowly, wondering if she would ever be able to find out what would restore him to his right mind; and, as she was watching him, the same little bairn who had played with the magic wand came up to her again. Only this time he was playing with a little bird.

And as he played, one of the dancers passed by, and, turning to her partner, said lightly, 'Three bites of that birdie would lift the Prince's sickness, and make him as well as he ever was.' Then she joined in the dance again, leaving Katherine sitting upright on her stone quivering with excitement.

If only she could get that bird the Prince might be cured! Very carefully she began to shake some nuts out of her pocket, and roll them across the floor towards the child.

He picked them up eagerly, letting go the bird as he did so; and, in an instant, Katherine caught it, and hid it under her apron.

In no long time after that the cock crew, and the Prince and she set out on their homeward ride. But this morning, instead of cracking nuts, she killed and plucked the bird; then she put it on a spit in front of the fire and began to roast it.

And soon it began to frizzle, and get brown, and smell deliciously, and the Prince, in his bed in the corner, opened his eyes and murmured faintly, 'How I wish I had a bite of that birdie.'

When she heard the words Katherine's heart jumped for joy, and as soon as the bird was roasted she cut a little piece from its breast and popped it into the Prince's mouth.

When he had eaten it his strength seemed to come back somewhat, for he rose on his elbow and looked at his nurse. 'Oh! if I had but another bite of that birdie!' he said. And his voice was certainly stronger.

So Katherine gave him another piece, and when he had eaten that he sat right up in bed.

'Oh! if I had but a third bite o' that birdie!' he cried. And now the colour was coming right back into his face, and his eyes were shining.

This time Katherine brought him the whole of the rest of the bird; and he ate it up greedily, picking the bones quite clean with his fingers; and when it was finished, he sprang out of bed and dressed himself, and sat down by the fire.

And when the King came in the morning, with his old housekeeper at his back, to see how the Prince was, he found him sitting cracking nuts with his nurse, for Katherine had brought home quite a lot in her apron pocket.

The King was so delighted to find his son cured that he gave all the credit to Katherine Crackernuts, as he called her, and he gave orders at once that the Prince should marry her. 'For,' said he, 'a maiden who is such a good nurse is sure to make a good queen.'

The Prince was quite willing to do as his father bade him; and, while they were talking together, his younger brother came in, leading Princess Velvet-Cheek by the hand, whose acquaintance he had made but yesterday, declaring that he had fallen in love with her, and that he wanted to marry her immediately.

So it all turned out very well, and everybody was quite pleased; and the two weddings took place at once, and, unless they be dead since that time, the young couples are living yet.

TAM LIN

Anon.

'O I forbid you, maidens a'   *a'*, all
That wear gowd on your hair,   *gowd*, gold
To come or gae by Carterhaugh,   *gae*, go
For young Tam Lin is there.

There's nane that gaes by   *nane*, none; *gaes*, goes
    Carterhaugh
But they leave him a wad,   *wad*, pledge, wager
Either their rings or green mantles
Or else their maidenhead.'

Janet has belted her green kirtle   *kirtle*, skirt
A little aboon her knee,   *aboon*, above
And she has braided her yellow hair
A little aboon her bree,   *bree*, brow
And she's awa to Carterhaugh
As fast as she can hie.   *hie*, go, speed

When she came to Carterhaugh,
Tam Lin was at the well;
And there she fand his steed standing   *fand*, found
But away was himsel'.

She hadna pu'd a double rose,   *pu'd*, pulled
A rose but only twa,   *twa*, two
Till up then started young Tam Lin,
Saying, 'Lady, don't pu' them a'.   *a'*, all

'Why pu's thou the rose, Janet?
And why breaks thou my
    wand?   *wand*, baton (symbolizing rule)
Or why comes thou to Carterhaugh
Withouten my command?'

'Carterhaugh it is my ain,
My daddie gave it me.
I'll come and gang at Carterhaugh
And ask nae leave of thee.'   *nae*, no

Janet has kilted her green kirtle
A little aboon her knee,
And she has snooded her yellow   *snooded*, bound
    hair
A little aboon her bree,
And she is to her father's ha'
As fast as she can hie.

Four and twenty ladies fair
Were playing at the ba',
When out came the fair Janet,
Aince the flower amang   *Aince*, Once; *amang*, among
    them a'.

Four and twenty ladies fair
Were playing at the chess,
And out then came the fair Janet,
As green as ony grass.   *ony*, any

Out then spak an auld grey   *spak*, spoke; *auld*, old
    knight,
Lent o'er the castle wa',
And says, 'Alas, fair Janet for thee,
But we'll be blamèd a'!'

'Haud your tongue, ye auld-faced   *Haud*, Hold
    knight,
Some ill death may ye die!
Father my bairn on whom I will,   *bairn*, baby
I'll father nane on thee.'   *nane*, none

Out then spak her father dear,
And he spak meek and mild:
'And ever alas, sweet Janet!' he says,
'I think thou gaes wi' child.'

'If that I gae wi' child, father,
Myself maun bear the blame.
There's ne'er a laird aboot your ha'
Shall give my bairn his name.

'If my love were an earthly knight,
As he's an elfin grey,
I wadna gie my ain true-love
For nae lord that ye hae.

'The steed that my true-love rides on
Is lighter than the wind.
Wi' siller he is shod before,   *siller*, silver
Wi' burning gowd behind.'   *gowd*, gold

Janet has kilted her green kirtle
A little aboon her knee,
And she has snooded her yellow hair
A little aboon her bree,
And she's awa' to Carterhaugh
As fast as she can hie.

When she came to Carterhaugh
Tam Lin was at the well,
And there she fand his steed standing,
But away was himsel'.

She hadna pu'd a double rose,
A rose but only twa,
Till up then started young Tam Lin,
Saying, 'Lady, don't pu' them a'.

'Why pu's thou the rose, Janet,
Amang the groves sae green,
And a' to kill the bonnie babe
That we gat us between?'

'O tell me, tell me, Tam Lin,' she says,
'For His sake that died on tree,
If e'er ye was in holy chapel
Or Christendom did see?'

'Roxburgh was my grandfather,
Took me with him to bide,   *bide*, live
And aince it fell upon a day   *aince*, once
That wae did me betide.   *wae*, woe

'And aince it fell upon a day,
A cauld day and a snell,   *snell*, bitter cold
When we were frae the hunting come,   *frae*, from
That frae my horse I fell.
The Queen o the Fairies she caught me
In yon green hill to dwell.

'And pleasant is the fairy land,
But an eerie tale to tell –
Aye, at the end o seven years
We pay a tiend to hell.   *tiend*, tithe, fee
I'm feared, being fair and fu' of flesh,
The tiend may be mysel'.

'But the night is Halloween, lady,   *the night*, tonight
The morn is Hallowday.   *the morn*, tomorrow
Then win me, win me, if you will,
For weel I ken ye may.   *ken*, know

'Just at the mirk and midnight hour,   *mirk*, dark
The fairy folk will ride.
And they that wad their true-love win
At Miles Cross they maun bide.'   *maun bide*, must wait

'But how shall I ken thee, Tam Lin,   *ken*, know
Or how my true-love know,
Amang sae mony unco knights,   *unco*, unfamiliar
The like I never saw?'

'O first let pass the black, lady,
And syne let pass the brown,   *syne*, then
But quickly run to the milk-white steed
And pu' his rider down.

'For I'll ride on the milk-white steed
And ay nearest the town,
Because I was an earthly knight
They gie me that renoun.   *renoun*, privilege

'My right hand will be gloved, lady,
My left hand will be bare,
Cocked up shall my bonnet be
And kaim'd down shall my hair,   *kaim'd*, combed
And thae's the tokens I gie to thee,   *thae's*, these are
Without doubt I'll be there.

'They'll turn me in your arms, lady,
Into an esk and adder;   *esk*, newt
But hold me fast, and fear me not,
I am your bairn's father.

'They'll turn me into a bear sae grim,   *sae*, so
And then a lion bold;
But hold me fast, and fear me not,
As ye shall love your child.

'Again they'll turn me in your arms
To a red-het gaud of airn;   *het*, hot; *gaud*, bar; *airn*, iron
But hold me fast, and fear me not,
and I'll do you nae harm.

'At last they'll turn me in your arms
Into the burning lead.
Then throw me into well water,
O throw me in wi' speed!

'And then I'll be your ain true love,
I'll turn a naked knight,
Then cover me wi' your green mantle,
And cover me out o sight.'

Gloomy, gloomy was the night,
And eerie was the way,
As fair Janet in her green mantle
To Miles Cross she did gae.

About the middle o the night
She heard the bridles ring.
This lady was as glad at that
As any earthly thing.

First she let the black pass by,
And syne she let the brown;
But quickly she ran to the milk-white steed
And pu'd the rider down.

Sae weel she minded what he'd said,
And young Tam Lin did win,
Syne covered him wi' her green mantle,
As blythe's a bird in spring.

Out then spak the Queen o Fairies,
Out of a bush o broom:
'Them that's gotten the young Tam Lin
Has gotten a stately groom.'

Out then spak the Queen o Fairies
And an angry queen was she:
'Shame betide her ill-fared face,
And an ill death may she dee!
For she's taen awa the bonniest knight   *taen*, taken
In a' my companie.

'But had I kend, Tam Lin,' she says,   *kend*, known
'What now this night I see,
I wad hae taen out thy twa grey een   *een*, eyes
And put in twa een o tree.'   *tree*, wood

THOMAS THE RHYMER

Anon.

True Thomas lay on Huntlie bank,
A ferlie he spied wi his ee;   *ferlie*, a strange sight
And there he saw a lady bright,
Come riding down by the Eildon Tree.

Her skirt was o the grass-green silk,
Her mantle o the velvet fine;
At ilka tett o her horse's mane   *ilka tett*, each tuft
Hung fifty siller bells and nine.   *siller*, silver

True Thomas, he pull'd aff his cap
And lowted low down to his knee,   *lowted*, bowed
'All hail, thou mighty Queen of Heaven,
For thy peer on earth I never did see!'

'O no, O no, Thomas,' she said,
'That name does not belang to me,
I am but the Queen of fair Elfland,
That am hither come to visit thee.

'Harp and carp, Thomas,' she said, *Harp and carp*, play
'Harp and carp along wi me;   and recite (as a minstrel)
And if you dare to kiss my lips,
Sure of your body I will be.'

'Betide me weel, betide me woe,
That weird shall never daunton   *weird*, fate; *daunton*, daunt
    me.'
Syne he has kiss'd her rosy lips   *Syne*, Thereupon, Then
All underneath the Eildon Tree.

'Now ye maun go wi me,' she said,   *maun*, must
'True Thomas, ye maun go wi me.
And ye maun serve me seven years,
Thro' weel or woe as may chance to be.'

She's mounted on her milk-white steed,
She's taen True Thomas up behind.   *taen*, taken
And aye whene'er her bridle rung,
The steed flew swifter than the wind.

O they rade on, and farther on,   *rade*, rode
The steed gaed swifter than the wind,   *gaed*, went
Until they reach'd a desert wide
And living land was left behind.

'Light down, light down now, true Thomas,
And lean your head upon my knee;
Abide and rest a little space
And I will show you ferlies three.

'O see ye not yon narrow road,
So thick beset with thorns and briars?
That is the path of righteousness,
Though after it but few enquires.

'And see ye not that braid, braid road   *braid*, broad
That lies across the lily leven?   *leven*, lawn
That is the path of wickedness,
Though some call it the road to Heaven.

'And see ye not that bonny road
That winds about the fernie brae?
That is the road to fair Elfland
Where thou and I this night maun gae.   *gae*, go

'But Thomas, ye maun hold your tongue,
Whatever you may hear or see.
If you speak word in Elflyn land
Ye'll ne'er get back to your ain countrie.'

O they rade on, and farther on,
And waded through rivers aboon   *aboon*, above
    the knee;
And they saw neither sun nor moon,
But they heard the roaring of the sea.

It was mirk, mirk night; there was   *mirk*, dark
    nae stern light,   *stern*, stars
And they waded thro' red blude to the knee.
For a' the blude that's shed on earth
Rins thro' the springs o that countrie.

Syne they came to a garden green,
And she pu'd an apple frae a tree –   *pu'd*, pulled
'Take this for thy wages, true Thomas;
It will give thee the tongue that can never lie.'

'My tongue's mine ain,' true Thomas said,
'A gudely gift ye wad gie to me!   *wad gie*, would give
I neither dought to buy nor sell   *dought*, could
At fair or tryst where I may be.   *tryst*, market

'I dought neither speak to prince nor peer,
Nor ask of grace from fair lady!' –
'Now hold thy peace!' the lady said,
'For as I say, so must it be.'

He has gotten a coat of the even cloth
And a pair of shoes of velvet green.
And till seven years were gane and past   *gane*, gone
True Thomas on earth was never seen.

THOMAS THE RHYMER, SON OF THE DEAD WOMAN

Margaret Fay Shaw

As I heard about it, there was once upon a time a tailor. In those days, as I myself remember, tailors used to go around the houses making clothes. And this tailor came to the house of a certain man who had three sons and one daughter; and the tailor was making suits for the three sons. And the girl told him she needed some clothes too and that she would be very glad if he would make them before he departed, after he had made the sons' clothes. The tailor replied that he couldn't wait to make clothes for her. 'Well,' she said, 'I want you to make clothes for me very much, and I'll pay you for them separately from the others.' 'What will you pay me?' said the tailor. 'Anything you like, as long as you make the clothes.' 'Will you give me leave to spend a night with you?' said the tailor. 'Make you the clothes,' said she, 'and you'll get that.'

So when the tailor had finished making the sons' clothes, he made the girl's too, and he did not ask her for any payment; he had only been joking with the girl anyway. He went away not long afterwards, and a little time later the girl fell ill and died, and that was all there was to it. But one night when the tailor was coming home, he met the girl after her death. He recognized the girl very well and he spoke to her, and she replied to him. 'Well,' she said, 'I never paid you what I promised for making the clothes.' 'Oh,' said the tailor, 'I never expected to get such payment, though I suggested it at the time.' 'Oh,' she said, 'what I promised must be done, or else I shall follow you everywhere.' So it was. 'Now,' she said, 'nine months after tonight you will come to my gravestone, and you will find a baby boy there, and he will be half above the earth and half under it, and', she said, 'you will call him Thomas. And you will find a red book beside him on the gravestone, and you are not to give it to him until he is fourteen years old.' They parted after this conversation and the tailor went home.

At the end of nine months the tailor went to the graveyard, as he had promised, and he found the baby boy as she had told him, and the red book. And the boy was lying half above the earth and half beneath it. The tailor took him home, and gave him to a wet nurse, and put away the book, later showing it to many learned men, of the kind who might be able to read it, but none of the learned men was able to make out a word of it. When the boy was fourteen years old, the tailor gave him the book, and there was not a word in it he couldn't read as if he had been studying it all his life.

Then his father started to teach him tailoring. He used to go around the houses with his father. One time, an old man of the village had died and the tailor was asked to make a shroud for the body. And he and his son went to the house where the dead man was, and when they went indoors they discovered that the people were making no great lamentation over the departed. But when Thomas came in after his father, he began to cry. And he was crying and lamenting all the time they were making the shroud, and his father was ashamed that Thomas was making such a lamentation for a man whom even the bereaved relations themselves were not lamenting very much. But that did not stop Thomas from his lamenting. Well, when they had finished, they went home, Thomas and his father.

Not long afterwards, another old man in the neighbourhood died, and Thomas and his father were asked to make his shroud too. They were sent for, and when they reached the house they found everyone lamenting the departed with much sorrow; but when Thomas came in he began to rejoice noisily and no one could keep up with his rejoicing and delight. And if his father was ashamed on the first occasion, he was utterly ashamed tonight, what with Thomas rejoicing in the middle of a house full of sorrowful lamentation. Then the tailor said to himself, 'There has to be some explanation for this strange behaviour, and before I get home tonight I'll find out what all this means.'

When they had finished, they walked home, and as they were walking the tailor said, 'Alas, alas, Thomas, how ashamed you made me tonight. What do you mean by laughing all the time, when everyone else was lamenting the man who had gone from them? Tell me what you mean before we go any further.' 'Oh,' said Thomas, 'you know that it takes very little to make me laugh. I was only thinking about all the things I had seen at the house.' 'No, no, that wasn't it at all, tell me what you meant, and don't prevaricate with me.'

Thomas didn't want to tell, and tried to distract his father, but his father wouldn't be distracted and insisted he explain himself. 'Well,' said Thomas, 'if you let me be until I'm sixteen years old I'll tell you then. And then I'll be with you and everyone I see in the world until the Day of Judgement. But if you make me tell you tonight you'll never see me again.' At this his father thought Thomas was still prevaricating, and he insisted on being told. 'Well, I'll tell you,' said Thomas, 'and it won't surprise you when you hear why I behaved as I did. The first house we visited to make the shroud for the dead man was without lamentation, because he wasn't worth it. But when I looked around the house,' he said, 'it was packed full of demons waiting to tear the dead man's soul to shreds; and I alone could see that. Do you wonder now why I was sorrowful and sad to see that? Whereas at the house we visited tonight,' he said, 'the people were very sad lamenting the death of a good man. And thicker than the crowd of demons in the first house was the crowd of angels waiting all around the second house for the dead man's soul. And was that not a great joy to me when I saw it? Didn't I have good cause to rejoice at the second house? And now,' said Thomas, 'I have to part from you, and you shall never see me again.'

And his father never saw Thomas again. Then it was that his father repented, and realized that Thomas had been telling him the truth all along.

GOLD-TREE AND
SILVER-TREE

Joseph Jacobs

Once upon a time there was a king who had a wife, whose name was Silver-tree, and a daughter, whose name was Gold-tree. On a certain day of the days, Gold-tree and Silver-tree went to a glen, where there was a well, and in it there was a trout.

Said Silver-tree, 'Troutie, bonny little fellow, am not I the most beautiful queen in the world?'

'Oh! indeed you are not.'

'Who then?'

'Why, Gold-tree, your daughter.'

Silver-tree went home, blind with rage. She lay down on the bed, and vowed she would never be well until she could get the heart and the liver of Gold-tree, her daughter, to eat.

At nightfall the King came home, and it was told him that Silver-tree, his wife, was very ill. He went where she was, and asked her what was wrong with her.

'Oh! only a thing which you may heal if you like.'

'Oh! indeed there is nothing at all which I could do for you that I would not do.'

'If I get the heart and the liver of Gold-tree, my daughter, to eat, I shall be well.'

Now it happened about this time that the son of a great king had come from abroad to ask Gold-tree for marrying. The King now agreed to this, and they went abroad.

The King then went and sent his lads to the hunting-hill for a he-goat, and he gave its heart and its liver to his wife to eat; and she rose well and healthy.

A year after this Silver-tree went to the glen, where there was the well in which there was the trout.

'Troutie, bonny little fellow,' said she, 'am not I the most beautiful queen in the world?'

'Oh! indeed you are not.'

'Who then?'

'Why, Gold-tree, your daughter.'

'Oh! well, it is long since she was living. It is a year since I ate her heart and liver.'

'Oh! indeed she is not dead. She is married to a great prince abroad.'

Silver-tree went home, and begged the King to put the long ship in order, and said, 'I am going to see my dear Gold-tree, for it is so long since I saw her.' The long ship was put in order, and they went away.

It was Silver-tree herself that was at the helm, and she steered the ship so well that they were not long at all before they arrived.

The Prince was out hunting on the hills. Gold-tree knew the long ship of her father coming.

'Oh!' said she to the servants, 'my mother is coming, and she will kill me.'

'She shall not kill you at all; we will lock you in a room where she cannot get near you.'

This was done; and when Silver-tree came ashore, she began to cry out: 'Come to meet your own mother, when she comes to see you.'

Gold-tree said that she could not, that she was locked in the room, and that she could not get out of it.

'Will you not put out,' said Silver-tree, 'your little finger through the keyhole, so that your own mother may give a kiss to it?'

She put out her little finger, and Silver-tree went and put a poisoned stab in it, and Gold-tree fell dead.

When the Prince came home, and found Gold-tree dead, he was in great sorrow, and when he saw how beautiful she was, he did not bury her at all, but he locked her in a room where nobody would get near her.

In the course of time he married again, and the whole house was under the management of this wife but one room, and he himself always kept the key of that room. On a certain day of the days he forgot to take the key with him, and the second wife got into the room. What did she see there but the most beautiful woman that she ever saw.

She began to turn and try to wake her, and she noticed the poisoned stab in her finger. She took the stab out, and Gold-tree rose alive, as beautiful as she was ever.

At the fall of night the Prince came home from the hunting-hill, looking very downcast.

'What gift,' said his wife, 'would you give me that I could make you laugh?'

'Oh! indeed, nothing could make me laugh, except if Gold-tree were to come alive again.'

'Well, you'll find her alive down there in the room.'

When the Prince saw Gold-tree alive he made great rejoicings, and he began to kiss her, and kiss her, and kiss her. Said the second wife, 'Since she is the first one you had it is better for you to stick to her, and I will go away.'

'Oh! indeed you shall not go away, but I shall have both of you.'

At the end of that year, Silver-tree went again to the glen, where there was the well, in which there was the trout.

'Troutie, bonny little fellow,' said she, 'am not I the most beautiful queen in the world?'

'Oh! indeed you are not.'

'Who then?'

'Why, Gold-tree, your daughter.'

'Oh! well, she is not alive. It is a year since I put the poisoned stab into her finger.'

'Oh! indeed she is not dead at all, at all.'

Silver-tree went home, and begged the King to put the long ship in order, for that she was going to see her dear Gold-tree, as it was so long since she saw her. The long ship was put in order, and they went away. It was Silver-tree herself that was at the helm, and she steered the ship so well that they were not long at all before they arrived.

The Prince was out hunting on the hills. Gold-tree knew her father's ship coming.

'Oh!' said she, 'my mother is coming again, and she will kill me.'

'Not at all,' said the second wife; 'we will go down to meet her.'

Silver-tree came ashore. 'Come down, Gold-tree, love,' said she, 'for your own mother has come to you with a precious drink.'

'It is a custom in this country,' said the second wife, 'that the person who offers a drink takes a draught out of it first.'

Silver-tree put her mouth to it, and the second wife went and struck it so that some of it went down her throat, and she was poisoned and fell dead. They had only to carry her home a dead corpse and bury her.

The Prince and his two wives were long alive after this, pleased and peaceful.

I left them there.

THE MAGIC
WALKING-STICK

John Buchan

When Bill came back for mid-term that autumn half he had before him a complex programme of entertainment. Thomas, the keeper, whom he revered more than anyone else in the world, was to take him in the afternoon to try for a duck in the big marsh called Alemoor. In the evening Hallowe'en would be celebrated in the nursery with his small brother Peter, and he would be permitted to sit up after dinner till ten o'clock. Next day, which was Sunday, would be devoted to wandering about with Peter, hearing from him all the appetizing home news, and pouring into his greedy ears the gossip of the foreign world of school. On Monday morning, after a walk with the dogs, he was to be driven up to London, lunch with Aunt Alice, go to a conjuring show, and then, after a noble tea, return to school in time for lock-up.

It seemed to Bill all that could be desired in the way of excitement. But he did not know just how exciting that mid-term was destined to be.

The first shadow of a cloud appeared after luncheon, when he had changed into his hunting gear, and Peter and the dogs were waiting at the gunroom door. Bill could not find his own proper stick. It was a long hazel staff, given him by the second stalker in a Scottish deer-forest the year before – a staff rather taller than Bill, of glossy hazel, with a shapely polished crook, and without a ferrule, like all stalking-sticks. He hunted for it high and low, but it could not be found. Without it in his hand Bill felt that an expedition lacked something vital, and he was not prepared to take instead one of his father's shooting-sticks, as Groves, the butler, recommended. Nor would he accept a knobbly cane proffered by Peter. Feeling a little aggrieved and imperfectly equipped, he rushed out to join Thomas. He would cut himself an ash-plant in the first hedge.

But as the two ambled down the lane which led to Alemoor, they came on an old man sitting under a hornbeam. He was a funny little wizened old man, in a shabby long green overcoat, which had once been black, and he wore on his head the oldest and tallest and greenest bowler hat that ever graced a human head. Thomas walked on as if he did not see him, and Gyp, the spaniel, and Shawn, the Irish setter, at the sight of him dropped their tails between their legs, and remembered an engagement a long way off. But Bill stopped, for he saw that the old man had a bundle under his arm, a bundle of ancient umbrellas and queer ragged sticks.

The old man smiled at him, and he had very bright eyes. He seemed to know what was wanted, for he at once took from his bundle a stick. You would not have said that it was the kind of stick Bill was looking for. It was short, and heavy, and made of some dark foreign wood, and instead of a crook it had a handle shaped like a crescent, cut out of some white substance which was neither bone nor ivory. Yet Bill, as soon as he saw it, felt that it was the one stick in the world for him.

'How much?' he asked.

'One penny,' said the old man, and his voice squeaked like a winter wind in a chimney.

Now a penny is not a common price for anything nowadays, but Bill happened to have one – a gift from Peter on his arrival that day, along with a brass cannon, five empty cartridges, a broken microscope, and a badly printed, brightly illustrated narrative called *Two Villains Foiled*. But a penny sounded too little, so Bill proffered one of his rare pounds.

'I said one penny,' said the old man rather snappily.

The small coin changed hands, and the little old wizened face seemed to light up with an elfish glee. ' 'Tis a fine stick, young sir,' he squeaked, 'a noble stick, when you gets used to the ways of it.'

Bill had to run to catch up Thomas, who was plodding along with the dogs, now returned from their engagement.

'That's a queer chap – the old stick-man, I mean,' he said.

'I ain't seen no old man, Maaster Bill,' said Thomas. 'What be 'ee talkin' about?'

'The fellow back there. I bought this stick off him.'

Thomas cast a puzzled glance at the stick. 'That be a craafty stick, Maaster Bill –' but he said no more, for Bill had shaken it playfully at the dogs. As soon as they saw it they set off to keep another engagement – this time, apparently, with a hare – and Thomas was yelling and whistling for ten minutes before he brought them to heel.

It was a soft grey afternoon, and Bill was stationed beside one of the deep dykes in the moor, well in cover of a thorn bush, while Thomas and the dogs went off on a long circuit to show themselves beyond the big mere, so that the duck might move in Bill's direction. It was rather cold, and very wet underfoot, for a lot of rain had fallen in the past week, and the mere, which was usually only a sedgy pond, had now grown to a great expanse of shallow flood-water. Bill began his vigil in high excitement. He drove his new stick into the ground, and used the handle as a seat, while he rested his gun in the orthodox way in the crook of his arm. It was a double-barrelled, sixteen bore, and Bill knew that he would be lucky if he got a duck with it; but a duck was to him a bird of mystery, true wild game, and he preferred the chance of one duck to the certainty of many rabbits.

The minutes passed, the grey afternoon sky darkened towards twilight, but no duck came. Bill saw a wedge of geese high up in the sky and longed to salute them; also he heard snipe, but could not locate them in the dim weather. Far away he thought he detected the purring noise which Thomas made to stir the duck, but no overhead beat of wings followed. Soon the mood of eager anticipation died away, and he grew bored and rather despondent. He scrambled up the bank of the dyke and strained his eyes over the moor between the bare boughs of the thorn. He thought he saw duck moving – yes, he was certain of it – they were coming from the direction of Thomas and the dogs. It was perfectly clear what was happening. There was far too much water on the moor, and the birds, instead of flying across the mere to the boundary slopes, were simply settling on the flood. From the misty grey water came the rumour of many wildfowl.

Bill came back to his wet stand grievously disappointed. He did not dare to leave it in case a flight did appear, but he had lost all hope. He tried to warm his feet by moving them up and down in the squelchy turf. His gun was now under his arm, and he was fiddling idly with the handle of the stick which was still embedded in earth. He made it revolve, and as it turned he said aloud: 'I wish I was in the middle of the big flood.'

Then a remarkable thing happened. Bill was not conscious of any movement, but suddenly his surroundings were completely changed. He had still his gun under his left arm and the stick in his right hand, but instead of standing on wet turf he was up to the waist in water . . . And all around him were duck – shovellers, pintail, mallard, teal, widgeon, pochard, tufted – and bigger things that might be geese – swimming or diving or just alighting from the air. In a second Bill realized that his wish had been granted. He was in the very middle of the flood water.

He got a right and left at mallards, missing with his first barrel. Then the birds rose in alarm, and he shoved in fresh cartridges and fired wildly into the air. His next two shots were at longer range, but he was certain that he had hit something. And then the duck vanished in the brume, and he was left alone with the grey waters running out to the dimness.

He lifted up his voice and shouted wildly for Thomas and the dogs, and looked about him to retrieve what he had shot. He had got two anyhow – a mallard drake and a young teal, and he collected them. Presently he heard whistling and splashing, and Gyp the spaniel appeared half swimming, half wading. Gyp picked up a second mallard, and Bill left it at that. He thought he knew roughly where the deeper mere lay so as to avoid it, and with his three duck he started for where he believed Thomas to be. The water was often up to his armpits and once he was soused over his head, and it was a very wet, breathless and excited boy that presently confronted the astounded keeper.

'Where in goodness ha' ye been, Maaster Bill? Them ducks was tigglin' out to the deep water and I was feared ye wouldn't get a shot. Three on 'em, no less! My word, ye 'ave poonished 'em.'

'I was in the deep water,' said Bill, but he explained no more,

for it had just occurred to him that he couldn't. It was a boy not
less puzzled than triumphant that returned to show his bag to
his family, and at dinner he was so abstracted that his mother
thought he was ill and sent him early to bed. Bill made no
complaint, for he wanted to be alone to think things out.

It was plain that a miracle had happened, and it must be
connected with the stick. He had wished himself in the middle of
the flood water – he remembered that clearly – and at the time
he had been doing something to the stick. What was it? It had
been stuck in the ground, and he had been playing with the
handle. Yes, that was it. He had been turning it round when he
uttered the wish. Bill's mind was better stored with fairy-tales
than with Latin and Greek, and he remembered many precedents.
The stick was in the rack in the hall, and he had half a mind to
slip downstairs and see if he could repeat the performance. But he
reflected that he might be observed, and that this was a business
demanding profound secrecy. So he resolutely composed himself
to sleep. He had been allowed for a treat to have his old bed in
the night-nursery, next to Peter, and he realized that he must be
up bright and early to frustrate that alert young inquirer.

He woke before dawn, and at once put on socks and shoes and
a dressing-gown, and tiptoed downstairs. He heard a housemaid
moving in the direction of the dining-room, and Groves opening
the library shutters, but the hall was deserted. He groped in the
rack and found the stick, struggled with the key of the garden
door, and emerged into the foggy winter half-light. It was very
cold, as he padded down the lawn to a shrubbery beside the pond,
and his shoes were soon soaked with hoar-frost. He shivered and
drew his dressing-gown around him, but he had decided what to
do. In this kind of weather he wished to be warm. He planted
his stick in the turf.

'I want to be on the beach in the Solomon Islands,' said Bill,
and three times twisted the handle.

In a second his eyes seemed to dazzle with excess of light and
something beat on his body like a blast from an open furnace . . .
He was standing on an expanse of blinding white sand at which
a lazy blue sea was licking. Behind him at a distance of perhaps

two hundred yards was a belt of high green forest, out of which stuck a tall crest of palms. A hot wind was blowing and tossing the tree-tops, but it only crisped the sea.

Bill gasped with joy to find his dream realized. He was in the far Pacific where he had always longed to be . . . But he was very hot, and could not endure the weight of winter pyjamas and winter dressing-gown. Also he longed to bathe in those inviting waters. So he shed everything and hopped gaily down to the tide's edge, leaving the stick still upright in the sand.

The sea was as delicious as it looked, but Bill, though a good swimmer, kept near the edge for fear of sharks. He wallowed and splashed, with the fresh salt smell which he loved in his nostrils. Minutes passed rapidly, and he was just on the point of striking out for a little reef, when he cast a glance towards the shore . . .

At the edge of the forest stood men – dark-skinned men, armed with spears.

Bill scrambled to his feet with a fluttering heart, and as he rose the men moved forward. He was, perhaps, fifty yards from the stick, which cast its long morning shadow on the sand, and they were two hundred yards on the farther side. At all costs he must get there first. He sprang out of the sea, and as he ran he saw to his horror that the men ran also – ran in great bounds – shouting and brandishing their spears.

Those fifty yards seemed miles, but Bill won the race. No time to put on his clothes. He seized his dressing-gown with one hand and the stick with the other, and as he twirled the handle a spear whizzed by his ear. 'I want to be home,' he gasped, and the next second he stood naked between the shrubbery and the pond, clutching his dressing-gown. The Solomon Islands had got his shoes and his pyjamas.

The cold of a November morning brought him quickly to his senses. He clothed his shivering body in his dressing-gown and ran by devious paths to the house. Happily the gunroom door was unlocked, and he was able to ascend by way of empty passages and back stairs to the nursery floor. He did not, how-ever, escape the eagle eye of Elsie, the nurse, who read the riot act over a boy who went out of doors imperfectly clad on such a morning. She prophesied pneumonia, and plumped him into a hot bath.

Bill applied his tongue to the back of his hand. Yes. It tasted salt, and the salt smell was still in his nose. It had not been a dream ... He hugged himself in the bath and made strange gurgling sounds of joy. Life had suddenly opened up for him in dazzling vistas of adventure.

His conduct in church that morning was exemplary, for while Peter at his side had his usual Sunday attack of St Vitus's Dance, Bill sat motionless as a mummy. On the way home his mother commented on it and observed that he seemed to have learned how to behave. But his thoughts during the service had not been devotional. The stick lay beside him on the floor, and for a moment he had a wild notion of twisting it during the sermon and disappearing for a few minutes to Kamchatka. Then prudence supervened. He must go very cautiously in this business, and court no questions. That afternoon he and Peter would seek a secluded spot and make experiments. He would take the stick back to school and hide it in his room – he had a qualm when he thought what a blunder it would be if a boy from the lower school appeared with it in public! For him no more hours of boredom. School would no longer be a place of exile, but a rapturous holiday. He would slip home now and then and see what was happening – he would go often to Glenmore – he would visit any spot in the globe which took his fancy. His imagination reeled at the prospect, and he cloaked his chortles of delight in a fervent Amen.

At luncheon it was decided that Peter and he should go for a walk together, and should join the others at a place called the Roman Camp. 'Let the boys have a chance of being alone,' his father had said. This exactly suited Bill's book, and as they left the dining-room he clutched his small brother. 'Shrimp,' he said in his ear, 'You're going to have the afternoon of your life.'

It was a mild, grey day, with the leafless woods and the brown ploughlands lit by a pale November sun. Peter, as he trotted beside him, jerked out breathless inquiries about what Bill proposed to do, and was told to wait and see.

Arriving at a clump of beeches which promised privacy, Bill first swore his brother to secrecy by the most awful oaths which he could imagine.

'Put your arm around my waist and hang on to my belt,' he told him. 'I'm going to take you to have a look at Glenmore.'

'Don't be silly,' said Peter. 'That only happens in summer, and we haven't packed yet.'

'Shut up and hold tight,' said Bill as he twirled the stick and spoke the necessary words . . .

The boys were looking not at the smooth boles of beeches, but at a little coppice of rowans and birches above the narrow glen of the hill burn. It was Glenmore in very truth. There was the strip of mossy lawn, the whitewashed gable end of the lodge; there to the left beside the walled garden was the smoking chimney of the keeper's cottage; there beyond the trees was the long lift of brown moorland and the blue top of Stob Ghabhar. To the boys Glenmore was the true home of the soul, but they had seen it only in the glory of late summer and early autumn. In its winter dress it seemed for a moment strange. Then the sight of an old collie waddling across the lawn gave the connecting link.

'There's Wattie,' Peter gasped, and lifted up his voice in an excited summons. His brother promptly made to throttle him.

'Don't be an ass, Shrimp,' he said fiercely. 'This is a secret, you fat-head. This is magic. Nobody must know we are here. Come on and explore.'

For an hour – it must have been an hour, Bill calculated afterwards, but it seemed like ten minutes – the two visited their favourite haunts. They found the robbers' cave in the glen where a raven nested, and the pool where Bill had caught his first pound trout, and the stretch in the river where their father that year had had the thirty-pound salmon. There were no blaeberries or crowberries in the woods, but there were many woodcock, and Bill had a shot with his catapult at a wicked old blackcock on a peat-stack. Also they waylaid Wattie, the collie, and induced him to make a third in the party. All their motions were as stealthy as an Indian's, and the climax of the adventure was reached when they climbed the garden wall and looked in at the window of the keeper's cottage.

Tea was laid before a bright peat fire in the parlour, so Mrs Macrae must be expecting company. It looked a very good tea, for there were scones and pancakes, and shortbread and currant-loaf and heather honey. Both boys felt suddenly famished at the sight.

'Mrs Macrae always gives me a scone and honey,' Peter bleated. 'I'm hungry. I want one.'

So did Bill. His soul longed for food, but he kept hold of his prudence.

'We daren't show ourselves,' he whispered. 'But, perhaps, we might pinch a scone. It wouldn't be stealing, for if Mrs Macrae saw us she would say "Come awa in, laddies, and get a jeely piece." I'll give you a back, Shrimp, and in you get.'

The window was open, and Peter was hoisted through, falling with a bang on a patchwork rug. But he never reached the table, for at that moment the parlour door opened and someone entered. After that things happened fast. Peter, urged by Bill's anguished whisper, turned back to the window, and was hauled through by the scruff of the neck. A woman's voice was heard crying, 'Mercy on us, it's the bairns,' as the culprits darted to the shelter of the gooseberry bushes.

Bill realized that there was no safety in the garden, so he dragged Peter over the wall by the way they had come, thereby seriously damaging a pear tree. But they had been observed, and as they scrambled out of a rose-bed, they heard cries and saw Mrs Macrae appearing around the end of the wall, having come through the stable yard. Also a figure, which looked like Angus, the river gillie, was running from the same direction.

There was nothing for it but to go. Bill seized Peter with one hand and the stick with the other, and spoke the words, with Angus not six yards away ... As he looked once more at the familiar beech boles, his ears were still full of the cries of an excited woman and the frenzied howling of Wattie, the dog.

The two boys, very warm and flustered and rather scratched about the hands and legs, confronted their father and mother and their sister, Barbara, who was sixteen and very proud.

'Hullo, hullo,' they heard their father say. 'I thought you'd be hiding somewhere hereabouts. You young rascals know how to take cover, for you seemed to spring out of the ground. You look as if you'd been playing football. Better walk home with us and cool down ... Bless my soul, Peter, what's that you've got? It's bog myrtle! Where on earth did you find it? I've never seen it before in Oxfordshire.'

Then Barbara raised a ladylike voice. 'Oh, Mummy, look at the mess they've made of themselves. They've been among the brambles, for Peter has two holes in his socks. Just look at Bill's hands!' And she wrinkled her finical nose, and sniffed.

Bill kept a diplomatic silence, and Peter, usually garrulous, did the same, for his small wrist was in his brother's savage clutch.

That night, before Peter went to bed, he was compelled once more to swear solemn oaths, and Bill was so abstracted that his mother thought that he was sickening for some fell disease. He lay long awake, planning out the best way to use his marvellous new possession. His thoughts were still on the subject next morning, and to his family's amazement he made no protest when, to suit his mother's convenience, it was decided to start for London soon after breakfast, and the walk with the dogs was cancelled. He departed in high spirits, most unlike his usual leave-takings, and his last words to Peter were fierce exhortations to secrecy.

All the way to London he was in a happy dream, and at luncheon he was so urbane that Aunt Alice, who had strong and unorthodox views about education, announced that in Bill's case, at any rate, the public school system seemed to answer, and gave him double her customary tip.

Then came the conjuring show at the Grafton Hall. Bill in the past had had an inordinate appetite for such entertainments, and even in his new ecstasy he looked forward to this one. But at the door of the hall he had a shock. Hitherto he had kept close to his stick, but it was now necessary to give it up and receive a metal check for it. To his mother's surprise he protested hotly. 'It won't do any harm,' he pleaded. 'It will stay beside me under the seat.' But the rule was inexorable and he had to surrender it. 'Don't be afraid, darling,' his mother told him. 'That funny new stick of yours won't be lost. The check is a receipt for it, and they are very careful.'

The show was not up to his expectations. What were all these disappearing donkeys and vanishing ladies compared to the performances he had lately staged? Bill was puffed up with a great pride. With the help of his stick he could make rings around this trumpery cleverness. He was the true magician ... He wished that the thing would end that he might feel the precious stick again in his hand.

At the counter there was no sign of the man who had given him the check. Instead there was a youth who seemed to be new to the business, and who was very slow in returning the sticks and umbrellas. When it came to Bill's turn he was extra slow, and presently announced that he could find no Number 229.

Bill's mother, seeing his distress, intervened, and sent the wretched youth to look again, while other people were kept waiting, but he came back with the same story. There was no duplicate Number 229, or any article to correspond to the check. After that he had to be allowed to attend to the others, and Bill, almost in tears, waited hysterically until the crowd had gone. Then there was a thorough search, and Bill and his mother were allowed to go behind the counter. But no Number 229 could be found, and there were no sticks left, only three umbrellas.

Bill was now patently in tears.

'Never mind, darling,' his mother said, 'we must be off now, or you will be late for lock-up. I promise that your father will come here tomorrow and clear up the whole business. Never fear – the stick will be found.'

But it is still lost.

When Bill's father went there next day, and cross-examined the wretched youth – for he had once been a barrister – he extracted a curious story. If the walking-stick was lost, so also was the keeper of the walking-sticks, for the youth was only an assistant. The keeper – his name was Jukes and he lived in Hammersmith – had not been seen since yesterday afternoon during the performance, and Mrs Jukes had come round and made a scene last night, and that morning the police had been informed. Mr Jukes, it appeared, was not a very pleasant character, and he had had too much beer at luncheon. When the audience had all gone in, he had been telling his assistant how fed up he was. The youth's testimony ran as follows: 'Mr Jukes, 'e was wavin' his arm something chronic and carryin' on about 'ow this was no billet for a man like 'im. He picks up a stick, and I thought he was goin' to 'it me. "Percy, me lad," says 'e, "I'm fed up – fed up to the back teeth." He starts twisting the stick, and says 'e, "I wish to 'eaven I was out of 'ere." After that I must 'ave come over faint, for when I looks again, 'e 'ad 'opped it.'

Mr Jukes' case is still a puzzle to Mrs Jukes and the police, but Bill understands only too clearly what happened. Mr Jukes and the stick have gone 'out of 'ere', and where that may be neither Bill nor I can guess.

But Bill lives in hope, and he wants me to broadcast this story in case the stick may have come back to earth. So let every boy and girl keep a sharp eye on shops where sticks are sold. The magic walking-stick is not quite four feet long, and about one inch and a quarter thick. It is made of a heavy dark-red wood, rather like the West Indian purple-heart. Its handle is in the shape of a crescent with the horns uppermost, made of some white substance which is neither bone nor ivory. If anyone sees such a stick, then Bill will give all his worldly wealth for news of it.

Failing that, he would like information about the man who sold it to him. He is very old, small and wizened, but his eyes are the brightest you ever saw in a human head. He wears a shabby, greeny-black overcoat which reaches down to his heels, and a tall, greeny-black bowler hat. It is possible that the stick may have returned to him. So if you meet anyone like him, look sharply at his bundle, and if it is there and he is willing to sell, *buy it – buy it – buy it*, or you will regret it all your days. For this purpose it is wise always to have a penny in your pocket, for he won't take anything else.

PART TWO

TALL TALES, GIANTS,
MONSTERS

THE TWO SHEPHERDS

John Francis Campbell

There were living in the country between Lochaber and Badenoch two shepherds who were neighbours to each other, and the one would often visit the other. One lived on the east side of the River Spean, and the other lived on the west. One evening, the one from the west side came to visit the one on the east side. He stayed till it was pretty late, and then he wished to go home.

'It's time I was going home,' said he.

'It's far too late, you can just stay here tonight,' said the other.

'I can't stay; the only bother is crossing the river, and once I'm over that, I'll be fine,' said the first man.

The host had a big, strong son, who said, 'If you insist on going home, I'll go with you, and see you safe over the river. But my father's right – you'd be better staying here for what's left of the night.'

'No, I must get back.'

'In that case, I'll go with you,' said the lad, who called his dog to accompany them.

When he had seen their visitor safe across the river, he set out to wade back over the water, carrying his boots and stockings in one hand. Suddenly the dog, which had been swimming alongside him quite happily, made a great splashing leap into the arms of the shepherd lad. Not wanting to get soaked, he threw her off, scolding her for wetting him. Thus they came back to their own side of the river. Then the shepherd lad noticed that he had somehow mislaid his hat. 'What a nuisance,' he said to himself. 'Did I lose it in the river when the dog jumped up, or did I leave it on the far side? I can't go home without my good hat.' So, for the third time that night, he crossed the river and soon saw, on the far bank, a big man seated right where he had said good night to his father's friend, and holding his bonnet in his hand. Now, as we said, the shepherd lad was a big, brawny, muscular boy, and fearlessly he went straight up to the big man. Catching hold of the bonnet, he took it from him.

'What business have you with that?' the lad asked. 'It belongs to me.' And putting the hat firmly on his head, he turned and made to cross the river for the fourth time that night. But the big man came after him, and put his arm under the arm of the shepherd lad, and began to drag him down into one of the deep pools of the river. The shepherd lad defended himself, and fought back bravely, wondering who on earth this silent stranger could be, and why he should wish to attack him. He felt himself losing his footing, and stretched his arm up to grip the branch of an oak tree which hung out over the water. But the big man was striving hard to pull the lad down into the water, and the shepherd's son could feel the tree start to give way and creak over towards the water. He panicked just a little then, as he heard the roots loosening and giving way on the riverbank. Just when he felt the last root give way, and he thought that all was lost, he heard the cocks crow in his father's farmyard. Then the shepherd lad realized that it was almost daybreak, for he saw a gleam of yellowish light in the eastern sky.

The big man had also heard the cocks crowing, and said to the lad, 'You've stood your ground well, son, and you're a bonny fechter. That's just as well, and you needed to defend yourself – or your bonnet would have cost you dear!' Then the big man left the scene, and has never been seen again from that day to this.

fechter, fighter

THE SPRIGHTLY TAILOR

Joseph Jacobs

A sprightly tailor was employed by the great Macdonald, in his castle at Saddell in Kintyre, in order to make the laird a pair of trews, as used in olden time. And trews being the vest and breeches united in one piece, and ornamented with fringes, were very comfortable, and suitable to be worn in walking or dancing. And Macdonald had said to the tailor as a sort of a dare, that if he would make the trews by night in the church, he would get a handsome reward. For it was thought that the old ruined church was haunted, and that fearsome things were to be seen there at night.

The tailor was well aware of this; but he was a sprightly man, and when the laird dared him to make the trews by night in the church, the tailor was not to be daunted, but took it in hand to gain the prize. So, when night came, away he went up the glen, about half a mile's distance from the castle, till he came to the old church. Then he chose him a nice gravestone for a seat and he lighted his candle, and put on his thimble, and set to work at the trews; playing his needle nimbly, and thinking about the prize that the laird would have to give him.

For some time he got on pretty well, until he felt the floor all of a tremble under his feet; and looking about him, but keeping his fingers at work, he saw the appearance of a massive human head rising up through the stone pavement of the church. And when the head had risen above the surface, there came from it a great, great voice. And the voice said: 'Do you see this great head of mine?'

'I see that, but I'll sew this!' replied the sprightly tailor; and he kept stitching away at the trews.

Then the head rose higher up through the pavement, until its neck appeared. And when its neck was shown, the thundering voice came again and said: 'Do you see this great neck of mine?'

'I see that, but I'll sew this!' said the sprightly tailor; and he kept stitching away at his trews.

Then the head and neck rose higher still, until the great shoulders and chest were shown above the ground. And again the mighty voice thundered: 'Do you see this great chest of mine?'

And again the sprightly tailor replied: 'I see that, but I'll sew this!' and he kept stitching away at his trews.

And still the monster kept rising through the pavement, until it shook a great pair of arms in the tailor's face, and said: 'Do you see these great arms of mine?'

'I see those, but I'll sew this!' answered the tailor; and he kept stitching hard at his trews, for he knew that he had no time to lose.

The sprightly tailor was doing the long stitches, when he saw the monster gradually rising and rising through the floor, until it lifted out a great leg, and stamping with it upon the pavement, said in a roaring voice: 'Do you see this great leg of mine?'

'Aye, aye: I see that, but I'll sew this!' cried the tailor; and his fingers flew with the needle, and he made such long stitches, that he was just coming to the end of the trews, when the monster was taking up its other leg. But before it could pull it out of the pavement, the sprightly tailor had finished his task; and, blowing out his candle, and springing from off his gravestone, he buckled up his coat, and ran out of the church with the trews under his arm. Then the fearsome thing gave a loud roar, and stamped with both his feet upon the pavement, and out of the church he went thundering after the sprightly tailor.

Down the glen they ran, faster than the stream when the flood rides it; but the tailor had got the start and a nimble pair of legs, and he did not choose to lose the laird's reward. And though the thing roared to him to stop, the sprightly tailor was not the man to be restrained by a monster if he could help it. So he held his trews tight, and let no darkness grow under his feet, until he had reached Saddell Castle. He had no sooner got inside the gate, and shut it, than the monster came up to it; and, enraged at losing his prize, struck the wall above the gate, and left there the mark of his five great fingers. You may see them plainly to this day, if you'll only peer close enough.

But the sprightly tailor gained his reward: for Macdonald was impressed by his courage and paid him handsomely for the trews, and never discovered that a few of the stitches were somewhat long.

THE LONELY GIANT

Alasdair MacLean

There was a giant once who was lonely. Most giants are, of
course, or would be if they stopped to think about it. A giant
needs a great deal of land to live off, which means that giants
have to space themselves out very thinly, something like one to
every shire. So the only time they see one another is on the rare
occasions when two neighbouring giants happen to arrive at the
borders of their territories at the same time. When that takes
place they usually play catch for a time with a boulder or have a
game of hide-and-seek among the mountains. Then they go their
separate ways. You can hear them shouting goodbye for miles.

They don't think about this loneliness, however, because thinking isn't something they go in for very much. Mostly they just
get on with the business of being giants, which takes up all their
time and which is very hard work because it is laid down in the
Rule Book for Giants that, when they aren't actually eating or
sleeping, they have to stamp around the countryside bellowing
at the tops of their voices and looking very fierce. Looking fierce
is hard work in itself as you'll find out if you try it for half an
hour. You keep forgetting that you're supposed to have a scowl
on your face and you find yourself smiling at something. Then
you have to start all over again.

Being kept so busy means that giants don't have much time
for thinking. When a giant does manage to get a few minutes to
himself he generally feels so tired that he just drops off to sleep.
He sits down first of all with his back against the nearest hill.
Then he opens his huge mouth and gives a huge yawn. Then he
spits out all the birds that have got sucked into his mouth while
the yawn was going on. Then off he goes to dream-land.

But the giant who was lonely was different. He had long since lost his rule book and had never bothered to get it replaced. He didn't go around stamping and roaring because he couldn't see much point in it. It only made your feet sore and gave you a headache. Besides that, it frightened people away and he didn't want to frighten people away. He wanted to be friendly.

What made him especially different from other giants, though, was that he was always thinking, and what he was always thinking about was how much alone he was. It was true that he did have one or two friends among the creatures. There was Goldentop, the eagle, for example. But the creatures as a rule weren't greatly interested in people big or little, considering them a very limited species, incapable of running at much more than a trot, or swimming farther than a few miles, or flying any higher than five or six feet and staying up any longer than one or two seconds, or burrowing underground, or carrying their houses on their backs or anything really worthwhile like that.

'As for people,' said Goldentop once to the lonely giant – whose name, by the way, was Angus Macaskill – 'all that they are good for, whether they are big or little and with very few exceptions, is making a noise or making places dirty or breaking things. And all that pink naked skin on them without a single feather! Ugh!' So all that Angus got from Goldentop, usually, was a dip of the wings in passing.

It was true, also, that Angus did have one or two friends among the ordinary-sized folk. There was Morag Matheson, for instance, the shoemaker's daughter. He sometimes had quite good conversations with her. But in order for them to talk either Angus had to lie down to get his ear to the level of her mouth, which usually struck him as such a comical proceeding that he burst into fits of laughter, or he had to pick her up and hold her to his ear, which usually struck her as such a comical proceeding that she burst into fits of laughter.

It is difficult, as you will know from your own experience, to have a sensible talk with someone who giggles all the time. You can hear properly only one or two words in every sentence and you have to guess at the rest. If you guess wrongly, of course, it produces even more laughter. Morag had once told Angus that her mother had been ordered by the doctor to eat two legs for breakfast every day. He was quite horrified until he discovered that she had really said 'eggs'.

One day Angus's loneliness became more than he could bear and he realized that he would have to do something about it. He thought that the wisest thing he could do would be to ask for advice and he decided to ask Morag first of all. He went along to her father's house and saw her in the distance, as he approached, sitting at the front door, spinning and singing, the sound and the thread flowing out with equal sweetness.

I wish I were not a giant, thought Angus, *then I could ask Morag to marry me. And if she said 'Yes' I would not be lonely any more.*

But he *was* a giant, therefore he put that thought away from him, as a peasant lad might put away a thought of the king's daughter. Instead, he picked Morag up so quickly that she was too much out of breath to start laughing.

'Morag,' he said, 'listen to me carefully because I need your advice. And don't laugh, please, because it's a very serious matter. The trouble is that I am lonely. What can I do about it? Is there any cure?'

'I wish you weren't a giant,' Morag answered. 'Or I wish that I were. I would soon cure your loneliness.'

'How?' asked Angus.

'Never mind,' replied Morag. She thought long and hard and sadly. 'The only cure for you, Angus,' she said at last, 'is to get married. You must find yourself a giantess somewhere.'

'Where?' asked Angus.

'Well, now, that I don't know,' Morag answered. 'Most of the people I have met in my life have been very small in one way or another. You'd better ask Goldentop the eagle. He's always boasting that he knows every mountain in the whole Land of Lorne.'

'Giants aren't mountains,' Angus pointed out.

'No,' agreed Morag. 'Giants are lighter coloured and more gentle. At least, some of them are.' She looked at the ground, where it dizzied away into the distance. 'But there are certain resemblances just the same.'

Angus in his turn looked down at the ground. Somewhere down there were daisies and primroses and violets. 'Yes,' he sighed. 'I know what you mean.' He put Morag down very gently and set off in search of Goldentop.

The eagle was sat on a favourite perch. One of his eyes was watching the approach of Angus and it was more or less blank. The other was fixed on some hills that stuck up above the horizon and it was a calculating eye, the sort of eye that added up figures and got one less every time.

'What are you watching with that left eye?' asked Angus.

'A flock of sheep leaving Hugh Henderson's sheep-fold in the village of Carraig in the parish of Cray,' answered Goldentop.

'You have good eyesight,' said Angus.

'I have an empty belly,' said the eagle. 'It clears the vision of trivialities.'

'Has this vision of yours ever rested on a giantess?' queried Angus. 'An unattached one, I mean.'

'Island of Alva,' replied Goldentop promptly. 'Walk north along the coast until you come to the Blue Bay. Then swim due west.'

'Ah, but are you sure she's unattached?' insisted Angus. 'There might have been a giant there when you weren't looking.'

'Somehow I do not think so,' remarked the eagle thoughtfully.

'Anyway, I can't go to this island,' Angus told him, 'even if I could swim that far. My mother told me on her deathbed never to go into the salt water.'

'Then you must balance the commands of the dead against the requirements of the living,' said Goldentop. 'It is an old dilemma. But not for eagles.' He left the perch and slid upwards, heading in the direction of the sheep.

Angus didn't know what to do. He decided that while he was making up his mind he might as well walk to the Blue Bay. He had never been there and it sounded like a pleasant spot. Besides, he knew that there is nothing like a good long walk for getting rid of sadness. It flows out of your feet into the ground, which of course is where it comes from in the first place, only it enters through your bottom while you are sitting down.

By the time he reached the Blue Bay he was feeling a lot better.

He knew it was the right place because the surrounding hills were blue and the sea was blue and the sky was blue. Also there was a small stunted signpost near by, growing crookedly between two rocks, and on it there said in blue letters, *This is the Blue Bay*.

The tide was out when he got there. Indeed it was so far out that it might well need the help of a signpost itself to get back. It had left behind it, as a pledge perhaps, a mile or more of ribbed sand and stranded right in the middle of this sand there was a whale. If you think it was anything other than a blue whale you have not been following my story as closely as you should.

Angus approached the whale circumspectly, which means that he stopped about fifty feet away. He could see that it had worn a hollow in the sand by threshing around. When it saw him it shouted 'Help!' in a tiny squeaky voice, whales having very small throats.

'What seems to be the trouble, Whale?' inquired Angus.

'The trouble, Giant,' replied the whale, 'is that I fell asleep on a sandbank in the middle of the bay. It was only a baby sandbank then but by the time I woke it had grown up. I am stranded. Unless I can get back to the water soon this hot white sun will shrivel my tender skin, which is used only to the coolness and moistness and greenness of the deep sea. I shall die. But what can I do? I cannot swim over the sand and I have neither legs to walk with nor wings to fly.'

It was plain that he spoke the truth, for already on his blue back two or three blisters were beginning to form.

'It seems to me,' remarked Angus, 'that you creatures aren't quite as superior as Goldentop is always saying you are. I may be only a giant but at least I would never get stuck in the middle of a flat piece of land. I have legs.'

'Goldentop is a snob,' said the whale. 'It comes of continually looking down on the rest of the world. And as for legs, unless they are put to the service of the community they remain a private luxury.'

'You are a heavy weight,' Angus told him. 'Even for me. But I think that with the help of my legs – and arms – I might just be able to pull you as far as the water's edge.'

He caught hold of the whale's tail and set to work. After a long hard struggle he managed to get it into the shallows, and with a flick of its powerful body it did the rest. It was so happy to be back where it belonged that it turned three underwater cart-wheels in succession.

'Look at me, Giant!' it shouted when it re-emerged. 'Where are your legs now? Can you swim like this?'

'I'm afraid I'm not very much of a swimmer,' replied Angus. 'If I were I might swim across to the Island of Alva, for on it there lives a giantess.'

'I know,' said the whale.

'Have you seen her?' Angus asked.

'I have seen her,' the whale agreed. 'And heard her too.'

'I am going to ask her to marry me,' Angus informed him.

'Have *you* seen her?' inquired the whale.

'No,' replied Angus. 'Why do you ask?'

'Never mind,' the whale answered. 'But I owe my life to you and if you truly wish to go there I will help you. Wade into the water and catch hold of my tail.'

'It's very kind of you,' Angus told him. 'But there's one more snag. My mother told me just before she died never to go into the sea.'

'And died, I suppose,' asked the whale, 'before she had time to say why?' Angus nodded. 'That's the trouble with Death,' the whale continued. 'He always comes when you're in the middle of something, even if it's only drawing breath. Well, it's up to you whether you want to take a chance or not. I'll give you five minutes to make up your mind.'

The whale set off on a slow tour round the bay, or what was left of it. Angus pondered. What was the mysterious salt-water fate that lay in store for giants? Was it some monster of the deep? Something big enough to swallow even him? And whatever the fate was could it be any worse than loneliness?

The sea looked lovely. Surely nothing too terrible could happen to him if he ventured in? There was the Giantess, too, to think about, on her island just below the horizon. Very likely she was waiting impatiently for just such a one as he was. He decided to take the risk.

'I'm going to the island!' he shouted to the whale. 'I'm ready now!'

They began their voyage, with Angus grasping the tail of his new friend and being towed through the water. Their progress, to be sure, was slow, for a giant is a considerable burden even for a whale. But the sun shone, the sea remained peaceful, no monsters appeared and one by one the miles slid past beneath them. Gradually they began to go a little faster.

Angus noticed this. 'You're getting used to me!' he called.

'I expect that's it,' the whale agreed.

On they went a mile or two farther and still the sea unrolled quietly before them like a great blue carpet. Their speed increased a little more.

Angus noticed this as well. 'Wonderful!' he shouted. 'You're going faster than ever!'

'I'm not sure that I am,' the whale said. 'There's something very strange going on. I don't understand it at all.' He sounded worried.

On they went again. Faster and still faster. Angus noticed that his hands didn't grasp the whale's tail as easily as they had when he started. 'That's because of the speed,' he told himself. But almost as soon as he said it he knew it wasn't true. His mother's warning sounded again in his ears. 'Don't go into the salt water, Angus!' And suddenly he realized what she had meant. He was slowly shrinking!

What could he do? He called out once more to his friend the whale, telling it what was happening.

'Yes, I thought you must be getting smaller,' the whale admitted. 'But I was afraid to say anything in case you dropped off through shock.'

'Should we turn back?' asked Angus.

'We're there,' replied the whale. Sure enough, the island loomed ahead, a large well-wooded one with the tallest tower that Angus had ever seen soaring above the tree-tops.

'That'll be the Giantess's tower, I suppose,' thought Angus. The island grew nearer and nearer and presently a great booming voice thundered out across the water.

'I am a giant, a female giant,
by nature bold and strong.
My eyes are quick, my club is thick,
my arms are extra long.

My voice is thunderously large,
a wondrous voice to hear,
and when I shout and stamp about,
the echoes take a year.

My towering height is something else
of which I'm very proud.
I scrape the sky when I pass by
and drink from every cloud.

A tailor who was measuring me
and swore he had the knack,
set off in haste to chalk my waist
and hasn't yet come back.

My future husband, I insist,
must be more huge than me,
or with one bound I'll swing him around
and hurl him out to sea.'

'Grammar never was her strong point,' said the whale, 'but she sounds in excellent form today.'

Angus had listened in trepidation to the great voice and to the awesome catalogue of attributes it had listed. He had tried to give himself courage by allowing ten per cent off the list for the usual giant's exaggeration. But even if she were only half of what she claimed, the Giantess must be a formidable woman indeed. Somehow it was difficult to imagine her darning socks. And apart from that there was the worrying discovery he had made in the sea just now. How much had he shrunk?

The whale glided into the shallow water of the creek. Angus released his hold, waded ashore and turned to face his friend. 'How much have I lost?' he inquired anxiously.

'A lot,' replied the whale, surveying him. 'An awful lot. You've dwindled by about half.'

The voice Angus had heard on approaching the island rolled out again, sounding louder and nearer all the time. He found himself thinking with longing of his home territory and of the clear eyes of Goldentop and the fringed ones of Morag Matheson.

'You know, I think perhaps I'll come back some other time,' he said to the whale. 'I don't feel in the right frame of mind for courting.'

'It's too late to back out now,' the whale told him. 'Here she comes!' He nodded with his head in the direction of Angus's right shoulder. 'Good luck!' he added and with a flick of his tail he was gone. Angus turned. The 'tower' he had seen above the tree-tops was advancing down the beach towards him. It was the Giantess!

'Good afternoon,' said Angus politely, the occasion obviously being one that called for politeness. The Giantess said nothing but she stooped suddenly and her huge hand shot out. Before he realized what she was about she had grasped him by the waist and swung him up to face level.

'Angus Macaskill is my name,' said Angus hurriedly. 'I'm a giant. At least, I was this morning. I'm from the mainland. I have quite a good little territory over there. Lots of butter and eggs and vegetables and that sort of thing. More than enough for two. I'm looking for a wife, I think. Will you marry me?'

The Giantess listened to this recital in complete silence. When it was finished she spoke just one word. 'Cheek!' she said. The hand that grasped Angus drew back quickly and then shot forward. He found himself flying out over the sea in a huge tumbling curve that arched slowly down towards the waves.

Goodbye, world! he thought. *Goodbye!* And splash! He hit the water. But before he could sink, there beside him was the whale.

'You landed just about where I thought you would,' he said to Angus. 'Hang on and I'll have you back at the Blue Bay in no time.'

Angus spat out a mouthful of salt water. 'If I shrink as much on the way back as I did when I came here,' he said, 'there'll be nothing left of me.'

'I'll go extra specially fast,' the whale promised. And so he did. He tore through the water at such a rate that Angus had to hold on with all his strength. Even so, he felt himself shrinking so much smaller that his clothes began to fall off. He had to clutch them desperately.

When they landed in the Blue Bay they went through the same routine as at the island. 'How much have I lost this time?' Angus asked, after he had waded ashore.

The whale looked him over carefully. 'Well, not as much as last time,' he answered. 'But still quite a lot. You're about ordinary-sized now. I shouldn't try it again.'

'Don't worry,' Angus told him. 'It's dry land for me from now on. Dry land and a bit more reverence for the wisdom of mothers. Thanks for rescuing me.'

'At least you can say one thing,' said the whale.

'What's that?' asked Angus.

'You're not the first man to shrink from courtship,' the whale answered. He dived under the water and vanished.

Angus made his way home as quickly as he could and the first person he went to see was Morag. He found her spinning and singing as before but more slowly and sadly than she used to.

'It's me!' he shouted when he reached her. 'I'm back!'

'Angus?' cried Morag. 'I recognize your voice but where are you?' She was so busy craning her neck skyward that she failed to notice him standing beside her.

'I'm down here,' he told her. 'The salt water shrank me. I'm just about your size now.'

'So you are,' she agreed. Her eyes dropped down from the clouds, rested on him briefly and kept on dropping till her gaze was fixed on the ground.

'Will you marry me, Morag?' he asked.

'Yes, I will,' she replied. So they got married and lived as happily as two people in love might reasonably expect to live. They had three ordinary-sized children, two girls and a boy, none of whom could ever be persuaded to go near the sea. Angus stopped being lonely.

THE MAN IN THE BOAT

Betsy Whyte

This story is aboot a laird awa in the Heilands ... and he had the Black Art ... but every year he used to gie a big ceilidh for aa the workers on his estate, an aa the fairm folk an aa the fairm hands, an he used tae had the ceilidh in a big barn. There wis a fire in this barn, and they'd put on a big pot of sowens. (Ye ken whit sowens are? No? Well, Scotland, it's always been a very poor country, and no that very long ago, jist aboot a hundred years ago, they used to soak ... the husks o the grain ... until they were soor, and then they strained it, and boiled up the liquid an this made a sort of porridge, and a lot o them had to exist on that.) So this big pot o sowens wis boilin away anywey, and everybody wis doin their thing: ye hed tae

> Tell a story,
> Sing a sang,
> Show yir bum
> Or oot ye gang!

They hed other things as well as singin an tellin stories an that: they hed sort of games, they'd games of strength an guesses an that sort o thing, an one o the things wis to see who could tell the biggest lie. So everybody wis gaun their roond an gaun their

laird, landowner.   *awa*, away.
Black Art, magic, the devil's work. The devil was often referred to as 'the black man'.
ceilidh, Gaelic name for a social gathering, often involving dance, music, songs, storytelling and other entertainment.
sowens, a type of porridge.   *soor*, sour.

roond, but every time it cam roond tae this cattleman he would aye say, 'Ye ken fine A cannae dae nothing, ye shouldnae ask me! Ye ken A cannae dae it.'

So this laird says, 'Look, ye can surely tell a lie.'

He says, 'No, A cannae.' Sandy wis a bit simple, ye ken, and he wisnae very good at nothin but lookin efter the coos.

So the laird says, 'Sandy, look, try an tell a story, or tell us a lie o some kind.'

He says, 'A cannae, A dinnae ken how tae.'

'Well,' the laird says, 'if ye dinnae ken how tae ye're no gaunnae be here. Awa ye go an mak yirsel useful some other place.'

He says, 'What am A gaunnae dae?'

An the laird says, 'A'll tell ye what tae dae. Awa ye go doon tae the water an clean ma boat, because A'll be usin it shortly. Awa ye go.' So Sandy's away, tramp, tramp, tramp, doon through the gutters tae this river, this big river. And he scraped aa the moss an dirt aff the boat, scrapin it oot, and there wis a baler lyin in the boat, an he wis balin oot the water, an balin oot the water, an he steps inside the boat so that he could finish balin it oot, ye see?

But didn't this boat take off wi him, an there's no wey he could stop it! An before he could get time to think, even, they're away in the middle o the water, an he couldnae swim. So he says, 'Ach, A'll jist sit an let it go wherever it wants tae go.' So he jist sat like this lookin up at the birds an things.

But he glanced doon again, an there he saw the loveliest wee green satin slippers; pure silk stockins; taffeta dress. He says, 'Whit's this? Whit's this?' An he felt his sel ower – oh! pappies an everything! 'Oh!' he says. 'Whit's happenin?' Curls an everything. An he looked ... ower the side o the boat, an there wis the bonniest lassie that he ever saw lookin back at him. 'What's happened?' he says. 'What's happened? (higher voice) *What's happened*?' His voice changed all of a sudden. Oh! So he says, 'Oh, my God!' – he was so stunned he jist sat there, an this boat, it got tae the other side, an he felt ... it was the boat scrapin the

pappies, breasts.

bottom that brought him back tae himsel, ye see – but he was a she now!

So she stands up in this lovely green claes, an she looked – she wondered how she was gonnae get oot o the boat withoot makin a mess o her shoes an everything. Now there was a young man walkin alang the bank o the river, and when he looked doon an sa this lassie in the boat, 'course he would run doon an help her oot. So he ran doon an cairried her oot o the boat till he got her on dry land, an he says, 'Where are ye going?'

'A don't know,' she says. 'A don't really know where A'm goin.'

He says, 'Well, where did ye come from?'

'Oh, A came from the other side o the water.'

'Are ye goin tae anybody?'

'A don't know.'

He says, 'Lassie, I think ye must have fell an bumped yir heid. I think ye've lost yir memory wi aa this "Don't knows, don't knows".'

She says, 'Well, mebbe something like that happened.' She says, 'A jist don't know where A'm goin here. Ye see, A know where A'm goin when A'm at the other side o the water, but A don't know where A'm goin here.'

'Well,' he says, 'A think A'll take ye home tae ma mother, an get her tae look after ye, see if ye get yir memory back.' So he took her home tae his mother, and she helped his mother in the hoose, an did this an that. But in time he got aafae fond o her, in fact he fell in love wi her, and the two of them got married. And within a couple o year they had two o the bonniest wee bairns ye ever saw, a wee toddler an one in the pram.

So one day, when they were oot walkin wi the bairns, an he was pushin his pram, quite proud o this wee laddie he's got, ye see . . . she says, 'Ye know, I think we'll go a walk down the river today.' She says, 'A haven't been back down that way since the day A came here.'

He says, 'Well, that's a good idea. It might bring back yir memory,' he says, 'if nothing else has all this time.'

She says, 'That's right.' So away they go down the riverside

claes, clothes.

and, sure enough, the wee boat wis still sittin there. 'Aw,' she says, 'Look at it! It's aa covered wi moss an lichen an aa kinds o dirt: A must go down an clean it.'

So she ran doon the bank, and she says: 'You keep the bairns here an A'll run down the bank an clean it.' Down she goes, an she's scrapin away at it, an the baler wis still lyin in it, an she startit tae bale oot the water. And in the end she stepped intae the boat to bale oot the last water, an ye can guess whit happen't! The boat's away wi her again, an it kept goin and kept goin, an the fella – there wis no wey he could stop it, it went so fast, an he couldnae swim efter it, so he jist had tae stand there an let it go.

Now halfway across the water when she lookit doon, there wis the auld tackety boots, the auld moleskin troosers covered wi coo shairn, the whiskers an baird an ... this auld sleeved waistcoat, an he looked ower intae the water an there wis this cattleman ... wi his teeth all broon wi tobacco juice an everything. 'Oh my God!' He started to roar an greet, an howl an greet, 'Oh, ma man an ma bairns! Ma man an ma bairns! Ma man an ma bairns . . .' and he jist sat like this and the tears trippin him, until the boat scraped the other side: an the boat took him right back tae where it had started aff.

Then Sandy jumpit oot the boat, an he ran an ran greetin an sobbin an sobbin an greetin. An when he ran up tae the fairm, this ceilidh's still gaun on, see? an the pot o sowens is still on the fire! An he cam in howlin an greetin an sobbin, an the laird says tae him, 'Whit's adae wi ye, Sandy?'

'Oh, dinnae speak tae me, dinnae speak tae me,' he says. 'Wheesht, leave me alane – wid ye leave me alane? Ma man an ma bairns! Ma man an ma bairns!'

'Man an bairns?' the laird says. 'Whit are ye speakin aboot?'

'Oh, would you wheesht?' he says.

'Sandy, come in here. Come on an sit doon beside . . . me here an tell us aa aboot it!' So Sandy came in, an he sat doon beside the laird, an between sobbin an greetin he tells them aa aboot his man an his bairns.

coo shairn, cow dung.   *Whit's adae*, What's wrong.

An the laird says, 'Well, Sandy, that's the biggest lie we've heard the nicht, so you've won the golden guinea!'

That's the end o that one. Ye see, the laird had pit a glamourie ower him, so that he thought aa this had happen't tae him, but actually he'd only been awa aboot twenty minutes.

pit a glamourie ower him, cast a spell over him.

ASSIPATTLE AND THE
MESTER STOORWORM

Elizabeth Grierson

In far bygone days, on the Mainland of Orkney, there lived a well-to-do farmer, who had seven sons and one daughter. And the youngest of these seven sons bore a very curious name; for he was called Assipattle, which means, 'He who grovels among the ashes'.

Perhaps Assipattle deserved his name, for he was rather a lazy boy, who never did any work on the farm as his brothers did, but ran about outdoors with ragged clothes and unkempt hair, and whose mind was ever filled with wondrous stories of trolls and giants, elves and goblins.

When the sun was hot in the long summer afternoons, when the bees droned drowsily and even the tiny insects seemed almost asleep, the boy was content to throw himself down on the ash-heap amongst the ashes, and lie there, lazily letting them run through his fingers, as one might play with sand on the sea-shore, basking in the sunshine and telling stories to himself.

And his brothers, working hard in the fields, would point to him with mocking fingers, and laugh, and say to each other how well the name suited him, and how little use he was in the world.

And when they came home from their work, they would push him about and tease him, and even his mother would make him sweep the floor, and draw water from the well, and fetch peats from the peat-stack, and do all the little odd jobs that nobody else would do.

So poor Assipattle had rather a hard life of it, and he would often have been very miserable had it not been for his sister, who loved him dearly, and who would listen quite patiently to all the stories that he had to tell; who never laughed at him or told him that he was telling lies, as his brothers did.

But one day a very sad thing happened – at least, it was a sad thing for poor Assipattle.

For it chanced that the King of these parts had one only daughter, the Princess Gemdelovely, whom he loved dearly, and to whom he denied nothing. And Princess Gemdelovely was in want of a waiting-maid, and as she had seen Assipattle's sister standing by the garden gate as she was riding by one day, and had taken a fancy to her, she asked her father if she might ask her to come and live at the castle and serve her.

Her father agreed at once, as he always did agree to any of her wishes; and sent a messenger in haste to the farmer's house to ask if his daughter would come to the castle to be the Princess's waiting-maid.

And, of course, the farmer was very pleased at the piece of good fortune which had befallen the girl, and so was her mother, and so were her six brothers, all except poor Assipattle, who looked with wistful eyes after his sister as she rode away, proud of her new clothes and of the slippers which her father had made her out of cowhide, which she was to wear in the Palace when she waited on the Princess, for at home she always ran barefoot.

Time passed, and one day a rider rode in hot haste through the country bearing the most terrible tidings. For the evening before, some fishermen, out in their boats, had caught sight of the Mester Stoorworm, which, as everyone in Orkney knows, was the largest, and the first, and the greatest of all sea serpents. It was that beast which, in the Good Book, is called the Leviathan, and if it had been measured in our day, its tail would have touched Iceland, while its snout rested at John-o'-Groat's Head.

And the fishermen had noticed that this fearsome monster had its head turned towards the mainland, and that it opened its mouth and yawned horribly, as if to show that it was hungry, and that, if it were not fed, it would kill every living thing upon the land, both man and beast, bird and creeping thing.

For it was well known that its breath was so poisonous that it consumed as with a burning fire everything that it lighted on. So that, if it pleased the awful creature to lift its head and put forth its breath, like noxious vapour, over the country, in a few weeks the fair farmland would be turned into a region of desolation.

As you may imagine, everyone was almost paralysed with terror at this awful calamity which threatened them; and the King called a solemn meeting of all his counsellors, and asked them if they could devise any way of warding off the danger.

And for three whole days they sat in Council, these grave, bearded men, and many were the suggestions which were made, and many the words of wisdom which were spoken; but, alas! no one was wise enough to think of a way by which the Mester Stoorworm might be driven back.

At last, at the end of the third day, when everyone had given up hope of finding a remedy, the door of the Council Chamber opened and the Queen appeared.

Now the Queen was the King's second wife, and she was not a favourite in the Kingdom, for she was a proud, insolent woman, who did not behave kindly to her stepdaughter, the Princess Gemdelovely. She spent much more of her time in the company of a great Sorcerer, whom everyone feared and dreaded, than she did in that of the King, her husband.

So the sober counsellors looked at her disapprovingly as she came boldly into the Council Chamber and stood up beside the King's Chair of State, and, speaking in a loud, clear voice, addressed them thus:

'Ye think that ye are brave men and strong, oh, ye Elders, and fit to be the Protectors of the People. And so it may be, when it is mortals that ye are called on to face. But ye are no match for the foe that now threatens our land. Before him your weapons are but as straw. 'Tis not through strength of arm, but through sorcery, that he will be overcome. So listen to my words, even though they be but those of a woman, and take counsel with the great Sorcerer, from whom nothing is hid, but who knows all the mysteries of the earth, and of the air, and of the sea.'

Now the King and his counsellors did not like this advice, for they hated the Sorcerer, who had, as they thought, too much influence with the Queen; but they were at their wits' end, and knew not to whom to turn for help, so they agreed to do as she said and summon the Wizard before them.

And when he obeyed the summons and appeared in their midst, they liked him none the better for his looks. For he was long, and thin, and awesome, with a beard that came down to his knees, and hair that wrapped him about like a mantle, and his face was the colour of mortar, as if he had always lived in darkness, and had been afraid to look on the sun.

But there was no help to be found in any other man, so they laid the case before him, and asked him what they should do. And he answered coldly that he would think over the matter, and come again to the Assembly the following day and give them his advice.

And his advice, when they heard it, was like to turn their hair white with horror.

For he said that the only way to satisfy the Monster, and to make it spare the land, was to feed it every Saturday with seven young maidens, who must be the fairest who could be found; and if, after this remedy had been tried once or twice, it did not succeed in mollifying the Stoorworm and inducing him to depart, there was but one other measure that he could suggest, but that was so horrible and dreadful that he would not rend their hearts by mentioning it in the meantime.

And as, although they hated him, they feared him also, the Council had to abide by his words, and they pronounced the awful doom.

And so it came about that, every Saturday, seven bonnie, innocent maidens were bound hand and foot and laid on a rock which ran into the sea, and the Monster stretched out his long, jagged tongue, and swept them into his mouth; while all the rest of the folk looked on from the top of a high hill – or, at least, the men looked – with cold, set faces, while the women hid theirs in their aprons and wept aloud.

'Is there no other way,' they cried, 'no other way than this, to save the land?'

But the men only groaned and shook their heads. 'No other way,' they answered; 'no other way.'

Then suddenly a boy's indignant voice rang out among the crowd. 'Is there no grown man who would fight that monster, and kill him, and save the lassies alive? I would do it; I am not feared for the Mester Stoorworm.'

It was the boy Assipattle who spoke, and everyone looked at him in amazement as he stood staring at the great sea serpent, his fingers twitching with rage, and his great blue eyes glowing with pity and indignation.

'The poor bairn's mad; the sight has turned his head,' they whispered one to another; and they would have crowded around him to pet and comfort him, but his elder brother came and gave him a heavy clout on the side of his head.

'*You* fight the Stoorworm!' he cried contemptuously. 'A likely story! Go home to your ash-pit, and stop speaking havers.' And, taking his arm, he drew him to the place where his other brothers were waiting, and they all went home together.

But all the time Assipattle kept on saying that he meant to kill the Stoorworm; and at last his brothers became so angry at what they thought was mere bragging, that they picked up stones and pelted him so hard with them that he took to his heels and ran away from them.

That evening the six brothers were threshing corn in the barn, and Assipattle, as usual, was lying among the ashes thinking his own thoughts, when his mother came out and bade him run and tell the others to come in for their supper.

The boy did as he was bid, for he was a willing enough little fellow; but when he entered the barn his brothers, in revenge for his having run away from them in the afternoon, set on him and pulled him down, and piled so much straw on top of him that, had his father not come from the farmhouse to see what they were all waiting for, he would certainly have been smothered.

But when, at supper-time, his mother was quarrelling with the other lads for what they had done, and saying to them that it was only cowards who set on bairns littler and younger than themselves, Assipattle looked up from the bowl of porridge which he was supping.

'Don't vex yourself, Mother,' he said, 'for I could have fought them all if I liked; ay, and beaten them, too.'

'Why didn't you try it then?' cried everybody at once.

'Because I knew that I would need all my strength when I go to fight the Giant Stoorworm,' replied Assipattle gravely.

And, as you may fancy, the others laughed louder than before.

Time passed, and every Saturday seven lassies were thrown to the Stoorworm, until at last it was felt that this state of things could not be allowed to go on any longer; for if it did, there would soon be no maidens at all left in Orkney.

So the Elders met once more, and, after long consultation, it was agreed that the Sorcerer should be summoned, and asked what his other remedy was. 'For, in truth,' said they, 'it cannot be worse than that which we are practising now.'

But, had they known it, the new remedy was even more dreadful than the old. For the cruel Queen hated her stepdaughter, Gemdelovely, and the wicked Sorcerer knew that she did, and that she would not be sorry to get rid of her, and, things being as they were, he thought that he saw a way to please the Queen. So he stood up in the Council, and, pretending to be very sorry, said that the only other thing that could be done was to give the Princess Gemdelovely to the Stoorworm, and then it would surely depart.

When they heard this sentence a terrible stillness fell upon the Council, and everyone covered his face with his hands, for no man dared look at the King.

But although his dear daughter was as the apple of his eye, he was a just and righteous monarch, and he felt that it was not right that other fathers should have been forced to part with their daughters, in order to try and save the country, if his child was to be spared.

So, after he had had speech with the Princess, he stood up before the Elders, and declared, with trembling voice, that both he and she were ready to make the sacrifice.

'She is my only child,' he said, 'and the last of her race. Yet it seems good to both of us that she should lay down her life, if by so doing she may save the land that she loves so well.'

Salt tears ran down the faces of the great bearded men as they heard their King's words, for they all knew how dear the Princess Gemdelovely was to him. But it was felt that what he said was wise and true, and that the thing was just and right; for it was better, surely, that one maiden should die, even though she were of royal blood, than that bands of other maidens should go to their death week by week, and all to no purpose.

So, amid heavy sobs, the aged deemster – the lawman who was the chief man of the Council – rose up to pronounce the Princess's doom. But, ere he did so, the King's kemper-man – or fighting-man – stepped forward.

'I ask that this doom should have a tail, just like the Stoor-worm! A tail with a sting in it, what's more! If, after devouring our dear Princess the monster has still not departed, the next thing that is offered to him will be no tender young maiden, but that tough, lean old Sorcerer.'

And at the kemper-man's words there was such a great shout of approval that the wicked Sorcerer seemed to shrink within himself, and his pale face grew even paler than it was before.

Now, three weeks were allowed between the time that the doom was pronounced upon the Princess and the time that it was carried out, so that the King might send ambassadors to all the neighbouring kingdoms to issue proclamations that, if any champion would come forward who was able to drive away the Stoorworm and save the Princess, he should have her for his wife.

And with her he should have the Kingdom of Orkney, as well as a very famous sword that was now in the King's possession, but which had belonged to the great god Odin, with which he had fought and vanquished all his foes.

The sword bore the name of Sickersnapper, and no man had any power against it.

The news of all these things spread over the length and breadth of the land, and everyone mourned for the fate that was likely to befall the Princess Gemdelovely. And the farmer, and his wife, and their six sons mourned also – all but Assipattle, who sat amongst the ashes and said nothing.

When the King's proclamation was made known throughout the neighbouring kingdoms, there was a fine stir among all the young gallants, for it seemed but a little thing to slay a sea monster; and a beautiful wife, a fertile kingdom and a trusty sword are not to be won every day.

So six-and-thirty champions arrived at the King's Palace, each hoping to gain the prize.

But the King sent them all out to look at the Giant Stoorworm lying in the sea with its enormous mouth open, and when they saw it, twelve of them were seized with sudden illness, and twelve of them were so afraid that they took to their heels and ran, and never stopped until they reached their own countries; and so only twelve returned to the King's Palace, and as for them, they were so downcast at the thought of the task that they swore they had no spirit left in them at all.

And none of them dared try to kill the Stoorworm; so the three weeks passed slowly by, until the night before the day on which the Princess was to be sacrificed. On that night the King, feeling that he must do something to entertain his guests, made a great supper for them.

But, as you may guess, it was a dreary feast, for everyone was thinking so much about the terrible thing that was to happen on the morrow, that no one could eat or drink.

And when it was all over, and everybody had retired to rest, save the King and his old kemper-man, the King returned to the great hall, and went slowly up to his Chair of State, high up on the dais. It was not like the Chairs of State that we know nowadays; it was nothing but a massive kist, in which he kept all the things which he treasured most.

The old monarch undid the iron bolts with trembling fingers, and lifted the lid, and took out the wondrous sword, Sicker-snapper, which had belonged to the great god Odin.

His trusty kemper-man, who had stood by him in a hundred fights, watched him with pitying eyes.

'Why lift out the sword,' he said softly, 'when your fighting days are done? Right nobly have you fought your battles in the past, oh, my Lord! when your arm was strong and sure. But when folk's years number four score and sixteen, as yours do, 'tis time to leave such work to other and younger men.'

The old King turned on him angrily, with something of the old fire in his eyes. 'Wheesht,' he cried, 'else will I turn this sword on

kist, wooden chest, box.

you. Do you think that I can see my only bairn devoured by a monster, and not lift a finger to try and save her when no other man will? I tell you – and I will swear it with my two thumbs crossed on Sickersnapper – that both the sword and I will be destroyed before so much as one of her hairs be touched. So go, if you love me, my old comrade, and order my boat to be ready, with the sail set and the prow pointed out to sea. I will go myself and fight the Stoorworm; and if I do not return, I will lay it on you to guard my cherished daughter. Peradventure, my life may redeem hers.'

Now that night everybody at the farm went to bed early, for next morning the whole family was to set out first thing, to go to the top of the hill near the sea, to see the Princess eaten by the Stoorworm. All except Assipattle, who was to be left at home to herd the geese.

The lad was so vexed at this – for he had great schemes in his head – that he could not sleep. And as he lay tossing and tumbling about in his corner among the ashes, he heard his father and mother talking in the great box-bed. And, as he listened, he found that they were having an argument.

' 'Tis such a long way to the hill overlooking the sea, I fear me I shall never walk it,' said his mother. 'I think I had better bide at home.'

'Nay,' replied her husband, 'that would be a bonny-like thing, when all the countryside is to be there. You will ride behind me on my good mare Go-swift.'

'I do not care to trouble you to take me behind you,' said his wife, 'for I think you don't love me as you used to do.'

'The woman's havering,' cried the Goodman of the house impatiently. 'What makes you think that I have ceased to love you?'

'Because you no longer tell me your secrets,' answered his wife. 'To go no further, think of this very horse, Go-swift. For five long years I have been begging you to tell me how it is that, when *you* ride her, she flies faster than the wind, while if any other man mount her, she hirples along like a broken-down nag.'

hirples, hobbles, limps.

The Goodman laughed. ''Twas not for lack of love for you that I kept that a secret, Goodwife,' he said, 'though it might be for lack of trust. For women's tongues wag but loosely; and I did not want other folk to ken my secret. But since my silence has vexed your heart, I'll tell you everything.

'When I want Go-swift to stand, I give her one clap on the left shoulder. When I would have her go like any other horse, I give her two claps on the right. But when I want her to fly like the wind, I whistle through the windpipe of a goose. And, as I never ken when I want her to gallop like that, I aye keep the bird's thrapple in the left-hand pocket of my coat.'

'So *that* is how you manage the beast,' said the farmer's wife, in a satisfied tone; 'and that is what becomes of all my goose thrapples. Oh! but you're a clever fellow, Goodman; and now that I ken the way of it I may go to sleep.'

Assipattle was not tumbling about in the ashes now; he was sitting up in the darkness, with glowing cheeks and sparkling eyes.

His opportunity had come at last, and he knew it.

He waited patiently till their heavy breathing told him that his parents were asleep; then he crept over to where his father's clothes were, and took the goose's windpipe out of the pocket of his coat, and slipped noiselessly out of the house. Once he was out of it, he ran like lightning to the stable. He saddled and bridled Go-swift, and threw a halter around her neck, and led her to the stable door.

The good mare, unaccustomed to her new groom, pranced, and reared, and plunged; but Assipattle, knowing his father's secret, clapped her once on the left shoulder, and she stood as still as a stone. Then he mounted her, and gave her two claps on the right shoulder, and the good horse trotted off briskly, giving a loud neigh as she did so.

The unwonted sound, ringing out in the stillness of the night, roused the household, and the Goodman and his six sons came tumbling down the wooden stairs, shouting to one another in confusion that someone was stealing Go-swift.

thrapple, throat.

The farmer was the first to reach the door; and when he saw, in the starlight, the vanishing form of his favourite steed, he cried at the top of his voice:

> 'Stop thief, ho!
> Go-swift, whoa!'

And when Go-swift heard that she pulled up in a moment. All seemed lost, for the farmer and his sons could run very fast indeed, and it seemed to Assipattle, sitting motionless on Go-swift's back, that they would very soon make up on him.

But, luckily, he remembered the goose's thrapple, and he pulled it out of his pocket and whistled through it. In an instant the good mare bounded forward, swift as the wind, and was over the hill and out of sight of its pursuers before they had taken ten steps more.

Day was dawning when the lad came within view of the sea; and there, in front of him, in the water, lay the enormous monster whom he had come so far to slay. Anyone would have said that he was mad even to dream of making such an attempt, for he was but a slim, unarmed youth, and the Mester Stoorworm was so big that men said it would reach the fourth part around the world. And its tongue was jagged at the end like a fork, and with this fork it could sweep whatever it chose into its mouth, and devour it at its leisure.

For all this, Assipattle was not afraid, for he had the heart of a hero underneath his tattered garments. 'I must be cautious,' he said to himself, 'and do by my wits what I cannot do by my strength.'

He climbed down from his seat on Go-swift's back, and tethered the good steed to a tree, and walked on, looking well about him, till he came to a little cottage on the edge of a little wood.

The door was not locked, so he entered, and found its occupant, an old woman, fast asleep in bed. He did not disturb her, but he took down an iron pot from the shelf, and examined it closely.

'This will serve my purpose,' he said; 'and surely the old dame would not grudge it if she knew it was to save the Princess's life.'

Then he lifted a live peat from the smouldering fire, and went his way.

Down at the water's edge he found the King's boat lying, guarded by a single boatman, with its sails set and its prow turned in the direction of the Mester Stoorworm.

'It's a cold morning,' said Assipattle. 'Are you not well-nigh frozen sitting there? If you'll come ashore, and run about, and warm yourself, I will get into the boat and guard it till you return.'

'A likely story,' replied the man. 'And what would the King say if he were to come, as I expect every moment he will do, and find me playing myself on the sand, and his good boat left to a wee laddie like you? 'Twould be as much as my head is worth.'

'As you will,' answered Assipattle carelessly, beginning to search among the rocks. 'In the mean time, I must be looking for a few mussels to roast for my breakfast.' And after he had gathered the mussels, he began to make a hole in the sand to put the live peat in. The boatman watched him curiously, for he, too, was beginning to feel hungry.

Presently the lad gave a wild shriek, and jumped high in the air. 'Gold, gold!' he cried. 'By the name of Thor, who would have looked to find gold here?'

This was too much for the boatman. Forgetting all about his head and the King, he jumped out of the boat, and, pushing Assipattle aside, began to scrape among the sand with all his might.

While he was doing so, Assipattle seized his pot, jumped into the boat, and pushed off. He was half a mile out to sea before the outwitted man, who, needless to say, could find no gold, noticed what he was about.

And, of course, he was very angry, and the old King was more angry still when he came down to the shore, attended by his nobles and carrying the great sword Sickersnapper, in the vain hope that he, poor feeble old man that he was, might be able in some way to defeat the monster and save his daughter.

But to make such an attempt was beyond his power now that his boat was gone. So he could only stand on the shore, along with the fast assembling crowd of his subjects, and watch what would befall.

And this was what befell.

Assipattle, sailing slowly over the sea, and watching the Mester Stoorworm intently, noticed that the terrible monster yawned occasionally, as if longing for his weekly feast. And as it yawned a great flood of sea-water went down its throat, and came out again at its huge gills.

So the brave lad took down his sail, and pointed the prow of his boat straight at the monster's mouth, and the next time it yawned he and his boat were sucked right in, and, like Jonah, went straight down its throat into the dark regions inside its body. On and on the boat floated; but as it went the water grew less, pouring out of the Stoorworm's gills, until at last it stuck, as it were, on dry land. And Assipattle jumped out, his pot in his hand, and began to explore.

Presently he came to the huge creature's liver, and, having heard that the liver of a fish is full of oil, he made a hole in it and put in the live peat.

Woe's me! but there was a conflagration! And Assipattle just got back to his boat in time; for the Mester Stoorworm, in its convulsions, threw the boat right out of its mouth again, and it was flung up, high and dry, on the bare land.

The commotion in the sea was so terrible that the King and his daughter – who by this time had come down to the shore dressed like a bride, in white, ready to be thrown to the monster – and all his courtiers, and all the country-folk, were fain to take refuge on the hilltop, out of harm's way, and stand and see what happened next.

And this was what happened next.

The poor, distressed creature – for it was now to be pitied, even although it was a great, cruel, awful Mester Stoorworm – tossed itself to and fro, twisting and writhing.

And as it tossed its awful head out of the water its tongue fell out, and struck the earth with such force that it made a great dent in it, into which the sea rushed. And that dent formed the crooked Straits which now divide Denmark from Norway and Sweden.

Then some of its teeth fell out and rested in the sea, and became the islands that we now call the Shetland Isles; and a little afterwards some more teeth dropped out, and they became what we now call the Faeroe Isles.

After that the creature twisted itself into a great lump and died; and this lump became the island of Iceland; and the fire which Assipattle had kindled with his live peat still burns on underneath it, and that is why there are mountains which throw out fire in that chilly land.

When at last it was plainly seen that the Mester Stoorworm was dead, the King could scarce contain himself with joy. He put his arms around Assipattle's neck, and kissed him, and called him his son. And he took off his own royal mantle and put it on the lad, and girded his good sword Sickersnapper around his waist. And he called his daughter, the Princess Gemdelovely, to him, and put her hand in his, and declared that when the right time came she should be his wife, and that he should be ruler over all the Kingdom of Orkney.

Then the whole company mounted their horses again, and Assipattle rode on Go-swift by the Princess's side; and so they returned, with great joy, to the King's Palace.

But as they were nearing the gate Assipattle's sister, she who was the Princess's maid, ran out to meet him, and signed to the Princess to lean down, and whispered something in her ear.

The Princess's face grew dark, and she turned her horse's head and rode back to where her father was, with his nobles. She told him the words that the maiden had spoken; and when he heard them his face, too, grew as black as thunder.

For the matter was this: the cruel Queen, full of joy at the thought that she was to be rid, once and for all, of her stepdaughter, had been making love to the wicked Sorcerer all the morning in the old King's absence.

'He shall be killed at once,' cried the monarch. 'Such behaviour cannot be overlooked.'

'You will have much ado to find him, your Majesty,' said the girl, 'for more than an hour since he and the Queen fled together on the fleetest horses that they could find in the stables.'

'But I can find him,' cried Assipattle; and he went off like the wind on his good horse Go-swift.

It was not long before he came within sight of the fugitives, and he drew his sword and shouted to them to stop.

They heard the shout and turned around, and they both laughed aloud in derision when they saw that it was only the boy who grovelled in the ashes who pursued them.

'The insolent brat! I will cut off his head for him! I will teach him a lesson!' cried the Sorcerer; and he rode boldly back to meet Assipattle. For although he was no fighter, he knew that no ordinary weapon could harm his enchanted body; therefore he was not afraid.

But he did not count on Assipattle having the sword of the great god Odin, with which he had slain all his enemies; and before this magic weapon the Sorcerer was powerless. And, at one thrust, the young lad ran it through his body as easily as if he had been any ordinary man, and he fell from his horse, dead.

Then the courtiers of the King, who had also set off in pursuit, but whose steeds were less fleet of foot than Go-swift, came up, and seized the bridle of the Queen's horse, and led it and its rider back to the Palace.

She was brought before the Council, and judged, and condemned to be shut up in a high tower for the remainder of her life. Which thing surely came to pass.

As for Assipattle, when the proper time came he was married to the Princess Gemdelovely, with great feasting and rejoicing. And when the old King died they ruled the kingdom for many a long year.

PART THREE

WANCHANCY APPARITIONS, SECOND SIGHT, WITCHES

TAM O' SHANTER: A TALE

Robert Burns

'*Of Brownyis and of Bogillis full is this Buke.*'
(*Gavin Douglas*)

When chapman billies leave the street, *chapman billies*, tradesmen laddies
And drouthy neebors neebors meet; *drouthy*, thirsty
As market days are wearing late,
An' folk begin to tak the gate; *gate*, road
While we sit bousing at the nappy, *nappy*, ale
An' gettin fou and unco happy, *fou*, mellow; *unco*, very
We think na on the lang Scots miles,
The mosses, waters, slaps, and stiles, *slaps*, gaps (in the hedges)
That lie between us and our hame,
Whare sits our sulky sullen dame,
Gathering her brows like gathering storm,
Nursing her wrath to keep it warm.

This truth fand honest Tam o' Shanter, *fand*, found
As he frae Ayr ae nicht did canter:
(Auld Ayr, wham ne'er a town surpasses
For honest men and bonny lasses).

O Tam! hads't thou but been sae wise
As taen thy ain wife Kate's advice!
She tauld thee weel thou wast a skellum *skellum*, rascal
A blethering, blustering, drunken
blellum; *blellum*, noisy drunk

That frae November till October
Ae market day thou was na sober,
That ilka melder wi' the miller   *ilka melder*, every meal-grinding
Thou sat as lang as thou had siller;
That every naig was ca'd a shoe on   *naig*, horse; *ca'd*, shod
The smith and thee gat roaring fou on;   *fou*, drunk
That at the Lord's house, ev'n on Sunday,
Thou drank wi' Kirkton Jean till Monday.
She prophesy'd that, late or soon,
Thou wad be found deep drown'd in Doon;
Or catch'd wi' warlocks in the   *warlocks*, wizards
          mirk   *mirk*, dark
By Alloway's auld haunted kirk.

Ah, gentle dames! it gars me greet   *gars*, makes; *greet*, weep
To think how mony counsels sweet,
How mony lengthen'd, sage advices
The husband from the wife despises!

But to our tale: — Ae market night,
Tam had got planted unco right;
Fast by an ingle, bleezing finely,   *bleezing*, blazing
Wi' reaming swats, that drank   *reaming swats*, foaming new beer
          divinely;
And at his elbow, Souter Johnny,   *Souter*, Cobbler
His ancient, trusty, drouthy crony;
Tam lo'ed him like a very brither;
They had been fou for weeks thegither.   *thegither*, together
The night drave on wi' sangs and clatter;
And ay the ale was growing better;
The landlady and Tam grew gracious
Wi favours secret, sweet and precious:
The Souter tauld his queerest stories;
The landlord's laugh was ready chorus:
The storm without might rair and rustle,   *rair*, roar
Tam did na mind the storm a whistle.

Care, mad to see a man sae happy,
E'en drown'd himself amang the nappy;
As bees flee hame wi' lades o' treasure,   *lades*, loads
The minutes wing'd their way wi' pleasure:
Kings may be blest, but Tam was glorious,
O'er a' the ills o' life victorious!

But pleasures are like poppies spread,
You seize the flow'r, its bloom is shed;
Or like the snow falls in the river,
A moment white – then melts for ever;
Or like the borealis race
That flit ere you can point their place;
Or like the rainbow's lovely form
Evanishing amid the storm.
Nae man can tether time or tide;
The hour approaches, Tam maun ride;   *maun*, must
That hour, o' night's black arch the   *black arch*, midnight
      key-stane,   *key-stane*, centrepiece
That dreary hour he mounts his beast in;
And sic a night he taks the road in   *sic*, such
As ne'er poor sinner was abroad in.

The wind blew as 'twad blawn its last   *'twad*, it would have
The rattling show'rs rose on the blast;
The speedy gleams the darkness swallow'd;
Loud, deep and lang the thunder bellow'd:
That night a child might understand
The Deil had business on his hand.   *Deil*, Devil

Weel mounted on his grey mare, Meg,
A better never lifted leg,
Tam skelpit on thro' dub and mire,   *skelpit*, hurried; *dub*, puddle
Despising wind, and rain, and fire;
Whiles holding fast his guid blue bonnet;   *Whiles*, Sometimes
Whiles crooning o'er some auld Scots sonnet;

Whiles glow'ring round wi' prudent cares
Lest bogles catch him unawares: *bogles*, goblins
Kirk-Alloway was drawing nigh
Where ghaists and houlets nightly cry.   *houlets*, owls

By this time he was 'cross the ford,
Where in the snaw the chapman
            smoor'd;   *smoor'd*, was smothered
And past the birks and meikle   *birks*, birches; *meikle stane*, big stone
            stane
Where drunken Charlie brak's neck-bane;   *brak's*, broke his
And thro' the whins, and by the cairn
Where hunters fand the murder'd bairn;   *bairn*, child
And near the thorn abune the well   *abune*, above
Where Mungo's mither hanged hersel.
Before him Doon pours all his floods,
The doubling storm roars thro' the woods;
The lightnings flash frae pole to pole;
Near and more near the thunders roll:
When, glimmering thro' the groaning trees,
Kirk-Alloway seem'd in a bleeze
Thro' ilka bore the beams were glancing,   *ilka bore*, every chink
And loud resounded mirth and dancing.

Inspiring bold John Barleycorn!   *John Barleycorn*, Whisky
What dangers thou canst make us scorn!
Wi' tippenny we fear nae evil,   *tippenny*, cheap (tuppenny) ale
Wi' usquabae we'll face the Devil!   *usquabae*, whisky (Gaelic)
The swats sae ream'd in Tammie's   *swats ... ream'd*, beer so frothed
            noddle,   *noddle*, head
Fair play, he car'd na deils a
            boddle.   *car'd ... boddle*, he didn't care tuppence
But Maggie stood right sair astonish'd
Till, by the heel and hand admonish'd,
She ventur'd forward on the light;
And vow, Tam saw an unco   *vow*, wow; *unco*, extraordinary
            sight!

Warlocks and witches in a dance;
Nae cotillion brent new frae   *Nae cotillion*, brand-new dance step
    France;
But hornpipes, jigs, strathspeys and reels,
Put life and mettle in their heels.
A winnock-bunker in the   *A winnock-bunker*, (On) a window-sill
    east,
There sat Auld Nick, in shape o' beast;
A towzie tyke, black, grim and   *towzie tyke*, dishevelled beast
    large,
To gie them music was his charge:
He screw'd the pipes and gart them skirl   *skirl*, shrill
Till roof and rafters a' did dirl.   *dirl*, clatter
Coffins stood round, like open presses   *presses*, cupboards
That shaw'd the dead in their last dresses;   *shaw'd*, showed
And, by some devilish cantraip sleight,   *cantraip*, weird trick
Each in its cauld hand held a licht –
By which heroic Tam was able
To note upon the haly table   *haly*, holy
A murderer's banes, in gibbet-airns;   *airns*, irons
Twa span-lang, wee unchristened bairns;   *span-lang*, hand-long
A thief, new-cutted frae a rape,   *rape*, rope
Wi' his last gasp his gab did gape;
Five tomahawks wi' blude red-rusted;
Five scymitars wi' murder crusted;
A garter which a babe had strangled;
A knife a father's throat had mangled –
Whom his ain son o' life bereft –
The grey hairs yet stack to the heft;   *stack*, stuck; *heft*, haft
Wi' mair o' horrible and awefu'
Which ev'n to name wad be unlawfu'.

As Tammie glowr'd, amaz'd and curious,
The mirth and fun grew fast and furious:
The piper loud and louder blew,
The dancers quick and quicker flew.

They reel'd, they set, they cross'd, they
    cleekit,   *cleekit*, linked hands
Till ilka carlin swat and reekit,   *carlin*, witch; *reekit*, steamed
And coost her duddies to the   *coost*, cast aside; *duddies*, clothes
    wark,   *wark*, work
And linket at it in her sark!   *linket*, went arm in arm; *sark*, vest

Now Tam, O Tam! had they been
    queans,   *queans*, young lasses
A' plump and strapping in their teens!
Their sarks, instead o' creeshie
    flannen,   *flannen*, dirty flannel
Been snaw-white seventeen-hunder   *seventeen-hunder*, fine-woven
    linen!–
Thir breeks o' mine, my only pair,   *breeks*, trousers
That aince were plush, o' gude blue hair,
I wad hae gi'en them off my hurdies   *hurdies*, buttocks
For ae blink o' the bonnie burdies!
But wither'd beldams, auld and droll,
Rigwoodie hags wad   *Rigwoodie*, Wizened
    spean a foal,   *wad spean*, would wean
Lowping and flinging on a   *Lowping*, Leaping
    crummock,   *crummock*, walking-stick
I wonder didna turn thy stomach.

But Tam kend what was what
    fu' brawlie: *fu' brawlie*, quite well
There was ae winsome wench an'   *winsome*, pleasant
    wawlie,   *wawlie*, nimble
That night enlisted in the core   *core*, corps (de danse)
(Lang after kend on Carrick shore,   *kend*, known
For mony a beast to dead she shot,   *dead*, death
And perish'd mony a bonny boat,
And shook both meikle corn and   *meikle*, much
    bere,   *bere*, barley
And held the countryside in fear).

Her cutty sark, o'
     Paisley harn   *cutty sark*, short shift; *Paisley harn*, coarse cloth
That while a lassie she had worn,
In longitude tho' sorely scanty,
It was her best and she was vauntie.   *vauntie*, proud (of it)
Ah! little ken'd thy reverend grannie,   *ken'd*, knew
That sark she coft for her wee Nannie,   *croft*, bought
Wi' twa pund Scots ('twas a' her riches),
Wad ever grac'd a dance of witches!

But here my Muse her wing
     maun cour,   *maun cour*, must cover
Sic flights are far beyond her power;
To sing how Nannie lap and flang   *lap*, leapt; *flang*, kicked
(A souple jade she was and strang),
And how Tam stood like ane bewitch'd
And thought his very een enrich'd;
Even Satan glowr'd, and fidg'd fu' fain,
And hotch'd and blew wi' might and main,   *hotch'd*, jerked
Till first ae caper, syne anither,   *syne*, then
Tam tint his reason a' thegither   *tint ... thegither*, altogether took
And roars out 'Weel done, Cutty-sark!'   leave of
And in an instant all was dark.
And scarcely had he Maggie rallied
When out the hellish legion sallied.

As bees bizz out wi' angry fyke   *bizz*, bustle; *fyke*, fuss
When plundering herds assail their   *herds*, herd-boys
     byke;   *byke*, hive
As open pussie's mortal foes,   *pussie's*, the hare's
When, pop! she starts before their nose;
As eager runs the market-crowd,
When 'Catch the thief!' resounds aloud:
So Maggie runs – the witches follow
Wi' mony an eldritch skreech and   *eldritch*, horrible
     hollo.   *hollo*, shout

Ah, Tam! Ah, Tam! thou'll get thy
    fairin',   *fairin'*, just deserts
In hell they'll roast thee like a herrin'!   *herrin'*, herring
In vain thy Kate awaits thy comin',
Kate soon will be a woefu' woman!
Now, do thy speedy utmost, Meg,
And win the key-stane of the brig.   *key-stane*, top or mid-stone
There, at them thou thy tail may toss,
A running stream they dare na cross.
But ere the key-stane she could make,
The fient a tail she had to shake!   *The fient . . .* , Never a tail
For Nannie, far before the rest,
Hard upon noble Maggie prest
And flew at Tam wi' furious ettle;   *ettle*, effort
But little wist she Maggie's mettle!
Ae spring brought off her master hale   *hale*, whole
But left behind her ain grey tail:
The carlin claught her by the rump   *claught*, clutched
And left poor Maggie scarce a stump.

Now, wha this tale o' truth shall read,
Ilk man and mother's son take heed:
Whene'er to drink you are inclin'd
Or cutty-sarks run in your mind,
Think! ye may buy the joys o'er dear,
Remember Tam o' Shanter's mare.

ADAM BELL

James Hogg

This tale, which may be depended on as in every part true, is singular, from the circumstance of its being insolvable, either from the facts that have been discovered relating to it, or by reason; for though events sometimes occur among mankind, which at the time seem inexplicable, yet there are always some individuals acquainted with the primary causes of these events, and they seldom fail of being brought to light before all the actors in them, or their confidants, are removed from this state of existence. But the causes which produced the events here related have never been accounted for in this world; even conjecture is left to wander in a labyrinth, unable to get hold of the thread that leads to the catastrophe.

Mr Bell was a gentleman of Annandale, in Dumfriesshire, in the south of Scotland, and proprietor of a considerable estate in that district, part of which he occupied himself. He lost his father when he was an infant, and his mother, dying when he was about twenty years of age, left him the sole proprietor of the estate, besides a large sum of money at interest, for which he was indebted, in a great measure, to his mother's parsimony during his minority. His person was tall, comely, and athletic, and his whole delight was in warlike and violent exercises. He was the best horseman and marksman in the county, and valued himself particularly upon his skill in the broadsword. Of this he often boasted aloud, and regretted that there was not one in the county whose skill was in some degree equal to his own.

In the autumn of 1745, after being for several days busily and silently employed in preparing for his journey, he left his own house, and went to Edinburgh, giving at the same time such directions to his servants as indicated his intention of being absent for some time.

A few days after he had left his home, one morning, while his housekeeper was putting the house in order for the day, her master, as she thought, entered by the kitchen door, the other being bolted, and passed her in the middle of the floor. He was buttoned in his greatcoat, which was the same he had on when he went from home; he likewise had the same hat on his head, and the same whip in his hand which he took with him. At sight of him she uttered a shriek, but recovering her surprise, instantly said to him, 'You have not stayed so long from us, Sir.' He made no reply, but went sullenly into his own room, without throwing off his greatcoat. After a pause of about five minutes, she followed him into the room. He was standing at his desk with his back towards her. She asked him if he wished to have a fire kindled, and afterwards if he was well enough; but he still made no reply to any of these questions. She was astonished, and returned into the kitchen. After tarrying about another five minutes, he went out at the front door, it being then open, and walked deliberately towards the bank of the River Kinnel, which was deep and wooded, and in that he vanished from her sight. The woman ran out in the utmost consternation to acquaint the men who were servants belonging to the house; and coming to one of the plough-men, she told him that their master was come home, and had certainly lost his reason, for he was wandering about the house and would not speak. The man loosed his horses from the plough and came home, listened to the woman's story, made her repeat it again and again, and then assured her that she was raving, for their master's horse was not in the stable, and of course he could not be come home. However, as she persisted in her claim, with every appearance of sincerity, he went down to the river to see what was become of his mysterious master. He was neither to be seen nor heard of in all the country. It was then concluded that the housekeeper had seen an apparition, and that something had befallen their master; but on consulting with some old people, skilled in these matters, they learned that when a 'wraith', or apparition of a living person, appeared while the sun was up, instead of being a prelude of instant death, it prognosticated very

long life; and, moreover, that it could not possibly be a ghost
that she had seen, for they always chose the night season for
making their visits. In short, though it was the general topic of
conversation among the servants and the people in the vicinity,
no reasonable conclusion could be formed on the subject.

The most probable conjecture was that as Mr Bell was known
to be so fond of arms, and had left his home on the very day
that Prince Charles Stuart and his Highlanders defeated General
Hawley on Falkirk Muir, he had gone either with him or the
Duke of Cumberland to the north. It was, however, afterwards
ascertained that he had never joined any of the armies. Week
passed after week, and month after month, but no word of Mr
Bell. A female cousin was his nearest living relation; her husband
took the management of his affairs; and concluding that he had
either joined the army, or drowned himself in the Kinnel, when
he was seen going down to the river, made no more inquiries
after him.

About this very time, a respectable farmer, whose surname
was McMillan, and who resided in the neighbourhood of Mussel-
burgh, happened to be in Edinburgh about some business. In the
evening he called upon a friend who lived near Holyrood House;
and being seized with an indisposition, they persuaded him to
tarry with them all night. About the middle of the night he grew
exceedingly ill, and, not being able to find any rest or ease in his
bed, imagined he would be the better of a walk. He put on his
clothes, and, that he might not disturb the family, slipped quietly
out at the back door, and walked in St Anthony's garden behind
the house. The moon shone so bright, that it was almost as light
as noonday, and he had scarcely taken a single turn, when he saw
a tall man enter from the other side, buttoned in a drab-coloured
greatcoat. It so happened that at that time McMillan stood in
the shadow of the wall, and perceiving that the stranger did not
observe him, a thought struck him that it would not be amiss to
keep himself concealed, that he might see what the man was
going to be about. The man walked backwards and forwards for
some time in apparent impatience, looking at his watch every
minute, until at length another man came in by the same way,
buttoned likewise in a greatcoat, and having a bonnet on his

head. He was remarkably stout made, but considerably lower in stature than the other. They exchanged only a single word; then turning both about, they threw off their coats, drew their swords, and began a most desperate and well-contested combat.

The tall gentleman appeared to have the advantage. He constantly gained ground on the other, and drove him half around the division of the garden in which they fought. Each of them strove to fight with his back towards the moon, so that it might shine full in the face of his opponent; and many rapid wheels were made for the purpose of gaining this position. The engagement was long and obstinate, and by the desperate thrusts that were frequently aimed on both sides, it was evident that they meant one another's destruction. They came at length within a few yards of the place where McMillan still stood concealed. They were both out of breath, and at that instant a small cloud chancing to overshadow the moon, one of them called out, 'Hold, we cannot see.' They uncovered their heads, wiped their faces, and as soon as the moon emerged from the cloud, each resumed his guard. Surely that was an awful pause! And short, indeed, was the stage between it and eternity with the one! The tall gentleman made a lunge at the other, who parried and returned it; and as the former sprung back to avoid the thrust, his foot slipped, and he stumbled forward towards his antagonist, who dextrously met his breast in the fall with the point of his sword, and ran him through the body. He made only one feeble convulsive struggle, as if attempting to rise, and expired almost instantaneously.

McMillan was petrified with horror; but conceiving himself to be in a perilous situation, having stolen out of the house at that dead hour of the night, he had so much presence of mind as to hold his peace, and to keep from interfering in the smallest degree.

The surviving combatant wiped his sword with great composure, put on his bonnet, covered the body with one of the greatcoats, took up the other, and departed. McMillan returned quietly to his chamber without awakening any of the family. His pains were gone, but his mind was shocked and exceedingly perturbed; and after deliberating until morning, he determined to say nothing of the matter, and to make no living creature acquainted with what he had seen, thinking that suspicion would infallibly rest on him. Accordingly, he kept his bed next morning, until his friend brought him the tidings that a gentleman had been murdered at the back of the house during the night. He then arose and examined the body, which was that of a young man, seemingly from the country, having brown hair, and fine manly features. He had neither letter, book, nor signature of any kind about him that could in the least lead to a discovery of who he was; only a common silver watch was found in his pocket, and an elegant sword was clasped in his cold bloody hand, which had an A and B engraved on the hilt. The sword had entered at his breast, and gone out at his back a little below the left shoulder. He had likewise received a slight wound on the sword arm.

The body was carried to the mortuary, where it lay for eight days, and though great numbers inspected it, yet none knew who or whence the deceased was, and he was at length buried among the strangers in Greyfriars churchyard.

Sixteen years elapsed before McMillan mentioned to any person the circumstance of his having seen the duel, but at that period, being in Annandale receiving some sheep that he had bought, and chancing to hear of the astonishing circumstances of Bell's disappearance, he divulged the whole. The time, the description of his person, his clothes, and, above all, the sword with the initials of his name engraved upon it, confirmed the fact beyond the smallest shadow of doubt that it was Mr Bell whom he had seen killed in the duel behind the abbey. But who the person was that slew him, how the quarrel commenced, or who it was that appeared to his housekeeper, remains to this day a profound secret, and is likely to remain so, until that day when every deed of darkness shall be brought to light.

Some have even ventured to blame McMillan for the whole, on account of his long concealment of facts, and likewise in consideration of his uncommon bodily strength and daring disposition, he being one of the boldest and most enterprising men of the age in which he lived; but all who knew him despised such insinuations, and declared them to be entirely inconsistent with his character, which was most honourable and disinterested; and besides, his tale has every appearance of truth.

THE GREY WOLF

George MacDonald

One evening-twilight in spring, a young English student, who had wandered northwards as far as the outlying fragments of Scotland called the Orkney and Shetland Islands, found himself on a small island of the latter group, caught in a storm of wind and hail, which had come on suddenly. It was in vain to look about for any shelter; for not only did the storm entirely obscure the landscape, but there was nothing around him save a desert moss.

At length, however, as he walked on for mere walking's sake, he found himself on the verge of a cliff, and saw, over the brow of it, a few feet below him, a ledge of rock, where he might find some shelter from the blast, which blew from behind. Letting himself down by his hands, he alighted upon something that crunched beneath his tread, and found the bones of many small animals scattered about in front of a little cave in the rock, offering the refuge he sought. He went in, and sat upon a stone. The storm increased in violence, and as the darkness grew he became uneasy, for he did not relish the thought of spending the night in the cave. He had parted from his companions on the opposite side of the island, and it added to his uneasiness that they must be full of apprehension about him. At last there came a lull in the storm, and the same instant he heard a footfall, stealthy and light as that of a wild beast, upon the bones at the mouth of the cave. He started up in some fear, though the least thought might have satisfied him that there could be no very dangerous animals upon the island. Before he had time to think, however, the face of a woman appeared in the opening. Eagerly the wanderer spoke. She started at the sound of his voice. He could not see her well, because she was turned towards the darkness of the cave.

'Will you tell me how to find my way across the moor to Shielness?' he asked.

'You cannot find it tonight,' she answered, in a sweet tone, and with a smile that bewitched him, revealing the whitest of teeth.

'What am I to do, then?' he asked.

'My mother will give you shelter, but that is all she has to offer.'

'And that is far more than I expected a minute ago,' he replied. 'I shall be most grateful.'

She turned in silence and left the cave. The youth followed.

She was barefooted, and her pretty brown feet went catlike over the sharp stones, as she led the way down a rocky path to the shore. Her garments were scanty and torn, and her hair blew tangled in the wind. She seemed about five and twenty, lithe and small. Her long fingers kept clutching and pulling nervously at her skirts as she went. Her face was very grey in complexion, and very worn, but delicately formed, and smooth-skinned. Her thin nostrils were tremulous as eyelids, and her lips, whose curves were faultless, had no colour to give sign of indwelling blood. What her eyes were like he could not see, for she had never lifted the delicate films of her eyelids.

At the foot of the cliff they came upon a little hut leaning against it, and having for its inner apartment a natural hollow within it. Smoke was spreading over the face of the rock, and the grateful odour of food gave hope to the hungry student. His guide opened the door of the cottage; he followed her in, and saw a woman bending over a fire in the middle of the floor. On the fire lay a large fish broiling. The daughter spoke a few words, and the mother turned and welcomed the stranger. She had an old and very wrinkled, but honest face, and looked troubled. She dusted the only chair in the cottage, and placed it for him by the side of the fire, opposite the one window, whence he saw a little patch of yellow sand over which the spent waves spread themselves out listlessly. Under this window there was a bench, upon which the daughter threw herself in an unusual posture, resting her chin upon her hand. A moment after the youth caught the first glimpse of her blue eyes. They were fixed upon him with a strange look of greed, amounting to craving, but as if aware that they belied or betrayed her, she dropped them instantly. The moment she veiled them, her face, notwithstanding its colourless complexion, was almost beautiful.

When the fish was ready, the old woman wiped the deal table, steadied it upon the uneven floor, and covered it with a piece of fine table-linen. She then laid the fish on a wooden platter, and invited the guest to help himself. Seeing no other provision, he pulled from his pocket a hunting knife, and divided a portion from the fish, offering it to the mother first.

'Come, my lamb,' said the old woman; and the daughter approached the table. But her nostrils and mouth quivered with disgust.

The next moment she turned and hurried from the hut.

'She doesn't like fish,' said the old woman, 'and I haven't anything else to give her.'

'She does not seem in good health,' he rejoined.

The woman answered only with a sigh, and they ate their fish with the help of a little rye-bread. As they finished their supper, the youth heard a sound like the pattering of a dog's feet upon the sand close to the door; but ere he had time to look out of the window, the door opened and the young woman entered. She looked better, perhaps from having just washed her face. She drew a stool to the corner of the fire opposite him. But as she sat down, to his bewilderment, and even horror, the student spied a single drop of blood on her white skin within her torn dress. The woman brought out a jar of whisky, put a rusty old kettle on the fire, and took her place in front of it. As soon as the water boiled, she proceeded to make some toddy in a wooden bowl.

Meantime the youth could not take his eyes off the young woman, so that at length he found himself fascinated, or rather bewitched. She kept her eyes for the most part veiled with the loveliest eyelids fringed with darkest lashes, and he gazed entranced; for the red glow of the little oil-lamp covered all the strangeness of her complexion. But as soon as he met a stolen glance out of those eyes unveiled, his soul shuddered within him.

Lovely face and craving eyes alternated fascination and repulsion.

The mother placed the bowl in his hands. He drank sparingly, and passed it to the girl. She lifted it to her lips, and as she tasted – only tasted it – looked at him. He thought the drink must have been drugged and have affected his brain. Her hair smoothed itself back, and drew her forehead backwards with it; while the lower part of her face projected towards the bowl, revealing, ere she sipped, her dazzling teeth in strange prominence. But the same moment the vision vanished; she returned the vessel to her mother and, rising, hurried out of the cottage.

Then the old woman pointed to a bed of heather in one corner with a murmured apology; and the student, wearied both with the fatigues of the day and the strangeness of the night, threw himself upon it, wrapped in his cloak. The moment he lay down, the storm began afresh, and the wind blew so keenly through the crannies of the hut, that it was only by drawing his cloak over his head that he could protect himself from its currents. Unable to sleep, he lay listening to the uproar which grew in violence, till the spray was dashing against the window. At length the door opened, and the young woman came in, made up the fire, drew the bench before it, and lay down in the same strange posture, with her chin propped on her hand and elbow, and her face turned towards the youth. He moved a little; she dropped her head, and lay on her face, with her arms crossed beneath her forehead. The mother had disappeared.

Drowsiness crept over him. A movement of the bench roused him, and he fancied he saw some four-footed creature as tall as a large dog trot quietly out of the door. He was sure he felt a rush of cold wind. Gazing fixedly through the darkness, he thought he saw the eyes of the damsel encountering his, but a glow from the falling together of the remnants of the fire revealed clearly enough that the bench was vacant. Wondering what could have made her go out in such a storm, he fell fast asleep.

In the middle of the night he felt a pain in his shoulder, came broad awake, and saw the gleaming eyes and grinning teeth of some animal close to his face. Its claws were in his shoulder, and its mouth in the act of seeking his throat. Before it had fixed its fangs, however, he had its throat in one hand, and sought his knife with the other. A terrible struggle followed; but regardless of the tearing claws, he found and opened his knife. He had made one futile stab, and was drawing it for a surer, when, with a spring of the whole body, and one wildly contorted effort, the creature twisted its neck from his hold, and with something betwixt a scream and a howl, darted from him. Again he heard the door open; again the wind blew in upon him, and it continued blowing; a sheet of spray dashed across the floor, and over his face. He sprung from his couch and bounded to the door.

It was a wild night – dark, but for the flash of whiteness from the waves as they broke within a few yards of the cottage; the wind was raving, and the rain pouring down the air. A gruesome sound as of mingled weeping and howling came from somewhere in the dark. He turned again into the hut and closed the door, but could find no way of securing it.

The lamp was nearly out, and he could not be certain whether the form of the young woman was upon the bench or not. Overcoming a strong repugnance, he approached it, and put out his hands – there was nothing there. He sat down and waited for the daylight: he dared not sleep any more.

When the day dawned at length, he went out yet again, and looked around. The morning was dim and gusty and grey. The wind had fallen, but the waves were tossing wildly. He wandered up and down the little strand, longing for more light.

At length he heard a movement in the cottage. By and by the voice of the old woman called to him from the door. 'You're up early, sir. I suppose you didn't sleep well.'

'Not very well,' he answered. 'But where is your daughter?'

'She's not awake yet,' said the mother. 'I'm afraid I have but a poor breakfast for you. But you'll take a dram and a bit of fish. It's all I've got.'

Unwilling to hurt her, though hardly in good appetite, he sat down at the table. While they were eating, the daughter came in, but turned her face away and went to the further end of the hut. When she came forward after a minute or two, the youth saw that her hair was drenched, and her face whiter than before. She looked ill and faint, and when she raised her eyes, all their fierceness had vanished, and sadness had taken its place. Her neck was now covered with a cotton handkerchief. She was modestly attentive to him, and no longer shunned his gaze. He was gradually yielding to the temptation of braving another night in the hut, and seeing what would follow, when the old woman spoke.

'The weather will be broken all day, sir,' she said. 'You had better be going, or your friends will leave without you.'

Ere he could answer, he saw such a beseeching glance on the face of the girl, that he hesitated, confused. Glancing at the mother, he saw the flash of wrath in her face. She rose and approached her daughter, with her hand lifted to strike her. The young woman stooped her head with a cry. He darted around the table to interpose between them. But the mother had caught hold of her; the handkerchief had fallen from her neck; and the youth saw five blue bruises on her lovely throat – the marks of the four fingers and the thumb of a left hand. With a cry of horror he darted from the house, but as he reached the door he turned. His hostess was lying motionless on the floor, and a huge grey wolf came bounding after him.

There was no weapon at hand; and if there had been, his inborn chivalry would never have allowed him to harm a woman even under the guise of a wolf. Instinctively, he set himself firm, leaning a little forward, with half outstretched arms, and hands curved ready to clutch again at the throat upon which he had left those pitiful marks. But the creature as she sprung eluded his grasp, and just as he expected to feel her fangs, he found a woman weeping on his bosom, with her arms around his neck. The next instant, the grey wolf broke from him, and bounded howling up the cliff. Recovering himself as he best might, the youth followed, for it was the only way to the moor above, across which he must now make his way to find his companions.

All at once he heard the sound of a crunching of bones – not as if a creature was eating them, but as if they were ground by the teeth of rage and disappointment: looking up, he saw close above him the mouth of the little cavern in which he had taken refuge the day before. Summoning all his resolution, he passed it slowly and softly. From within came the sounds of a mingled moaning and growling.

Having reached the top, he ran at full speed for some distance across the moor before venturing to look behind him. When at length he did so, he saw, against the sky, the girl standing on the edge of the cliff, wringing her hands. One solitary wail crossed the space between. She made no attempt to follow him, and he reached the opposite shore in safety.

BLACK ANDIE'S TALE OF TOD LAPRAIK

Robert Louis Stevenson

It was in the year seeventeen hunner and sax that the Bass Rock cam in the hands o the Da'rymples, and there was twa men soucht the chairge of it. Baith were weel qualified, for they had baith been sodgers in the garrison, and kent the gate to handle solans, and the seasons and values of them. Forby that they were baith – or they baith seemed – earnest professors and men of comely conversation. The first of them was just Tam Dale, my faither. The second was ane Lapraik, whom folk ca'd Tod Lapraik maistly, but whether for his name or his nature I could never hear tell. Weel, Tam gaed to see Lapraik upon this business, and took me, that was a toddlin' laddie, by the hand. Tod has his dwallin' in the lang loan benorth the kirkyaird. It's a dark uncanny loan, forby that the kirk has aye had an ill name since the days o James the Saxt and the deevil's cantrips played therein when the Queen was on the seas; and as for Tod's house, it was in the mirkest end, and was little liked by some that kenned the best. The door was on the sneck that day, and me and my faither gaed straught in. Tod was a wabster to his trade; his loom stood in the but. There he sat, a muckle fat, white hash of a man like

soucht, sought.   *chairge*, custody.   *kent the gate*, knew the way.
solans, solan geese, gannets.   *Forby*, moreover, besides.
Tod, Fox (sometimes a nickname).   *dwallin*, dwelling.
lang loan, long street.   *benorth*, to the north of.   *uncanny*, eerie, creepy.
deevil's cantrips, devil's tricks. Folklore had it that the Devil tried to shipwreck Anne of Denmark here, as she sailed to Leith in 1589 after her marriage to King James VI of Scotland in Oslo.
mirkest, darkest.   *kenned*, knew.   *on the sneck*, unlatched, unlocked.
wabster, weaver.   *but*, kitchen.

creish, wi a kind of a holy smile that gart me scunner. The hand of him aye cawed the shuttle, but his een was steeket. We cried to him by his name, we skirled in the deid lug of him, we shook him by the shou'ther. Nae mainner o service! There he sat on his dowp, an cawed the shuttle and smiled like creish.

'God be gude to us,' says Tam Dale, 'this is no canny!'

He had jimp said the word, when Tod Lapraik cam to himsel. 'Is this you, Tam?' says he. 'Haith, man! I'm blythe to see ye. I whiles fa' into a bit dwam like this,' he says; 'it's frae the stamach.'

Weel, they began to crack about the Bass and which of them twa was to get the warding o't, and by little and little cam to very ill words, and twined in anger. I mind weel, that as my faither and me gaed hame again, he cam ower and ower the same expression, how little he likit Tod Lapraik and his dwams.

'Dwams!' says he. 'I think folk hae brunt far dwams like yon.'

Aweel, my faither got the Bass and Tod had to go wantin'. It was remembered sinsyne what way he had ta'en the thing. 'Tam,' says he, 'ye hae gotten the better o me aince mair, and I hope,' says he, 'ye'll find aw that ye expeckit at the Bass.' Which have since been thought remarkable expressions.

At last the time came for Tam Dale to take young solans. This was a business he was weel used wi, he had been a craigsman frae a laddie, and trustit nane but himsel. So there was he hingin' by a line an' speldering on the craig face, whaur it's hieest and steighest. Fower tenty lads were on the tap, hauldin' the line and mindin' for his signals. But whaur Tam hung there was naething

---

creish, tallow-fat.   *gart me scunner*, made me sick.
cawed, pulled, moved.   *steeket*, stuck shut.   *skirled*, yelled.
deid lug, dead ear.   *Nae mainner o service!*, Nothing doing!
dowp, backside.   *jimp*, hardly.   *blythe*, happy.
fa' into a bit dwam, fall into a bit of a daydream.
stamach, stomach.   *crack*, chat.   *twined*, parted.
brunt far, burnt for.   *sinsyne*, since then.   *craigsman*, rock climber.
speldering, sprawling.   *craig face*, rockface.
hieest and steighest, highest and steepest.   *tenty*, watchful, attentive.
mindin for, looking out for.

but the craig, and the sea belaw, and the solans skirling and flying. It was a braw spring morn, and Tam whustled as he claught in the young geese. Mony's the time I heard him tell of this experience, and aye the swat ran upon the man.

It chanced, ye see, that Tam keeked up, and he was awaur of a muckle solan, and the solan pyking at the line. He thought this by-ordinar and outside the creature's habits. He minded that ropes was unco saft things, and the solan's neb and the Bass Rock unco hard, and that twa hunner feet were rather mair than he would care to fa'.

'Shoo!' says Tam. 'Awa, bird! Shoo, awa wi ye!' says he.

The solan keekit doun into Tam's face, and there was something unco in the creature's ee. Just the ae keek it gied, and back to the rope. But now it wroucht and warstl't like a thing dementit. There never was the solan made that wroucht as that solan wroucht; and it seemed to understand its employ brawly, birzing the saft rope between the neb of it and a crunkled jag o stane.

There gaed a cauld stend o fear into Tam's heart. 'This thing is nae bird,' thinks he. His een turnt backward in his heid and the day gaed black about him. 'If I get a dwam here,' he thoucht, 'it's by wi Tam Dale.' And he signalled for the lads to pu' him up.

And it seemed the solan understood about signals. For nae sooner was the signal made than he let be the rope, spried his wings, squawked out loud, took a turn flying, and dashed straucht at Tam Dale's een. Tam had a knife, he gart the cold steel glitter. And it seemed the solan understood about knives, for nae suner did the steel glint in the sun than he gied the ae squawk, but laigher, like a body disappointit, and flegged aff about the roundness of the craig, and Tam saw him nae mair.

claught, dragged. *swat*, sweat. *keeked*, looked. *muckle*, big.
pyking, pecking. *by-ordinar*, extraordinary, unusual. *neb*, beak, nose.
unco, (1) exceedingly, very; (2) strange, not right. *ae keek*, one look.
wroucht, worked. *warstl't*, wrestled. *dementit*, gone crazy.
brawly, well. *birzing*, grinding. *crunkled*, wrinkled. *gaed*, went.
stend, thrill. *spried*, spread. *straucht*, straight. *een*, eyes.
gart, made. *laigher*, lower. *flegged*, flew.

And as sune as the thing was gane, Tam's heid drapt upon his shouther, and they pu'd him up like a deid corp, dadding on the craig.

A dram of brandy (which he never went without) broucht him to his mind, or what was left of it. Up he sat.

'Rin, Geordie, rin to the boat, mak' sure of the boat, man — rin!' he cries, 'or yon solan'll have it awa,' says he.

The fower lads stared at ither, an' tried to whilly-wha him to be quiet. But naething would satisfy Tam Dale, till ane o them had startit on aheid to stand sentry on the boat. The ithers askit if he was for down again.

'Na,' he says, 'and neither you nor me,' says he, 'and as sune as I can win to stand on my twa feet we'll be aff frae this craig o Sawtan.'

Sure eneuch, nae time was lost, and that was ower muckle; for before they won to North Berwick Tam was in a crying fever. He lay aw the simmer; and wha was sae kind as come speiring for him, but Tod Lapraik! Folk thocht afterwards that ilka time Tod cam near the house the fever had worsened. I kenna for that; but what I ken the best, that was the end of it.

It was about this time o the year; my grandfaither was out at the white fishing; and like a bairn I wanted but to gang wi' him. We had a grand take, I mind, and the way that the fish lay broucht us near in by the Bass, whaur we foregaithered wi anither boat that belanged to a man Sandie Fletcher in Castleton. He's no lang deid neither, or ye could speir at himsel. Weel, Sandie hailed.

'What's yon on the Bass?' says he.

'On the Bass?' says grandfaither.

'Ay,' says Sandie, 'on the green side o it.'

'Whatten kind of a thing?' says grandfaither. 'There cannae be naething on the Bass but just the sheep.'

---

corp, body.   *dadding*, bouncing.   *broucht*, brought.   *Rin*, Run.
at ither, at each other.   *whilly-wha*, coax.   *Sawtan*, Satan.
ower muckle, too much.   *won*, reached.   *speiring for*, asking after.
ilka, each.   *I kenna for that*, I don't know about that.
I wanted but to gang, I wanted only to go.   *take*, catch of fish.

'It looks unco like a body,' quo Sandie, who was nearer in.

'A body!' says we, and we nane of us likit that. For there was nae boat that could have broucht a man, and the key o' the prison yett hung ower my faither's heid at hame in the press bed.

We keept the twa boats close for company, and crap in nearer hand. Grandfaither had a gless, for he had been a sailor, and the captain of a smack, and had lost her on the sands of Tay. And when we took the gless to it, sure eneuch there was a man. He was in a crunkle o' green brae, a wee below the chaipel, aw by his lee lane, and he lowped and flang and danced like a daft quean at a waddin'.

'It's Tod,' says grandfaither, and passed the gless to Sandie.

'Ay, it's him,' says Sandie.

'Or ane in the likeness o him,' says grandfaither.

'Sma' is the differ,' quo Sandie. 'Deil or warlock, I'll try the gun at him,' quo he, and broucht up a fowling-piece that he aye carried, for Sandie was a notable famous shot in aw that country.

'Haud yer hand, Sandie,' says grandfaither, 'we maun see clearer first,' says he, 'or this may be a dear day's wark to the baith of us.'

'Hout!' says Sandie, 'this is the Lord's judgements surely, and be damned to it!' says he.

'Maybe ay, and maybe no,' says my grandfaither, worthy man! 'But have you a mind of the Procurator Fiscal, that I think ye'll have forgaithered wi before,' says he.

This was ower true, and Sandie was a wee thing set ajee. 'Aweel, Edie,' says he, 'and what would be your way of it?'

'Oh, just this,' says grandfaither. 'Let me that has the fastest boat gang back to North Berwick, and let you bide here and keep

---

quo, said, quoth.   *yett*, prison-gate.   *press bed*, box-bed.
crap, crept.   *gless*, telescope.   *smack*, small fishing boat.
crunkle, fold.   *a wee below*, just below.   *chaipel*, chapel.
aw by his lee lane, all by himself.   *lowped*, leapt.   *flang*, flung.
daft quean, silly lass.   *waddin'*, wedding.   *warlock*, male witch.
a wee thing set ajee, slightly disturbed.   *bide*, stay.

an eye on Thon. If I cannae find Lapraik, I'll join ye and the twa of us'll have a crack wi him. But if Lapraik's at hame, I'll rin up a flag at the harbour, and ye can try Thon Thing wi the gun.'

Aweel, so it was agreed between them twa. I was just a bairn, an' clum in Sandie's boat, whaur I thocht I would see the best of the employ. My grandsire gied Sandie a siller tester to pit in his gun wi' the leid draps, bein' mair deidly against bogles. And then the ae boat set aff for North Berwick, and the tither lay whaur it was and watched the wanchancy thing on the braeside.

Aw the time we lay there it lowped and flang and capered and span like a teetotum, and whiles we could hear it skelloch as it span. I hae seen lassies, the daft queans, that would lowp and dance a winter's nicht, and still be lowping and dancing when the winter's day cam in. But there would be folk there to hauld them company, and the lads to egg them on; and this thing was its lee-lane. And there would be a fiddler diddling his elbock in the chimney-side; and this thing had nae music but the skirling of the solans. And the lassies were bits o young things wi the reid life dinnling and stending in their members; and this was a muckle, fat, creishy man, and him fa'n in the vale o years. Say what ye like, I maun say what I believe. It was joy was in the creature's heart; the joy o' hell, I daursay: joy whatever. Mony a time have I askit mysel why witches and warlocks should sell their sauls (whilk are their maist dear possessions) and be auld, duddy, wrunkl't wives or auld, feckless, doddered men; and then I mind upon Tod Lapraik dancing aw they hours by his lane in the black glory of his heart. Nae doubt they burn for it in muckle hell, but they have a grand time here of it whatever! – and the Lord forgie us!

Thon, That.   _crack_, word, chat.   _clum_, climbed.
best of the employ, best of the action.   _siller tester_, silver sixpence.
leid draps, lead shot.   _bogles_, evil spirits.   _ae_, one.
wanchancy, dangerous, scary.   _span like a teetotum_, spun like a top.
skelloch, screech, cry.   _elbock_, elbow.
dinnling and stending, tingling and throbbing.
creishy, flabby.   _fa'n_, fallen.   _duddy_, ragged.   _wrunkl't_, wrinkled.
forgie, forgive.

Weel, at the hinder end, we saw the wee flag yirk up to the mast-heid upon the harbour rocks. That was aw Sandie waited for. He up wi the gun, took a deleeberate aim, an pu'd the trigger. There cam' a bang and then ae waefu' skirl frae the Bass. And there were we rubbin' our een and lookin' at ither like daft folk. For wi the bang and the skirl the thing had clean disappeared. The sun glintit, the wund blew, and there was the bare yaird whaur the Wonder had been lowping and flinging but ae second syne.

The hale way hame I roared and grat wi the terror of that dispensation. The grawn folk were nane sae muckle better; there was little said in Sandie's boat but just the name of God; and when we won in by the pier, the harbour rocks were fair black wi the folk waitin' us. It seems they had fund Lapraik in ane of his dwams, cawing the shuttle and smiling. Ae lad they sent to hoist the flag, and the rest abode there in the wabster's house. You may be sure they liked it little; but it was a means of grace to severals that stood there praying in to themsels (for nane cared to pray out loud) and looking on thon awesome thing as it cawed the shuttle. Syne, upon a suddenty, and wi the ae dreidfu' skelloch, Tod sprang up frae his hinderlands and fell forrit on the wab, a bloody corp.

When the corp was examined the leid draps hadnae played buff upon the warlock's body; sorrow a leid drap was to be fund; but there was grandfaither's siller tester in the puddock's heart of him.

---

at the hinder end, in due course, later.
yirk, jerk.   *that dispensation*, that outcome.
grawn, adult, grown-up.   *severals*, several (people).
ae dreidfu' skelloch, one dreadful shriek.
hinderlands, backside.   *wab*, web.   *puddock*, frog.

THROUGH THE VEIL

Sir Arthur Conan Doyle

He was a great shock-headed, freckle-faced Borderer, the lineal
descendant of a cattle-thieving clan in Liddesdale. In spite of his
ancestry he was as solid and sober a citizen as one would wish
to see, a town councillor of Melrose, an elder of the Church, and
the chairman of the local branch of the Young Men's Christian
Association. Brown was his name – and you saw it printed up as
'Brown and Handiside' over the great grocery stores in the High
Street. His wife, Maggie Brown, was an Armstrong before her
marriage, and came from an old farming stock in the wilds
of Teviothead. She was small, swarthy, and dark-eyed, with a
strangely nervous temperament for a Scotswoman. No greater
contrast could be found than the big tawny man and the dark
little woman, but both were of the soil as far back as any memory
could extend.

One day – it was the first anniversary of their wedding – they
had driven over together to see the excavations of the Roman
fort at Newstead. It was not a particularly picturesque spot. From
the northern bank of the Tweed, just where the river forms a
loop, there extends a gentle slope of arable land. Across it run
the trenches of the excavators, with here and there an exposure
of old stonework to show the foundations of the ancient walls.
It had been a huge place, for the camp was fifty acres in extent,
and the fort fifteen. However, it was all made easy for them since
Mr Brown knew the farmer to whom the land belonged. Under
his guidance they spent a long summer evening inspecting the
trenches, the pits, the ramparts, and all the strange variety of
objects which were waiting to be transported to the Edinburgh
Museum of Antiquities. The buckle of a woman's belt had been

dug up that very day, and the farmer was discoursing upon it when his eyes fell upon Mrs Brown's face.

'Your good leddy's tired,' said he. 'Maybe you'd best rest a wee before we gang further.'

Brown looked at his wife. She was certainly very pale, and her dark eyes were bright and wild.

'What is it, Maggie? I've wearied you. I'm thinkin' it's time we went back.'

'No, no, John, let us go on. It's wonderful! It's like a dreamland place. It all seems so close and so near to me. How long were the Romans here, Mr Cunningham?'

'A fair time, mam. If you saw the kitchen midden-pits you would guess it took a long time to fill them.'

'And why did they leave?'

'Well, mam, by all accounts they left because they had to. The folk around could thole them no longer, so they just up and burned the fort aboot their lugs. You can see the fire marks on the stanes.'

The woman gave a quick little shudder. 'A wild night – a fearsome night,' said she. 'The sky must have been red that night – and these grey stones, they may have been red also.'

'Aye, I think they were red,' said her husband. 'It's a queer thing, Maggie, and it may be your words that have done it; but I seem to see that business aboot as clear as ever I saw anything in my life. The light shone on the water.'

'Aye, the light shone on the water. And the smoke gripped you by the throat. And all the savages were yelling.'

The old farmer began to laugh. 'The leddy will be writin' a story aboot the old fort,' said he. 'I've shown many a one ower it, but I never heard it put so clear afore. Some folk have the gift.'

They had strolled along the edge of the foss, and a pit yawned upon the right of them.

'That pit was fourteen foot deep,' said the farmer. 'What d'ye think we dug oot from the bottom o't? Weel, it was just the skeleton of a man wi' a spear by his side. I'm thinkin' he was grippin' it when he died. Now, how cam' a man wi' a spear doon

thole, tolerate.

a hole fourteen foot deep? He wasna' buried there, for they aye burned their dead. What make ye o' that, mam?'

'He sprang doon to get clear of the savages,' said the woman.

'Weel, it's likely enough, and a' the professors from Edinburgh couldna gie a better reason. I wish you were aye here, mam, to answer a' oor deeficulties sae readily. Now, here's the altar that we foond last week. There's an inscreeption. They tell me it's Latin, and it means that the men o this fort give thanks to God for their safety.'

They examined the old worn stone. There was a large deeply cut 'VV' upon the top of it.

'What does "VV" stand for?' asked Brown.

'Naebody kens,' the guide answered.

'*Valeria Victrix*,' said the lady softly. Her face was paler than ever, her eyes far away, as one who peers down the dim aisles of over-arching centuries.

'What's that?' asked her husband sharply.

She started as one who wakes from sleep. 'What were we talking about?' she asked.

'About this "VV" upon the stone.'

'No doubt it was just the name of the Legion which put the altar up.'

'Aye, but you gave some special name.'

'Did I? How absurd! How should I ken what the name was?'

'You said something – "*Victrix*", I think.'

'I suppose I was guessing. It gives me the queerest feeling, this place, as if I were not myself, but someone else.'

'Aye, it's an uncanny place,' said her husband, looking around with an expression almost of fear in his bold grey eyes. 'I feel it mysel'. I think we'll just be wishin' you good evenin', Mr Cunningham, and get back to Melrose before the dark sets in.'

Neither of them could shake off the strange impression which had been left upon them by their visit to the excavations. It was as if some miasma had risen from those damp trenches and passed into their blood. All the evening they were silent and thoughtful, but such remarks as they did make showed that the same subject was in the minds of each. Brown had a restless night, in which he dreamed a strange connected dream, so vivid that he woke sweating and shivering like a frightened horse. He tried to convey it all to his wife as they sat together at breakfast in the morning.

'It was the clearest thing, Maggie,' said he. 'Nothing that has ever come to me in my waking life has been more clear than that. I feel as if these hands were sticky with blood.'

'Tell me of it – tell me slow,' said she.

'When it began, I was oot on a braeside. I was laying flat on the ground. It was rough, and there were clumps of heather. All around me was just darkness, but I could hear the rustle and the breathin' of men. There seemed a great multitude on every side of me, but I could see no one. There was a low chink of steel sometimes, and then a number of voices would whisper, "Hush!" I had a ragged club in my hand, and it had spikes o' iron near the end of it. My heart was beatin' quickly, and I felt that a moment of great danger and excitement was at hand. Once I dropped my club, and again from all around me the voices in the darkness cried, "Hush!" I put oot my hand, and it touched the foot of another man lying in front of me. There was someone at my very elbow on either side. But they said nothin'.

'Then we all began to move. The whole braeside seemed to be crawlin' downwards. There was a river at the bottom and a high-arched wooden bridge. Beyond the bridge were many lights – torches on a wall. The creepin' men all flowed towards the bridge. There had been no sound of any kind, just a velvet stillness. And then there was a cry in the darkness, the cry of a man who has been stabbed suddenly to the hairt. That one cry swelled out for a moment, and then the roar of a thoosand furious voices. I was runnin'. Everyone was runnin'. A bright red light shone out, and the river was a scarlet streak. I could see my companions now. They were more like devils than men, wild figures clad in skins, with their hair and beards streamin'. They were all mad with rage, jumpin' as they ran, their mouths open, their arms wavin', the red light beatin' on their faces. I ran, too, and yelled out curses like the rest. Then I heard a great cracklin' of wood, and I knew that the palisades were doon. There was a

braeside, hillside.

loud whistlin' in my ears, and I was aware that arrows were flyin' past me. I got to the bottom of a dyke, and I saw a hand stretched doon from above. I took it, and was dragged to the top. We looked doon, and there were silver men beneath us holdin' up their spears. Some of our folk sprang on to the spears. Then we others followed, and we killed the soldiers before they could draw the spears oot again. They shouted loud in some foreign tongue, but no mercy was shown them. We went ower them like a wave, and trampled them doon into the mud, for they were few, and there was no end to our numbers.

'I found myself among buildings, and one of them was on fire. I saw the flames spoutin' through the roof. I ran on, and then I was alone among the buildings. Someone ran across in front o' me. It was a woman. I caught her by the arm, and I took her chin and turned her face so as the light of the fire would strike it. Whom think you that it was, Maggie?'

His wife moistened her dry lips. 'It was I,' she said.

He looked at her in surprise. 'That's a good guess,' said he. 'Yes, it was just you. Not merely like you, you understand. It was you – you yourself. I saw the same soul in your frightened eyes. You looked white and bonny and wonderful in the firelight. I had just one thought in my head – to get you awa' with me; to keep you all to mysel' in my own home somewhere beyond the hills. You clawed at my face with your nails. I heaved you over my shoulder, and I tried to find a way oot of the light of the burning hoose and back into the darkness.

'Then came the thing that I mind best of all. You're ill, Maggie. Shall I stop? My God! you have the very look on your face that you had last night in my dream. You screamed. He came runnin' in the firelight. His head was bare; his hair was black and curled; he had a naked sword in his hand, short and broad, little more than a dagger. He stabbed at me, but he tripped and fell. I held you with one hand, and with the other –'

His wife had sprung to her feet with writhing features.

'Marcus!' she cried. 'My beautiful Marcus! Oh, you brute! you brute! you brute!' There was a clatter of teacups as she fell forward senseless upon the table.

*

They never talk about that strange isolated incident in their married life. For an instant the curtain of the past had swung aside, and some strange glimpse of a forgotten life had come to them. But it closed down, never to open again. They live their narrow round – he in his shop, she in her household – and yet new and wider horizons have vaguely formed themselves around them since that summer evening by the crumbling Roman fort.

PART FOUR

A CLASSIC VICTORIAN
FAIRY TALE

THE GOLD OF FAIRNILEE

Andrew Lang

CHAPTER I

The Old House

You may still see the old Scots house where Randal was born, so long ago. Nobody lives there now. Most of the roof has fallen in, there is no glass in the windows, and all the doors are open. They were open in the days of Randal's father – nearly five hundred years have passed since then – and everyone who came was welcome to his share of beef and broth and ale. But now the doors are not only open, they are quite gone, and there is nobody within to give you a welcome.

So there is nothing but emptiness in the old house where Randal lived with Jean, four hundred and sixty years or so before you were born. It is a high old house, and wide, with the broken slates still on the roof. At the corner there are little round towers, like pepperboxes, with sharp peaks. The stems of the ivy that covers the walls are as thick as trees. There are many trees crowding all around, and there are hills around it too; and far below you hear the Tweed whispering all day. The house is called Fairnilee, which means 'the Fairies' Field'; for people believed in fairies, as you shall hear, when Randal was a boy, and even when my father was a boy.

Randal was all alone in the house when he was a little fellow – alone with his mother, and Nancy the old nurse, and Simon Grieve the butler, who wore a black velvet coat and a big silver chain. Then there were the maids, and the grooms, and the farm folk, who were all friends of Randal's. He was not lonely, and he did not feel unhappy, even before Jean came, as you shall be told. But the grown-up people were sad and silent at Fairnilee. Randal had no father; his mother, Lady Ker, was a widow. She was still quite young, and Randal thought her the most beautiful person in the world. Children think these things about their mothers, and Randal had seen no ladies but his mother only. She had brown hair and brown eyes and red lips, and a grave kind face, which looked serious under her great white widow's cap with the black hood over it. Randal never saw his mother cry; but when he was a very little child indeed, he had heard her crying in the night: this was after his father went away.

CHAPTER II

How Randal's Father Came Home

Randal remembered his father going to fight the English, and how he came back again. It was a windy August evening when he went away: the rain had fallen since morning. Randal had watched the white mists driven by the gale down through the black pine wood that covers the hill opposite Fairnilee. The mist looked like armies of ghosts, he thought, marching, marching through the pines, with their white flags flying and streaming. Then the sun came out red at evening, and Randal's father rode away with all his men. He had a helmet on his head, and a great axe hanging from his neck by a chain, and a spear in his hand. He was riding his big horse, Sir Hugh, and he caught Randal up to the saddle and kissed him many times before he clattered out of the courtyard. All the tenants and men about the farm rode with him, all with spears and a flag embroidered with a crest in gold. His mother watched them from the tower till they were out of sight. And Randal saw them ride away, not on hard, smooth roads like ours, but along a green grassy track, the water splashing up to their stirrups where they crossed the marshes.

Then the sky turned as red as blood, in the sunset, and next it grew brown, like the rust on a sword; and the Tweed below, when they rode the ford, was all red and gold and brown.

Then time went on; that seemed a long time to Randal. Only the women were left in the house, and Randal played with the shepherd's children. They sailed boats in the mill-pond, and they went down to the boat-pool and watched to see the big copper-coloured salmon splashing in the still water. One evening Randal looked up suddenly from his play. It was growing dark. He had been building a house with the round stones and wet sand by the river. He looked up, and there was his own father! He was riding all alone, and his horse, Sir Hugh, was very lean and lame, and scarred with the spurs. The spear in his father's hand was broken, and he had no sword; and he looked neither to right nor to left. His eyes were wide open, but he seemed to see nothing.

Randal cried out to him, 'Father! Father!' but he never glanced at Randal. He did not look as if he heard him; or knew he was there, and suddenly he seemed to go away, Randal did not know how or where.

Randal was frightened.

He ran into the house, and went to his mother.

'Oh, mother,' he said, 'I have seen father! He was riding all alone, and he would not look at me. Sir Hugh was lame!'

'Where has he gone?' said Lady Ker, in a strange voice.

'He went away out of sight,' said Randal. 'I could not see where he went.'

Then his mother told him it could not be, that his father would not have come back alone. He would not leave his men behind him in the war.

But Randal was so sure, that she did not scold him. She knew he believed what he said.

He saw that she was not happy.

All that night, which was the fourth of September, in the year 1513, the day of Flodden fight, Randal's mother did not go to bed. She kept moving about the house. Now she would look from the tower window up Tweed; and now she would go along the gallery and look down Tweed from the other tower. She had lights burning in all the windows. All next day she was never still. She climbed, with two of her maids, to the top of the hill above Yair, on the other side of the river, and she watched the roads down Ettrick and Yarrow. Next night she slept little, and rose early. About noon, Randal saw three or four men riding wearily, with tired horses. They could scarcely cross the ford of Tweed, the horses were so tired. The men were Simon Grieve the butler, and some of the tenants. They looked very pale; some of them had their heads tied up, and there was blood on their faces. Lady Ker and Randal ran to meet them.

Simon Grieve lighted from his horse, and whispered to Randal's mother.

Randal did not hear what he said, but his mother cried, 'I knew it! I knew it!' and turned quite white.

'Where is he?' she said.

Simon pointed across the hill. 'They are bringing the corp,' he said. Randal knew 'the corp' meant the dead body.

He began to cry. 'Where is my father?' he said. 'Where is my father?'

His mother led him into the house. She gave him to the old nurse, who cried over him, and kissed him, and offered him cakes, and made him a whistle with a branch of plane tree. So in a short while Randal only felt puzzled. Then he forgot, and began to play. He was a very little boy.

Lady Ker shut herself up in her own room – her 'bower', the servants called it.

Soon Randal heard heavy steps on the stairs, and whispering. He wanted to run out, and his nurse caught hold of him, and would not have let him go, but he slipped out of her hand, and looked over the staircase.

They were bringing up the body of a man stretched on a shield.

It was Randal's father.

He had been slain at Flodden, fighting for the king. An arrow had gone through his brain, and he had fallen beside James IV, with many another brave knight, all the best of Scotland, the Flowers of the Forest.

What was it Randal had seen, when he thought he met his father in the twilight, three days before?

He never knew. His mother said he must have dreamed it all.

The old nurse used to gossip about it to the maids. 'He's an unco' bairn, oor Randal; I wush he may na be fey.'

She meant that Randal was a strange child, and that strange things would happen to him.

CHAPTER III

How Jean was brought to Fairnilee

The winter went by very sadly. At first the people about Fairnilee expected the English to cross the Border and march against them. They drove their cattle out on the wild hills, and into marshes where only they knew the firm paths, and raised walls of earth and stones – *barmkyns*, they called them – around the old house; and made many arrows to shoot out of the narrow windows at the English. Randal used to like to see the arrow-making beside the fire at night. He was not afraid; and said he would show the English what he could do with his little bow. But weeks went on and no enemy came. Spring drew near, the snow melted from the hills. One night Randal was awakened by a great noise of shouting; he looked out of the window, and saw bright torches moving about. He heard the cows 'routing', or bellowing, and the women screaming. He thought the English had come. So they had; not the English army, but some robbers from the other side of the Border. At that time the people on the south side of Scotland and the north side of England used to steal each other's cows time about. When a Scots squire, or 'laird', like Randal's father, had been robbed by the neighbouring English, he would wait his chance and drive away cattle from the English side. This time most of Randal's mother's herds were seized, by a sudden attack in the night, and were driven away through the forest to England. Two or three of Lady Ker's men were hurt by the English, but old Simon Grieve took a prisoner. He did this in a curious way. He shot an arrow after the robbers as they rode off, and the arrow pinned an Englishman's leg to the saddle, and even into his horse. The horse was hurt and frightened, and ran away right back to Fairnilee, where it was caught, with the rider and all, for of course he could not dismount.

They treated him kindly at Fairnilee, though they laughed at him a good deal. They found out from him where the English had come from. He did not mind telling them, for he was really a gypsy from Yetholm, where the gypsies live, and Scot or Southron was all one to him.

When old Simon Grieve knew who the people were that had taken the cows, he was not long in calling the men together, and trying to get back what he had lost. Early one April morning, a grey morning, with snow in the air, he and his spearmen set out, riding down through the forest, and so into Liddesdale. When they came back again, there were great rejoicings at Fairnilee. They drove most of their own cows before them, and a great many other cows that they had not lost; cows of the English farmers. The byres and yards were soon full of cattle, lowing and roaring, very uneasy, and some of them with marks of the spears that had goaded them across many a ford, and up many a rocky pass in the hills.

Randal jumped downstairs to the great hall, where his mother sat. Simon Grieve was telling her all about it.

'Sae we drave oor ain kye hame, my lady,' he said, 'and aiblins some orra anes that was na oor ain. For-bye we raikit a' the plenishing oot o' the ha' o' Hardriding, and a bonny burden o' tapestries, and plaids, and gear we hae, to show for our ride.'*

Then he called to some of his men, who came into the hall, and cast down great piles of all sorts of spoil and booty, silver plate, and silken hangings, and a heap of rugs, and carpets, and plaids, such as Randal had never seen before, for the English were much richer than the Scots.

Randal threw himself on the pile of rugs and began to roll on it.

'Oh, mother,' he cried suddenly, jumping up and looking with wide-open eyes, 'there's something living in the heap! Perhaps it's a doggie, or a rabbit, or a kitten.'

---

* 'We drove our own cattle home, and perhaps some others that were not ours. And we took all the goods out of the hall at Hardriding, and a pretty load of tapestries, and rugs, and other things we have to show for our ride.'

Then Randal tugged at the cloths, and then they all heard a little shrill cry.

'Why, it's a bairn!' said Lady Ker, who had sat very grave all the time, pleased to have done the English some harm; for they had killed her husband, and were all her deadly foes. 'It's a bairn!' she cried, and pulled out of the great heap of cloaks and rugs a little beautiful child, in its white nightdress, with its yellow curls all tangled over its blue eyes.

Then Lady Ker and the old nurse could not make too much of the pretty English child that had come here in such a wonderful way.

How did it get mixed up with all the spoil? And how had it been carried so far on horseback without being hurt? Nobody ever knew. It came as if the fairies had sent it. English it was, but the best Scot could not hate such a pretty child. Old Nancy Dryden ran up to the old nursery with it, and laid it in a great wooden tub full of hot water, and was giving it warm milk to drink, and dandling it, almost before the men knew what had happened.

'Yon bairn will be a bonny mate for you, Maister Randal,' said old Simon Grieve. 'Deed, I dinna think her kin will come speering after her at Fairnilee. The red cock's crawing ower Hardriding Ha' this day, and when the womenfolk come back frae the wood, they'll hae other things to do forbye looking for bairns.'

When Simon Grieve said that the red cock was crowing over his enemies' home, he meant that he had set it on fire after the people who lived in it had run away.

Lady Ker grew pale when she heard what he said. She hated the English, to be sure, but she was a woman with a kind heart. She thought of the dreadful danger that the little English girl had escaped, and she went upstairs and helped the nurse to make the child happy.

speering, asking.

CHAPTER IV

Randal and Jean

The little girl soon made everyone at Fairnilee happy. She was
far too young to remember her own home, and presently she was
crawling up and down the long hall and making friends with
Randal. They found out that her name was Jane Musgrave,
though she could hardly say Musgrave; and they called her Jean,
with their Scots tongues, or 'Jean o' the Kye', because she came
when the cows were driven home again.

Soon the old nurse came to like her near as well as Randal,
'her ain bairn' (her own child), as she called him. In the summer
days, Jean, as she grew older, would follow Randal about like a
little doggie. They went fishing together, and Randal would pull
the trout out of Caddon Burn, or the Burn of Peel; and Jeanie
would be very proud of him, and very much alarmed at the big,
wide jaws of the yellow trout. And Randal would plait helmets
with green rushes for her and him, and make spears of bulrushes,
and play at tilts and tournaments. There was peace in the country;
or if there was war, it did not come near the quiet valley of the
Tweed and the hills that lie around Fairnilee. In summer they
were always on the hills and by the burnsides.

You cannot think, if you have not tried, what pleasant company a burn is. It comes out of the deep, black wells in the moss,
far away on the tops of the hills, where the sheep feed, and the
fox peers from his hole, and the ravens build in the crags. The
burn flows down from the lonely places, cutting a way between
steep, green banks, tumbling in white waterfalls over rocks, and
lying in black, deep pools below the waterfalls. At every turn it
does something new and plays a fresh game with its brown
waters. The white pebbles in the water look like gold: often
Randal would pick one out and think he had found a gold-mine,
till he got it into the sunshine, and then it was only a white stone,
what he called a 'chucky-stane'; but he kept hoping for better
luck next time. In the height of summer, when the streams were
very low, he and the shepherd's boys would build dams of stones

and turf across a narrow part of the burn, while Jean sat and watched them on a little round knoll. Then, when plenty of water had collected in the pool, they would break the dam and let it all run downhill in a little flood; they called it a 'hurly gush'. And in winter they would slide on the black, smooth ice of the boat-pool, beneath the branches of the alders.

Or they would go out with Yarrow, the shepherd's dog, and follow the track of wild creatures in the snow. The rabbit makes marks like this `•.•`, and the hare makes marks like this `•:•`; but the fox's track is just as if you had pushed a piece of wood through the snow – a number of cuts in the surface, going straight along. When it was very cold, the grouse and blackcocks would come into the trees near the house, and Randal and Jean would put out porridge for them to eat. And the great white swans floated in from the frozen lochs on the hills, and gathered around open reaches and streams of the Tweed. It was pleasant to be a boy then in the North. And at Hallowe'en they would duck for apples in tubs of water, and burn nuts in the fire, and look for the shadow of the lady Randal was to marry, in the mirror; but he only saw Jean looking over his shoulder.

The days were very short in winter, so far north, and they would soon be driven into the house. Then they sat by the nursery fire; and those were almost the pleasantest hours, for the old nurse would tell them old Scots stories of elves and fairies, and sing them old songs. Jean would crawl close to Randal and hold his hand, for fear the Red Etin, or some other awful bogle, should get her; and in the dancing shadows of the firelight she would think she saw Whuppity Stoorie, the wicked old witch with the spinning-wheel; but it was really nothing but the shadow of the wheel that the old nurse drove with her foot – *birr, birr* – and that whirred and rattled as she span and told her tale. For people span their cloth at home then, instead of buying it from shops; and the old nurse was a great woman for spinning.

She was a great woman for stories, too, and believed in fairies, and 'bogles', as she called them. Had not her own cousin, Andrew

---

bogle, ghost, spectre.
Whuppity Stoorie, the name of a witch or bad fairy in Border folklore.

Tamson, passed the Cauldshiels Loch one New Year morning? And had he not heard a dreadful roaring, as if all the cattle on Faldonside Hill were routing at once? And then did he not see a great black beast roll down the hillside, like a black ball, and run into the loch, which grew white with foam, and the waves leaped up the banks like a tide rising? What could that be except the kelpie that lives in Cauldshiels Loch, and is just a muckle big water bull? 'And what for should there no be water kye, if there's land kye?'

Randal and Jean thought it was very likely there were 'kye', or cattle, in the water. And some Highland people think so still, and believe they have seen the great kelpie come roaring out of the lake; or Shellycoat, whose skin is all crusted like a rock with shells, sitting beside the sea.

The old nurse had other tales, that nobody believes any longer, about Brownies. A Brownie was a very useful creature to have in a house. He was a kind of fairy-man, and he came out in the dark, when everybody had gone to bed, just as mice pop out at night. He never did anyone any harm, but he sat and warmed himself at the kitchen fire. If any work was unfinished he did it, and made everything tidy that was left out of order. It is a pity there are no such bogles now! If anybody offered the Brownie any payment, even if it was only a silver penny or a new coat, he would take offence and go away.

Other stories the old nurse had, about hidden treasures and buried gold. If you believed her, there was hardly an old stone on the hillside that didn't have gold under it. The very sheep that fed upon the Eildon Hills, which Randal knew well, had yellow teeth because there was so much gold under the grass. Randal had taken two scones, or rolls, in his pocket for dinner, and ridden over to the Eildon Hills. He had seen a rainbow touch one of them, and there he hoped he would find the treasure that always lies at the tail of the rainbow. But he got very soon tired of digging for it with his little dirk, or dagger. It blunted the dagger, and he found nothing. Perhaps he had not marked quite the right place, he thought. But he looked at the teeth of the sheep, and they were yellow; so he had no doubt that there was a gold-mine under the grass, if he could find it.

The old nurse knew that it was very difficult to dig up fairy gold. Generally something happened just when people heard their pickaxes clink on the iron pot that held the treasure. A dreadful storm of thunder and lightning would break out; or the burn would be flooded, and rush down all red and roaring, sweeping away the tools and drowning the digger; or a strange man, that nobody had ever seen before, would come up, waving his arms, and crying out that the Castle was on fire. Then the people would hurry up to the Castle, and find that it was not on fire at all. When they returned, all the earth would be just as it was before they began, and they would give up in despair. Nobody could ever see the man again that gave the alarm.

'Who could he be, nurse?' Randal asked.

'Just one of the good folk, I'm thinking; but it's no weel to be speaking o' *them*.'

Randal knew that the 'good folk' meant the fairies. The old nurse called them the good folk for fear of offending them. She would not speak much about them, except now and then, when the servants had been making merry.

'And is there any treasure hidden near Fairnilee, nursie?' asked little Jean.

'Treasure, my bonny doo! Mair than a' the men about the toon could carry away frae morning till nicht. Do ye no ken the auld rhyme?

> Atween the wet ground and the dry
> The gold of Fairnilee doth lie.

'And there's the other auld rhyme:

> Between the Camp o' Rink
> And Tweed-water clear,
> Lie nine kings' ransoms
> For nine hundred year!'

Randal and Jean were very glad to hear so much gold was near them as would pay nine kings' ransoms. They took their small spades and dug little holes in the Camp of Rink, which is a great old circle of stonework, surrounded by a deep ditch, on the top of a hill above the house. But Jean was not a very good digger, and even Randal grew tired. They thought they would wait till they grew bigger, and *then* find the gold.

CHAPTER V

The Good Folk

'Everybody knows there's fairies,' said the old nurse one night when she was bolder than usual. What she said we will put in English, not Scots as she spoke it. 'But they do not like to be called fairies. So the old rhyme runs:

> *If ye call me imp or elf,*
> *I warn you look well to yourself;*
> *If ye call me fairy,*
> *Ye'll find me quite contrary;*
> *If good neighbour you call me,*
> *Then good neighbour I will be;*
> *But if you call me kindly sprite,*
> *I'll be your friend both day and night.*

'So you must always call them "good neighbours" or "good folk", when you speak of them.'

'Did *you* ever see a fairy, nurse?' asked Randal.

'Not myself, but my mother knew a woman – they called her Tibby Dickson, and her husband was a shepherd, and she had a bairn, as bonny a bairn as ever you saw. And one day she went to the well to draw water, and as she was coming back she heard a loud scream in her house. Then her heart leaped, and fast she ran and flew to the cradle; and there she saw an awful sight – not her own bairn, but a withered imp, with hands like a mole's, and a face like a frog's, and a mouth from ear to ear, and two great staring eyes.'

'What was it?' asked Jeanie, in a trembling voice.

'A fairy's bairn that had not thriven,' said nurse; 'and when their bairns do not thrive, they just steal honest folk's children and carry them away to their own country.'

'And where's that?' asked Randal.

'It's under the ground,' said nurse, 'and there they have gold and silver and diamonds; and there's the Queen of them all, that's as beautiful as the day. She has yellow hair down to her feet, and she has blue eyes, like the sky on a fine day, and her voice like all the mavises singing in the spring. And she is aye dressed in green, and all her court in green; and she rides a white horse with golden bells on the bridle.'

'I would like to go there and see her,' said Randal.

'Oh, never say that, my bairn; you never know who may hear you! And if you go there, how will you come back again? And what will your mother do, and Jean here, and me that's carried you many a time in weary arms when you were a babe?'

'Can't people come back again?' asked Randal.

'Some say "Yes", and some say "No". There was Tam Hislop, that vanished away the day before all the lads and your own father went forth to that weary war at Flodden, and the English, for once, by guile, won the day. Well, Tam Hislop, when the news came that all must arm and mount and ride, he could nowhere be found. It was as if the wind had carried him away. High and low they sought him, but there was his clothes and his armour, and his sword and his spear, but no Tam Hislop. Well, no man heard more of him for seven whole years, not till last year, and then he came back: sore tired he looked, ay, and older than when he was lost. And I met him by the well, and I was frightened; and, "Tam," I said, "where have ye been this weary time?" "I have been with them that I will not speak the name of," says he. "Ye mean the good folk," said I. "Ye have said it," says he. Then I went up to the house, with my heart in my mouth, and I met Simon Grieve. "Simon," I says, "here's Tam Hislop come home from the good folk." "I'll soon send him back to them," says he. And he takes a great stick and lays it about Tam's

mavises, song-thrushes.

shoulders, calling him coward loon, that ran away from the fighting. And since then Tam has never been seen about the place. But the Laird's man, of Gala, knows them that say Tam was in Perth the last seven years, and not in Fairyland at all. But it was Fairyland he told me, and he would not lie to his own mother's half-brother's cousin.'

Randal did not care much for the story of Tam Hislop. A fellow who would let old Simon Grieve beat him could not be worthy of the Fairy Queen.

Randal was about thirteen now, a tall boy, with dark eyes, black hair, a brown face with the red on his cheeks. He had grown up in a country where everything was magical and haunted; where fairy knights rode on the leas after dark, and challenged men to battle. Every castle had its tale of Redcap, the sly spirit, or of the woman of the hairy hand. Every old mound was thought to cover hidden gold. And all was so lonely; the green hills rolling between river and river, with no men on them, nothing but sheep, and grouse, and plover. No wonder that Randal lived in a kind of dream. He would lie and watch the long grass until it looked like a forest, and he thought he could see elves dancing between the green grass stems, that were like fairy trees. He kept wishing that he, too, might meet the Fairy Queen, and be taken into that other world where everything was beautiful.

CHAPTER VI

The Wishing Well

'Jean,' said Randal one midsummer day, 'I am going to the Wishing Well.'

'Oh, Randal,' said Jean, 'it is so far away!'

'I can walk it,' said Randal, 'and you must come, too; I want you to come, Jeanie. It's not so very far.'

'But mother says it is wrong to go to Wishing Wells,' Jean answered.

loon, rascal.

'Why is it wrong?' said Randal, switching at the tall foxgloves with a stick.

'Oh, she says it is a wicked thing, and forbidden by the Church. People who go to wish there, sacrifice to the spirits of the well; and Father Francis told her that it was very wrong.'

'Father Francis is a shaveling,' said Randal. 'I heard Simon Grieve say so.'

'What's a shaveling, Randal?'

'I don't know: a man that does not fight, I think. I don't care what a shaveling says: so I mean just to go and wish, and I won't sacrifice anything. There can't be any harm in that!'

'But, oh, Randal, you've got your green doublet on!'

'Well! Why not?'

'Do you not know it angers the fair– I mean the good folk – that anyone should wear green on the hill but themselves?'

'I cannot help it,' said Randal. 'If I go in and change my doublet, they will ask what I do that for. I'll chance it, green or grey, and wish my wish for all that.'

'And what are you going to wish?'

'I'm going to wish to meet the Fairy Queen! Just think how beautiful she must be, dressed all in green, with gold bells on her bridle, and riding a white horse shod with gold! I think I see her galloping through the woods and out across the hill, over the heather.'

'But you will go away with her, and never see me any more,' said Jean.

'No, I won't; or if I do, I'll come back, with such a horse, and a sword with a gold handle. I'm going to the Wishing Well. Come on!'

Jean did not like to say 'No', so off they went.

Randal and Jean started without taking anything with them to eat. They were afraid to go back to the house for food. Randal said they would be sure to find something somewhere. The Wishing Well was on the top of a hill between Yarrow and Tweed. So they took off their shoes, and waded the Tweed at the shallowest part, and then they walked up the green grassy bank on the other side, until they came to the Burn of Peel. Here they passed the old square tower of Peel, and the shepherd dogs came out and barked at them. Randal threw a stone at them, and they ran away with their tails between their legs.

'Don't you think we had better go into Peel, and get some bannocks to eat on the way, Randal?' said Jean.

But Randal said he was not hungry; and, besides, the people at Peel would tell the Fairnilee people where they had gone.

'We'll *wish* for things to eat when we get to the Wishing Well,' said Randal. 'All sorts of good things – cold venison pasty, and everything you like.'

So they began climbing the hill, and they followed the Peel Burn. It ran in and out, winding this way and that, and when they did get to the top of the hill, Jean was very tired and very hungry. And she was very disappointed. For she expected to see some wonderful new country at her feet, and there was only a low strip of sunburnt grass and heather, and then another hill-top! So Jean sat down, and the hot sun blazed on her, and the flies buzzed about her and tormented her.

'Come on, Jean,' said Randal; 'it must be over the next hill!'

So poor Jean got up and followed him, but he walked far too fast for her. When she reached the crest of the next hill, she found a great cairn, or pile of grey stones; and beneath her lay, far, far below, a deep valley covered with woods, and a stream running through it that she had never seen before.

That stream was the Yarrow.

Randal was nowhere in sight, and she did not know where to look for the Wishing Well. If she had walked straight forward through the trees she would have come to it; but she was so tired, and so hungry, and so hot, that she sat down at the foot of the cairn and cried as if her heart would break.

Then she fell asleep.

When Jean woke, it was as dark as it ever is on a midsummer night in Scotland.

It was a soft, cloudy night; not a clear night with a silver sky.

Jeanie heard a loud roaring close to her, and the red light of a great fire was in her sleepy eyes.

In the firelight she saw strange black beasts, with horns, plung-

bannocks, oatcakes.

ing and leaping and bellowing, and dark figures rushing about
the flames. It was the beasts that made the roaring. They were
bounding about close to the fire, and sometimes in it, and were
all mixed in the smoke.

Jeanie was dreadfully frightened, too frightened to scream.

Presently she heard the voices of men shouting on the hill
below her. The shouts and the barking of dogs came nearer and
nearer.

Then a dog ran up to her, and licked her face, and jumped
about her.

It was her own sheep-dog, Yarrow.

He ran back to the men who were following him, and came
again with one of them.

It was old Simon Grieve, very tired, and so much out of breath
that he could scarcely speak.

Jean was very glad to see him, and not frightened any longer.

'Oh, Jeanie, my doo,' said Simon, 'where hae ye been? A
muckle gliff ye hae gien us, and a weary spiel up the weary braes.'

Jean told him all about it: how she had come with Randal to
see the Wishing Well, and how she had lost him, and fallen
asleep.

'And sic a nicht for you bairns to wander on the hill,' said
Simon. 'It's the nicht o' St John, when the guid folk hae power.
And there's a' the lads burning the Bel fires, and driving the nowt
through them: nae less will serve them. Sic a nicht!'

This was the cause of the fire Jean saw, and of the noise of the
cattle. On Midsummer Night the country people used to light
these fires, and drive the cattle through them. It was an old, old
custom come down from heathen times.

Now the other men from Fairnilee had gathered around Jean.
Lady Ker had sent them out to look for Randal and her on the
hills. They had heard from the good wife at Peel that the children
had gone up the burn, and Yarrow had tracked them until Jean
was found.

gliff, fright.   *spiel*, shout.   *nowt*, cattle.

CHAPTER VII

Where is Randal?

Jean was found, but where was Randal? She told the men who had come out to look for her, that Randal had gone on to look for the Wishing Well. So they rolled her up in a big shepherd's plaid, and two of them carried Jean home in the plaid, while all the rest, with lighted torches in their hands, went to look for Randal through the wood.

Jean was so tired that she fell asleep again in her plaid before they reached Fairnilee. She was wakened by the men shouting as they drew near the house, to show that they were coming home. Lady Ker was waiting at the gate, and the old nurse ran down the grassy path to meet them.

'Where's my bairn?' she cried as soon as she was within call.

The men said, 'Here's Mistress Jean, and Randal will be here soon; they have gone to look for him.'

'Where are they looking?' cried nurse.

'Just about the Wishing Well.'

The nurse gave a scream, and hobbled back to Lady Ker.

'Ma bairn's tint!' she cried. 'Ma bairn's tint! They'll find him never. The good folk have stolen him away from that weary Wishing Well!'

'Hush, nurse,' said Lady Ker, 'do not frighten Jean.'

She spoke to the men, who had no doubt that Randal would soon be found and brought home.

So Jean was put to bed, where she forgot all her troubles; and Lady Ker waited, waited, all night, until the grey light began to come in, about two in the morning.

Lady Ker kept very still and quiet, telling her beads, and praying. But the old nurse would never be still, but was always wandering out, down to the river's edge, listening for the shouts of the shepherds coming home. Then she would come back again, and moan and wring her hands, crying for her 'bairn'.

tint, lost.

About six o'clock, when it was broad daylight and all the birds were singing, the men returned from the hill.

But Randal did not come with them.

Then the old nurse set up a great cry, as the country people do over the bed of someone who has just died.

Lady Ker sent her away, and called Simon Grieve to her own room.

'You have not found the boy yet?' she said, very stately and pale. 'He must have wandered over into Yarrow; perhaps he has gone as far as Newark, and passed the night at the castle, or with the shepherd at Foulshiels.'

'No, my Lady,' said Simon Grieve, 'some o' the men went over to Newark, and some to Foulshiels, and other some down to Sir John Murray's at Philiphaugh; but there's never a word o' Randal in a' the countryside.'

'Did you find no trace of him?' said Lady Ker, sitting down suddenly in the great armchair.

'We went first through the wood, my Lady, by the path to the Wishing Well. And he had been there, for the whip he carried in his hand was lying on the grass. And we found *this*.'

He put his hand in his pouch, and brought out a little silver crucifix, that Randal used always to wear around his neck on a chain.

'This was lying on the grass beside the Wishing Well, my Lady –'

Then he stopped, for Lady Ker had swooned away. She was worn out with watching and with anxiety about Randal.

Simon went and called the maids, and they brought water and wine, and soon Lady Ker came back to herself, with the little silver crucifix in her hand.

The old nurse was crying, and making a great noise.

'The good folk have taken ma bairn,' she said, 'this nicht o' a' the nichts in the year, when the fairy folk – preserve us frae them! – have power. But they could nae take the blessed rood o' grace; it was beyond their strength. If gypsies, or robber folk frae the Debatable Land, had carried away the bairn, they would hae

Debatable Land, a no-man's land at the head of the Solway Firth, between England and Scotland.

taken him, cross and a'. But the guid folk have gotten him, and Randal Ker will never, never mair come hame to bonny Fairnilee.'

What the old nurse said was what everybody thought. Even Simon Grieve shook his head, and did not like it.

But Lady Ker did not give up hope. She sent horsemen through all the countryside: up Tweed to the Crook, and to Talla; up Yarrow, past Catslack Tower, and on to the Loch of St Mary; up Ettrick to Thirlestane and Buccleuch, and over to Gala, and to Branxholme in Teviotdale; and even to Hermitage Castle, far away by Liddel water.

They rode far and rode fast, and at every cottage and every tower they asked, 'Has anyone seen a boy in green?' But nobody had seen Randal through all the countryside. Only a shepherd lad, on Foulshiels Hill, had heard bells ringing in the night, and a sound of laughter go past him, like a breeze of wind over the heather.

Days went by, and all the country was out to look for Randal. Down in Yetholm they sought him, among the gypsies; and across the Eden in merry Carlisle; and through the Land Debatable, where the robber Armstrongs and Grahames lived; and far down Tweed, past Melrose, and up Jed water, far into the Cheviot Hills.

But there never came any word of Randal. He had vanished as if the earth had opened and swallowed him. Father Francis came from Melrose Abbey, and prayed with Lady Ker, and gave her all the comfort he could. He shook his head when he heard of the Wishing Well, but he said that no spirit of earth or air could have power for ever over a Christian soul. But, even when he spoke, he remembered that, once in seven years, the fairy folk have to pay a dreadful tax, one of themselves, to the King of a terrible country of Darkness; and what if they had stolen Randal, to pay the tax with him!

This was what troubled good Father Francis, though, like a wise man, he said nothing about it, and even put the thought away out of his own mind.

But you may be sure that the old nurse had thought of this tax on the fairies too, and that *she* did not hold her peace about it, but spoke to everyone that would listen to her, and would have spoken to the mistress if she had been allowed. But when she tried to begin, Lady Ker told her that she had put her own trust in Heaven, and in the saints. And she gave the nurse such a look when she said that, 'if ever Jean hears of this, I will send you away from Fairnilee, out of the country,' that the old woman was afraid, and was quiet.

As for poor Jean, she was perhaps the most unhappy of them all. She thought to herself, if she had refused to go with Randal to the Wishing Well, and had run in and told Lady Ker, then Randal would never have gone to find the Wishing Well.

And she put herself in great danger, as she fancied, to find him. She wandered alone on the hills, seeking all the places that were believed to be haunted by fairies. At every Fairy Knowe, as the country people called the little round green knolls in the midst of the heather, Jean would stoop her ear to the ground, trying to hear the voices of the fairies within. For it was believed that you might hear the sound of their speech, and the trampling of their horses, and the shouts of the fairy children. But no sound came, except the song of the burn flowing by, and the hum of gnats in the air, and the *gock, gock*, the cry of the grouse, when you frighten them in the heather.

Then Jeanie would try another way of meeting the fairies, and finding Randal. She would walk nine times around a Fairy Knowe, beginning from the left side, because then it was fancied that the hillside would open, like a door, and show a path into Fairyland. But the hillside never opened, and she never saw a single fairy; not even old Whuppity Stoorie sitting with her spinning-wheel in a green glen, spinning grass into gold, and singing her fairy song:

> 'I once was young and fair,
> My eyes were bright and blue,
> As if the sun shone through,
> And golden was my hair.
>
> Down to my feet it rolled
> Ruddy and ripe like corn,
> Upon an autumn morn,
> In heavy waves of gold.

Now am I grey and old,
And so I sit and spin,
With trembling hand and thin,
This metal bright and cold.

I would give all the gain,
These heaps of wealth untold
Of hard and glittering gold,
Could I be young again!'

CHAPTER VIII

The Ill Years

So autumn came, and all the hillsides were golden with the heather; and the red coral berries of the rowan trees hung from the boughs, and were wet with the spray of the waterfalls in the burns. And days grew shorter, and winter came with snow, but Randal never came back to Fairnilee. Season after season passed, and year after year. Lady Ker's hair grew white like snow, and her face thin and pale – for she fasted often, as was the rule of her Church; all this was before the Reformation. And she slept little, praying half the night for Randal's sake. And she went on pilgrimages to many shrines of the saints: to St Boswells and St Rules, hard by the great Cathedral of St Andrews on the sea. Nay, she went across the Border as far as the Abbey of St Albans, and even to St Thomas's shrine of Canterbury, taking Jean with her. Many a weary mile they rode over hill and dale, and many an adventure they had, and ran many dangers from robbers, and soldiers disbanded from the wars.

But at last they had to come back to Fairnilee; and a sad place it was, and silent without the sound of Randal's voice in the hall, and the noise of his hunting-horn in the woods. None of the people wore mourning for him, though they mourned in their hearts. For to put on black would look as if they had given up all hope. Perhaps most of them thought they would never see him again, but Jeanie was not one who despaired.

The years that had turned Lady Ker's hair white, had made Jean a tall, slim lass – 'very bonny', everyone said; and the country people called her the Flower of Tweed. The Yarrow folk had their Flower of Yarrow, and why not the folk of Tweedside? It was now six years since Randal had been lost, and Jeanie was grown a young woman, about seventeen years old. She had always kept a hope that if Randal was with the Fairy Queen he would return perhaps in the seventh year. People said in the countryside that many a man and woman had escaped out of Fairyland after seven years' imprisonment there.

Now the sixth year since Randal's disappearance began very badly, and got worse as it went on. Just when spring should have been beginning, in the end of February, there came the most dreadful snowstorm. It blew and snowed, and blew again, and the snow was as fine as the dust on a road in summer. The strongest shepherds could not hold their own against the tempest, and were 'smoored' in the waste. The flocks moved down from the hillsides, down and down, until all the sheep on a farm would be gathered together in a crowd, under the shelter of a wood in some deep dip of the hills. The storm seemed as if it would never cease; for thirteen days the snow drifted and the wind blew. There was nothing for the sheep to eat, and if there had been hay enough, it would have been impossible to carry it to them. The poor beasts bit at the wool on each other's backs, and so many of them died that the shepherds built walls with the dead bodies to keep the wind and snow away from those that were left alive.

There could be little work done on the farm that spring; and summer came in so cold and wet that the corn could not ripen, but was levelled to the ground. Then autumn was rainy, and the green sheaves lay out in the fields, and sprouted and rotted; so that little corn was reaped, and little flour could be made that year. Then in winter, and as spring came on, the people began to starve. They had no grain, and there were no potatoes in those days, and no rice; nor could corn be brought in from foreign

smoored, smothered.

THE GOLD OF FAIRNILEE

174

THE GOLD OF FAIRNILEE

countries. So men and women and children might be seen in the fields, with white pinched faces, gathering nettles to make soup, and digging for roots that were often little better than poison. They ground the bark of the fir trees, and mixed it with the little flour they could get; and they ate such beasts as never are eaten except in time of famine.

It is said that one very poor woman and her daughter always looked healthy and plump in these dreadful times, until people began to suspect them of being witches. And they were taken, and charged before the Sheriff with living by witchcraft, and very likely they would have been burned. So they confessed that they had fed ever since the famine began – on snails! But there were not snails enough for all the countryside; even if people had cared to eat them. So many men and women died, and more were very weak and ill.

Lady Ker spent all her money in buying food for her people. Jean and she lived on as little as they could, and were as careful as they could be. They sold all the beautiful silver plate, except the cup that Randal's father used to drink out of long ago. But almost everything else was sold to buy corn.

So the weary year went on, and Midsummer Night came round – the seventh since the night when Randal was lost.

Then Jean did what she had always meant to do. In the afternoon she slipped out of the house of Fairnilee, taking a little bread in a basket, and saying that she would go to see the farmer's wife at Peel, which was on the other side of Tweed. But her mind was to go to the Wishing Well. There she would wish for Randal back again, to help his mother in the evil times. And if she, too, passed away as he had passed out of sight and hearing, then at least she might meet him in that land where he had been carried. How strange it seemed to Jean to be doing everything over again that she had done seven years before! Then she had been a little girl, and it had been hard work for her to climb up the side of the Peel Burn. Now she walked lightly and quickly, for she was tall and well grown. Soon she reached the crest of the first hill, and remembered how she had sat down there and cried, when she was a child, and how the flies had tormented her. They were buzzing and teasing still; for good times or bad make no difference to them, as long as the sun shines. Then she reached the cairn at the top of the next hill, and far below her lay the forest, and deep within it ran the Yarrow, glittering like silver.

Jean paused a few moments, and then struck into a green path which led through the wood. The path wound beneath dark pines; their topmost branches were red in the evening light, but the shade was black beneath them. Soon the path reached a little grassy glade, and there among cold, wet grasses was the Wishing Well. It was almost hidden by the grass, and looked very black, and cool, and deep. A tiny trickle of water flowed out of it and flowed down to join the Yarrow. The trees about it had scraps of rags and other things pinned to them, offerings made by the country people to the spirit of the well.

CHAPTER IX

The White Roses

Jeanie sat down beside the well. She wished her three wishes: to see Randal, to win him back from Fairyland, and to help the people in the famine. Then she knelt on the grass, and looked down into the well-water. At first she saw nothing but the smooth black water, with little waves trembling in it. Then the water began to grow bright within, as if the sun was shining far, far below. Then it grew as clear as crystal, and she saw through it, like a glass, into a new country – a beautiful country with a wide green plain, and in the midst of the plain a great castle, with golden flags floating from the tops of all the towers. Then she heard a curious whispering noise that thrilled and murmured, as if the music of all the trees that the wind blows through the world were in her ears, as if the noise of all the waves of every sea, and the rustling of heather-bells on every hill, and the singing of all birds were sounding, low and sweet, far, far away. Then she saw a great company of knights and ladies, dressed in green, ride up to the castle; and one knight rode apart from the rest, on a milk-white steed. They all went into the castle gates; but this

knight rode slowly and sadly behind the others, with his head
bowed on his breast.

Then the musical sounds were still, and the castle and the plain
seemed to waver in the water. Next they quite vanished, and the
well grew dim, and then grew dark and black and smooth as it
had been before. Still she looked, and the little well bubbled up
with sparkling foam, and so became still again, like a mirror,
until Jeanie could see her own face in it, and beside her face came
the reflection of another face, a young man's, dark, and sad, and
beautiful. The lips smiled at her, and then Jeanie knew it was
Randal. She thought he must be looking over her shoulder, and
she leaped up with a cry, and glanced around.

But she was all alone, and the wood about her was empty and
silent. The light had gone out of the sky, which was pale like
silver, and overhead she saw the evening star.

Then Jeanie thought all was over. She had seen Randal as if it
had been in a glass, and she hardly knew him: he was so much
older, and his face was so sad. She sighed, and turned to go away
over the hills, back to Fairnilee.

But her feet did not seem to carry her the way she wanted to
go. It seemed as if something within her were moving her in a
kind of dream. She felt herself going on through the forest, she
did not know where. Deeper into the wood she went, and now
it grew so dark that she saw scarcely anything; only she felt the
fragrance of brier-roses, and it seemed to her that she was guided
towards these roses. Then she knew there was a hand in her
hand, though she saw nobody, and the hand seemed to lead her
on. And she came to an open place in the forest, and there the
silver light fell clear from the sky, and she saw a great shadowy
rose tree, covered with white wild roses.

The hand was still in her hand, and Jeanie began to wish for
nothing so much in the world as to gather some of these roses.
She put out her hand and she plucked one, and there before her
stood a strange creature – a dwarf, dressed in yellow and red,
with a very angry face.

'Who are you,' he cried, 'that pluck my roses without my will?'

'And who are *you*?' said Jeanie, trembling, 'and what right
have you on the hills of this world?'

Then she made the holy sign of the cross, and the face of the elf grew black, and the light went out of the sky.

She only saw the faint glimmer of the white flowers, and a kind of shadow standing where the dwarf stood.

'I bid you tell me,' said Jeanie, 'whether you are a Christian man, or a spirit that dreads the holy sign,' and she crossed him again.

Now all grew dark as the darkest winter's night. The air was warm and deadly still, and heavy with the scent of the fairy flowers.

In the blackness and the silence, Jeanie made the sacred sign for the third time. Then a clear fresh wind blew on her face, and the forest boughs were shaken, and the silver light grew and gained on the darkness, and she began to see a shape standing where the dwarf had stood. It was far taller than the dwarf, and the light grew and grew, and a star looked down out of the night, and Jean saw Randal standing by her. And she kissed him, and he kissed her, and he put his hand in hers, and they went out of the wood together. They came to the crest of the hill and the cairn. Far below them they saw the Tweed shining through an opening among the trees, and the lights in the farm of Peel, and they heard the night-birds crying, and the bells of the sheep ringing musically as they wandered through the fragrant heather on the hills.

CHAPTER X

Out of Fairyland

You may fancy, if you can, what joy there was in Fairnilee when Randal came home. They quite forgot the hunger and the hard times, and the old nurse laughed and cried over her bairn that had grown into a tall, strong young man. And to Lady Ker it was all one as if her husband had come again, as he was when first she knew him long ago; for Randal had his face, and his eyes, and the very sound of his voice. They could hardly believe he was not a spirit, and they clasped his hands, and hung on his neck, and could not keep their eyes off him. This was the end of all their sorrow, and it was as if Randal had come back from the dead; so that no people in the world were ever so happy as they were next day, when the sun shone down on the Tweed and the green trees that rustle in the wind around Fairnilee. But in the evening, when the old nurse was out of the way, Randal sat between his mother and Jean, and they each held his hands, as if they could not let him go, for fear he should vanish away from them again. And they would turn round anxiously if anything stirred, for fear it should be the two white deer that sometimes were said to come for people escaped from Fairyland, and then these people must rise and follow them, and never return any more. But the white deer never came for Randal.

So he told them all his adventures, and all that had happened to him since that Midsummer Night, seven long years ago.

It had been with him as it was with Jean. He had gone to the Wishing Well, and wished to see the Fairy Queen and Fairyland. And he had seen the beautiful castle in the well, and a beautiful woman's face had floated up to meet his on the water. Then he had gathered the white roses, and then he heard a great sound of horses' feet, and of bells jingling, and a lady rode up, the very lady he had seen in the well. She had a white horse, and she was dressed in green, and she beckoned to Randal to mount on her horse, with her before him on the pillion. And the bells on the bridle rang, and the horse flew faster than the wind.

So they rode and rode through the summer night, and they came to a desert place, and living lands were left far behind. Then the Fairy Queen showed him three paths, one steep and narrow, and beset with briers and thorns: that was the road to goodness and happiness, but it was little trodden or marked with the feet of people that had come and gone.

And there was a wide smooth road that went through fields of lilies, and that was the path of easy living and pleasure.

The third path wound about the wild hillside, through ferns and heather, and that was the way to Elfland, and that way they rode. And still they rode through a country of dark night, and they crossed great black rivers, and they saw neither sun nor moon, but they heard the roaring of the sea. From that country they came into the light, and into the beautiful garden that lies around the castle of the Fairy Queen. There they lived in a noble company of gallant knights and fair ladies. All seemed very mirthful, and they rode, and hunted and danced; and it was never dark night, nor broad daylight, but like early summer dawn before the sun has risen.

There Randal said that he had quite forgotten his mother and Jean, and the world where he was born, and Fairnilee.

But one day he happened to see a beautiful golden bottle of a strange shape, all set with diamonds, and he opened it. There was in it a sweet-smelling water, as clear as crystal, and he poured it into his hand, and passed his hand over his eyes. Now this water had the power to destroy the 'glamour' in Fairyland, and make people see it as it really was. And when Randal touched his eyes with it, lo, everything was changed in a moment. He saw that nothing was what it had seemed. The gold vanished from the embroidered curtains, the light grew dim and wretched like a misty winter day. The Fairy Queen, that had seemed so happy and beautiful in her bright dress, was a weary, pale woman in black, with a melancholy face and melancholy eyes. She looked as if she had been there for thousands of years, always longing for the sunlight and the earth, and the wind and rain. There were sleepy poppies twisted in her hair, instead of a golden crown. And the knights and ladies were changed. They looked but half alive; and some, in place of their bright green robes, were dressed in rusty mail, pierced with spears and stained with blood. And some were in burial robes of white, and some in dresses torn or dripping with water, or marked with the burning of fire. All were dressed strangely in some ancient fashion; their weapons were old-fashioned, too, unlike any that Randal had ever seen on earth. And their banquets were not of dainty meats, but of cold, tasteless flesh, and of beans, and pulses, and such things as the old heathens, before the coming of the Gospel, used to offer to the dead. It was dreadful to see them at such feasts, and dancing and riding, and pretending to be merry with hollow faces and unhappy eyes.

pulses, lentils.

And Randal wearied of Fairyland, which now that he saw it clearly looked like a great unending stretch of sand and barren grassy country, beside a grey sea where there was no tide. All the woods were of black cypress trees and poplar, and a wind from the sea drove a sea-mist through them, white and cold, and it blew through the open courts of the fairy castle.

So Randal longed more and more for the old earth he had left, and the changes of summer and autumn, and the streams of Tweed, and the hills, and his friends. Then the voice of Jeanie had come down to him, sounding from far away. And he was sent up by the Fairy Queen in a fairy form, as a hideous dwarf, to frighten her away from the white roses in the enchanted forest.

But her goodness and her courage had saved him, for he was a christened knight, and not a man of the fairy world. And he had taken his own form again beneath her hand, when she signed him with the Cross, and here he was, safe and happy, at home at Fairnilee.

CHAPTER XI

The Fairy Bottle

We soon grow used to the greatest changes, and almost forget the things that we were accustomed to before. In a day or two, Randal had nearly forgotten what a dull life he had lived in Fairyland, after he had touched his eyes with the strange water in the fairy bottle. He remembered the long, grey sands, and the cold mist, and the white faces of the strange people, and the gloomy queen, no more than you remember the dream you dreamed a week ago. But he did notice that Fairnilee was not the happy place it had been before he went away. Here, too, the faces were pinched and white, and the people looked hungry. And he missed many things that he remembered: the silver cups, and plates, and tankards. And the dinners were not like they had been, but only a little thin soup, and some oatmeal cakes, and trout taken from the Tweed. The beef and ale of old times were not to be found, even in the houses of the richer people.

Very soon Randal heard all about the famine; you may be sure the old nurse was ready to tell him all the saddest stories.

> Full many a place in evil case
> Where joy was wont afore, oh!
> Wi' Humes that dwell in Leader braes,
> And Scotts that dwell in Yarrow!

And the old woman would croon her old prophecies, and tell them how Thomas the Rymer, that lived in Ercildoune, had foretold all this. And she would wish they could find these hidden treasures that the rhymes were full of, and that maybe were lying – who knew – quite near them on their own lands.

'Where is the gold of Fairnilee?' she would cry; and, 'Oh, Randal! can you no dig for it, and find it, and buy corn out of England for the poor folk that are dying at your doors?

> Atween the wet ground and the dry
> The gold of Fairnilee doth lie!

'There it is, with the sun never glinting on it; there it may bide, till the Judgment Day, and no man the better for it.

> Between the Camp o' Rink
> And Tweed-water clear,
> Lie nine kings' ransoms
> For nine hundred year!'

'I doubt it's fairy gold, nurse,' said Randal. 'It would all turn black when it saw the sun. It would just be like this bottle, the only thing I brought with me out of Fairyland.'

Then Randal put his hand in his velvet pouch, and brought out a curious small bottle. It was made of something that none of them had ever seen before. It was black, and you could see the light through it, and there were green and yellow spots and

streaks on it. In bottles like this, the old Romans once kept their
tears for their dead friends.

'That ugly bottle looked like gold and diamonds when I found
it in Fairyland,' said Randal, 'and the water in it smelled as sweet
as roses. But when I touched my eyes with it, a drop that ran
into my mouth was as salt as the sea, and immediately everything
changed: the gold bottle became this glass thing, and the fairies
became like folk dead, and the sky grew grey, and all turned
waste and ugly. That's the way with fairy gold, nurse; and even
if you found it, it would all be dry leaves and black bits of coal
before the sun set.'

'Maybe so, and maybe no,' said the old nurse. 'The gold o'
Fairnilee may no be fairy gold, but just wealth o' this world that
folk buried here lang syne. But noo, Randal, ma bairn, I maun
gang out and see ma sister's son's dochter, that's lying sair sick
o' the kin-cough at Rink, and take her some of the medicine that
I gae you and Jean when you were bairns.'

So the old nurse went out, and Randal and Jean began to be
sorry for the child she was going to visit. For they remembered
the taste of the medicine that the old nurse made by boiling the
bark of elder-tree branches; and I remember it too, for it was the
very nastiest thing that ever was tasted, and did nobody any good
after all.

Then Randal and Jean walked out, strolling along without
much noticing where they went, and talking about the pleasant
days when they were children.

CHAPTER XII

At the Catrail

They had climbed up the slope of a hill, and they came to a broad
old ditch, beneath the shade of a wood of pine trees. Below them
was a wide marsh, all yellow with marsh flowers, and above
them was a steep slope made of stones. Now the dry ditch, where

kin-cough, whooping cough.

they sat down on the grass, looking towards the Tweed, with their backs to the hill, was called the Catrail. It ran all through that country, and must have been made by men very long ago. Nobody knows who made it, nor why. They did not know in Randal's time, and they do not know now. They do not even know what the name Catrail means, but that is what it has always been called. The steep slope of stone above them was named the Camp of Rink; it is a round place, like a ring, and no doubt it was built by the old Britons, when they fought against the Romans, many hundreds of years ago. The stones of which it is built are so large that we cannot tell how men moved them. But it is a very pleasant, happy place on a warm summer day, like the day when Randal and Jean sat there, with the daisies at their feet, and the wild doves cooing above their heads, and the rabbits running in and out among the ferns.

Jean and Randal talked about this and that, chiefly of how some money could be got to buy corn and cattle for the people. Randal was in favour of crossing the Border at night, and driving away cattle from the English side, according to the usual custom.

'Every day I expect to see a pair of spurs in a dish for all our dinner,' said Randal.

That was the sign the lady of the house in the forest used to give her men, when all the beef was done, and more had to be got by fighting.

But Jeanie would not hear of Randal taking spear and jack, and putting himself in danger by fighting the English. They were her own people after all, though she could not remember them and the days before she was carried out of England by Simon Grieve.

'Then,' said Randal, 'am I to go back to Fairyland, and fetch more gold like this ugly thing?' and he felt in his pocket for the fairy bottle.

But it was not in his pocket.

'What have I done with my fairy treasure?' cried Randal, jumping up. Then he stood still quite suddenly, as if he saw something strange. He touched Jean on the shoulder, making a sign to her not to speak.

Jean rose quietly, and looked where Randal pointed, and this was what she saw.

She looked over a corner of the old grassy ditch, just where the marsh and the yellow flowers came nearest to it.

Here there stood three tall grey stones, each about as high as a man. Between them, with her back to the single stone, and between the two others facing Randal and Jean, the old nurse was kneeling.

If she had looked up, she could hardly have seen Randal and Jean, for they were within the ditch, and only their eyes were on the level of the rampart.

Besides, she did not look up; she was groping in the breast of her dress for something, and her eyes were on the ground.

'What can the old woman be doing?' whispered Randal. 'Why, she has got my fairy bottle in her hand!'

Then he remembered how he had shown her the bottle, and how she had gone out without giving it back to him.

Jean and he watched, and kept very quiet.

They saw the old nurse, still kneeling, take the stopper out of the black strange bottle, and turn the open mouth gently on her hand. Then she carefully put in the stopper, and rubbed her eyes with the palm of her hand. Then she crawled along in their direction, very slowly, as if she were looking for something in the grass.

Then she stopped, still looking very closely at the grass.

Next she jumped to her feet with a shrill cry, clapping her hands; and then she turned, and was actually *running* along the edge of the marsh, towards Fairnilee.

'Nurse!' shouted Randal, and she stopped suddenly, in a fright, and let the fairy bottle fall.

It struck on a stone, and broke to pieces with a jingling sound, and the few drops of strange water in it ran away into the grass.

'Oh, ma bairns, ma bairns, what have you made me do?' cried the old nurse pitifully. 'The fairy gift is broken, and maybe the gold of Fairnilee, that my eyes have looked on, will ne'er be seen again.'

CHAPTER XIII

The Gold of Fairnilee

Randal and Jean went to the old woman and comforted her, though they could not understand what she meant. She cried and sobbed, and threw her arms about; but, by degrees, they found out all the story.

When Randal had told her how all he saw in Fairyland was changed after he had touched his eyes with the water from the bottle, the old woman remembered many tales that she had heard about some charm known to the fairies, which helped them to find things hidden, and to see through walls and stones. Then she had got the bottle from Randal, and had stolen out, meaning to touch her eyes with the water, and try whether *that* was the charm and whether she could find the treasure spoken of in the old rhymes. She went

> Between the Camp o' Rink
> And Tweed-water clear,

and to the place which lay

> Atween the wet ground and the dry,

that is, between the marsh and the Catrail.

Here she had noticed the three great stones, which made a kind of chamber on the hillside, and here she had anointed her eyes with the salt water of the bottle of tears.

Then she had seen through the grass, she declared, and through the upper soil, and she had beheld great quantities of gold. And she was running with the bottle to tell Randal, and to touch his eyes with the water that he might see it also. But, out of Fairyland, the strange water only had its magical power while it was still wet on the eyelashes. This the old nurse soon found; for she went back to the three standing stones, and looked and saw nothing, only grass and daisies. And the fairy bottle was broken, and all the water spilt.

This was her story, and Randal did not know what to believe. But so many strange things had happened to him, that one more did not seem impossible. So he and Jean took the old nurse home, and made her comfortable in her room, and Jean put her to bed, and got her a little wine and an oatcake.

Then Randal very quietly locked the door outside, and put the key in his pocket. It would have been of no use to tell the old nurse to be quiet about what she thought she had seen.

By this time it was late and growing dark. But that night there would be a moon.

After supper, of which there was very little, Lady Ker went to bed. But Randal and Jean slipped out into the moonlight. They took a sack with them, and Randal carried a pickaxe and a spade. They walked quickly to the three great stones, and waited for a while to hear if all was quiet. Then Jean threw a white cloak around her, and stole about the edges of the camp and the wood. She knew that if any wandering man came by, he would not stay long where such a figure was walking. The night was cool, the dew lay on the deep fern; there was a sweet smell from the grass and from the pine-wood.

In the mean time, Randal was digging a long trench with his pickaxe, above the place where the old woman had knelt, as far as he could remember it.

He worked very hard, and when he was in the trench up to his knees, his pickaxe struck against a stone. He dug around it with the spade, and came to a layer of black burnt ashes of bones. Beneath these, which he scraped away, was the large flat stone on which his pick had struck. It was a wide slab of red sandstone, and Randal soon saw that it was the lid of a great stone coffin, such as the ploughshare sometimes strikes against when men are ploughing the fields in the Border country.

Randal had seen these before, when he was a boy, and he knew that there was never much in them, except ashes and one or two rough pots of burnt clay.

He was much disappointed.

It had seemed as if he was really coming to something, and, behold, it was only an old stone coffin!

However, he worked on until he had cleared the whole of the stone coffin-lid. It was a very large stone chest, and must have been made, Randal thought, for the body of a very big man.

With the point of his pickaxe he raised the lid.

In the moonlight he saw something of a strange shape.

He put down his hand, and pulled it out.

It was an image, in metal, about a foot high, and represented a beautiful woman, with wings on her shoulders, sitting on a wheel.

Randal had never seen an image like this; but in an old book, which belonged to the monks of Melrose, he had seen, when he was a boy, a picture of such a woman.

The monks had told him that she was Dame Fortune, with her swift wings that carry her from one person to another, as luck changes, and with her wheel that she turns with the turning of chance in the world.

The image was very heavy. Randal rubbed some of the dirt and red clay off, and found that the metal was yellow. He cut it with his knife; it was soft. He cleaned a piece, which shone bright and unrusted in the moonlight, and touched it with his tongue. Then he had no doubt any more. The image was *gold*!

Randal now knew that the old nurse had not been mistaken. With the help of the fairy water she had seen *the gold of Fairnilee*. He called very softly to Jeanie, who came glimmering in her white robes through the wood, looking herself like a fairy. He put the image in her hand, and set his finger on his lips to show that she must not speak.

Then he went back to the great stone coffin, and began to grope in it with his hands. There was much earth in it that had slowly sifted through during the many years that it had been buried. But there was also a great round bowl of metal and a square box.

Randal got out the bowl first. It was covered with a green rust, and had a lid; in short, it was a large ancient kettle, such as soldiers use in camp. Randal got the lid off, and, behold, it was all full of very ancient gold coins, not Greek, nor Roman, but like those used in Britain before Julius Caesar came.

The square box was of iron, and was rusted red. On the lid, in the moonlight, Jeanie could read the letters SPQR, but she did not know what they meant. The box had been locked, and chained, and clamped with iron bars. But all was so rusty that the bars were easily broken, and the lid torn off.

Then the moon shone on bars of gold, and on great plates and dishes of gold and silver, marked with letters, and with what Randal thought were crests. Many of the cups were studded with red and green and blue stones. And there were beautiful plates and dishes, purple, gold, and green; and one of these fell, and broke into a thousand pieces, for it was of some strange kind of glass. There were three gold sword-hilts, carved wonderfully into the figures of strange beasts with wings, and heads like lions.

Randal and Jean looked at it and marvelled, and Jean sang in a low, sweet voice:

> 'Between the Camp o' Rink
> And Tweed-water clear,
> Lie nine kings' ransoms
> For nine hundred year!'

Nobody ever saw so much treasure in all broad Scotland.

Jean and Randal passed the rest of the night in hiding what they had found. Part they hid in the secret chamber of Fairnilee, of which only Jean and Lady Ker and Randal knew. The rest they stowed away in various places. Then Randal filled the earth into the trench, and cast wood on the place, and set fire to the wood, so that next day there was nothing there but ashes and charred earth.

You will not need to be told what Randal did, now that he had treasure in plenty. Some he sold in France, to the king, Henry II, and some in Rome, to the Pope; and with the money which they gave him he bought corn and cattle in England, enough to feed all his neighbours, and stock the farms, and sow the fields for next year. And Fairnilee became a very rich and fortunate house,

for Randal married Jean, and soon their children were playing
on the banks of the Tweed, and rolling down the grassy slope to
the river, to bathe on hot days. And the old nurse lived long and
happy among her new bairns, and often she told them how it
was *she* who really found the gold of Fairnilee.

You may wonder what the gold was, and how it came there?
Probably Father Francis, the good Melrose monk, was right. He
said that the iron box and the gold image of Fortune, and the
kettle full of coins, had belonged to some regiment of the Roman
army: the kettle and the coins they must have taken from the
Britons; the box and all the plate were their own, and brought
from Italy. Then they, in their turn, must have been defeated by
some of the fierce tribes beyond the Roman wall, and must
have lost all their treasure. That must have been buried by the
victorious enemy; and *they*, again, must have been driven from
their strong camp at Rink, either by some foes from the north,
or by a new Roman army from the south. So all the gold lay at
Fairnilee for many hundred years, never quite forgotten, as the
old rhyme showed, but never found until it was discovered, in
their sore need, by the old nurse and Randal and Jean.

As for Randal and Jean, they lived to be old, and died on one
day, and they are buried at Dryburgh in one tomb, and a green
tree grows over them; and the Tweed goes murmuring past their
grave, and past the grave of Sir Walter Scott.

PART FIVE

LETTING GO?

THE KELPIE

Violet Jacob

I'm feared o' the road ayont the glen,   *ayont*, beyond
I'm sweir to pass the place   *sweir*, scared
Whaur the water's rinnin', for aa fowk ken   *aa*, all
There's a kelpie sits at the fit   *kelpie*, water horse; *fit*, foot, bottom
     o' the den,
And there's them that's seen his face.

But whiles he watches and whiles he hides   *whiles*, sometimes
And whiles, gin na wind manes,   *gin*, when; *na*, no; *manes*, moans
Ye can hear him roarin' frae whaur he bides
An' the soond o' him splashin' agin the sides
O' the rocks an' the muckle stanes.

When the mune gaes doon at the arn-tree's   *arn-tree*, alder
     back
In a wee, wee weary licht,   *licht*, light
My bed claes up to my lugs I tak',   *claes*, clothes; *lugs*, ears
For I mind the swirl o' the water black
An the cry i' the fearsome nicht.   *nicht*, night

An' lang an' fell is yon road to me   *fell*, fierce, cruel
As I come frae the schule;   *schule*, school
I daurna think what I'm like to see   *daurna*, dare not
When dark fa's early on buss an' tree   *fa's*, falls; *buss*, bush
At Martinmas and Yule.   *Martinmas*, 11 November

Aside the crusie my mither reads,   *crusie*, oil-lamp
'My bairn,' says she, 'ye've heard
The Lord is mindful of aa oor needs
An' his shield an' buckler's abune the heids   *abune*, above
O' them that keeps His word.'

But I'm a laddie that's no that douce,   *douce*, good, pleasant
An fechtin's a bonnie game.   *fechtin'*, fighting
The dominie's pawmies are   *dominie*, teacher; *pawmies*, canings
     little use,
An' mony's the Sawbath I'm   *mony*, many; *Sawbath*, Sabbath
     rinnin' loose
When a'body thinks I'm hame!   *a'body*, everybody

Dod, noo we're nearin' the shorter days,   *Dod*, God
It's canny I'll hae to gang,   *hae to gang*, have to go
An' keep frae fechtin' an sic-like ways   *sic-like*, suchlike
And no be tearin' my Sawbath claes
Afore the nichts grow lang.   *Afore*, Before

Richt guid an' couthie   *guid*, good; *couthie*, biddable, agreeable
     I'll need to be
(But it's leein' to say I'm glad),   *leein'*, lying
I ken there's troubles that   *ken*, know
     fowk maun dree,   *fowk maun dree*, folk must dread
An' the kelpie's no like to shift   *no like to shift*, unlikely to move
     for me,
Sae, gin thae warlocks are fear't o' Thee,   *Sae*, So; *gin*, if
Lord, mak' me a better lad!

THE ROWAN

Violet Jacob

When the days were still as deith	*deith*, death
And ye couldna see the kye	*kye*, cattle
Though ye'd maybe hear their breith	*breith*, breath
I' the mist oot-by;	*oot-by*, outside
When I mind the lang	*mind*, remember; *lang*, long
grey een	*een*, eyes
O' the warlock by the hill	
And sit fleggit like a wean	*fleggit*, terrified; *wean*, child
Gin a whaup cried shrill;	*whaup*, curlew
Tho' the hert wad dee in me	*dee*, die
At a fitstep on the floor,	*fitstep*, footstep
There was aye the rowan tree	
Wi' its airm across the door.	*airm*, arm

But that is far, far past	
And a'thing's just the same,	*a'thing*, everything
There's a whisper up the blast	*blast*, gale
O' a dreid I daurna name;	*dreid*, dread; *daurna*, dare not
And the shilpit sun is thin,	*shilpit*, feeble, unreliable
Like an auld man deein' slow	
And a shade comes creepin' in	
When the fire is fa'in' low;	*fa'in'*, falling
Then I feel thae lang een set	*thae lang een*, those long eyes
Like a doom upon ma heid,	
For the warlock's livin' yet –	
But the rowan's deid!	

THE MAN IN THE LOCHAN

Eona MacNicol

My mother's girlhood home was a croft above Clachanree proper, over its skyline, in the middle of the moor. A solitary place; I doubt if there were any other houses within view. Only the smoke from the houses of Tallurach and perhaps the schoolhouse behind the Planting gave hint of neighbours at all. We looked on to a sheer hill face called the Leitir, which overshadowed Loch Laide, famous for its trout and for the waterfowl that lived secretly among its reeds.

A solitary place. When once I spent a whole summer there I found it too solitary. When I grew tired of watching women's ploys about the house I had to go about with my grandfather, tending his fields or rounding up his sheep. It must have been on an expedition with him that I discovered behind the Leitir a habitation I had never known about before.

It was a tiny croft, an islet of cultivation in the middle of the heather. There were only three fields, one of hay, one of turnips, one of potatoes, with a little grassland heavily encroached upon by tufts of bulrushes, even starred here and there by bog-cotton flowers. But in my eyes the smallness was its charm. On the greensward around the little house some half-dozen hens daintily strutted. A cow and her calf munched nearby, and a pony lay taking his ease in shelter of the single tutelary rowan tree. An old woman could be seen busy on one of the fields, singling turnips.

I do not think it was the custom in Clachanree for women to

croft, upland smallholding, found especially in the Highlands and islands.
single tutelary rowan tree, a rowan often guarded a house or cottage door. It was supposed to keep evil spirits away, and protect the occupants of the house.
singling, thinning out.

work much in the fields. True, they would help out at harvest or
lambing time. Here was a woman who every time I passed that
way with my grandfather was at man's work. I admired her
greatly. She was only of average height, but stalwart and strong.
How nonchalantly would she swing a hammer down upon a
post in her fence; how confidently catch and harness her pony;
with what careless ease cut rushes for his bed. Her clothes were
the dark long-sleeved blouse and the full skirt that all elderly
women wore, but she had man's boots, stout hobnailed affairs,
and I thought her worthy of them.

I persuaded my grandfather one day to pass near enough the
house to hail her. 'Well, well then, Oonagh, and how are you the
day?' She dropped her hoe and came silent, though smiling, to
meet us. She wore her hair, of a silvery gold colour, in a pile on
the top of her head, as the fashion then was or had been. Her
face was brown with the sun, the corners of her eyes wrinkled
from squinting against it.

I got into the habit of giving my grandfather the slip and
spending with Oonagh the time I was supposed to be under his
care. I made advances to her, and she accepted my presence in
her silent way. I had the privilege of assisting her out of doors:
gathering her cut hay, or making a mixture of milk and meal for
her calf. Soon I was permitted entry into her house. Its thatch
was adorned by a plume of heather sprouting all joco from it.
Inside it consisted of only one room – well, one and a half, for
the box-bed was virtually a room in itself. Everything was as
spick-and-span as if Oonagh expected company. The coverlet
of patchwork, though frayed, was immaculately clean; the table
was covered in a shiny, bright-coloured stuff called, I think,
baize; the bowls and jugs upon the dresser made as brave a
display, proportionately to the size of the dwelling, as did
ours in the croft house of Druim. Even the rag rug before the
hearth was clean – clean, I began to realize, because few feet trod
on it. There was no plant on the window sill; instead there was
a brown jam-jar of pink-spotted flowers with a heavy clinging
scent which vied with the usual smells of damp and peat-reek.

all joco, all jovial (jocose) and pleased with oneself.

I had not at that time seen orchids. Oonagh in a few words explained to me that she found them away out on the moor, among the peat bogs. I resolved I would go myself and find some.

Only one thing seemed to me to spoil the charm of the little dwelling; for joined on to the one room, like an envious poor neighbour, was the other half of the original house, now in a ruinous state. When I asked Oonagh why she did not have the old walls carried away, she laughed, colour rose in her face, and she said in a rare burst of talk, 'Who knows, *m'eudail*, but some day there will be need of them?'

She was not only silent, but strange. Yet I found it pleasanter to be with her than in jollier homes where there was always the likelihood of tedious talk, likening one's face to this and that past member of the family. Oonagh did not tease me with talk at all. In friendly silence we worked together, or rested; for sometimes she would fetch me out a glass of milk and a hunk of oatcake, and would herself sit down, her legs in the dark skirt spread comfortably upon the grass. She might hum to herself, or sing, more often in Gaelic but sometimes in English learnt at school. One song was a ballad of great length the chorus of which I picked up:

> '*I wish I were,*
> *But I wish in vain,*
> *I wish I were*
> *A young lass again.*
> *But such a thing*
> *Can never be*
> *Till an Aipple grows*
> *On an Oarange tree.*'

Other times she might bring out of her pocket a clay pipe, and light up and puff away as good as any man.

One day, as I was making my way to Oonagh's, I heard a creaking sound, as of wheels on a rough rocky road. It was

---

m'eudail, my dear (Gaelic, a term of endearment).

Oonagh going up on the high moor to turn her peats. And the sound was like a fairy pipe to me. I longed to be up on the heights in the sea of heather. Maybe too I should find those exotic pink-spotted flowers. The cart had got a start on me, yet it was going slowly, the pony straining with the effort of pulling, Oonagh walking beside.

I took short cuts and made up on them. I called a greeting to Oonagh, who said nothing in reply but looked as if she were not averse to my presence. She was smoking her clay pipe, curls of grey smoke floating backwards in the wind. We plodded uphill behind the pony, who kept nodding his head, poor thing, as if endorsing our unspoken complaints about the steepness of our way. At last we gained the peat moor, and Oonagh got busy turning, puffing the while at her pipe, saying nothing.

I for my part was content; there was so much to see. Among the heather grew blaeberry bushes with their vivid green, and staghorn moss paved that hidden world which is inhabited by lizards and beetles. But I found no flowers. And after a while I came back to Oonagh where she was turning the wet sides of the peat to the wind. The wind had teased out strands of her grey-gold hair, and she squinted against sun and smoke. An old woman, with little power to amuse. I began to think it was time for getting home.

But Oonagh took her pipe out of her mouth and said, 'Sheep.' I gathered she was uneasy about their whereabouts and wanted to scan the hill grazing ground. We left the pony patiently switching from his flanks the flies that settled whenever the wind dropped. We went around a hillock. I gasped with delight.

There lay a lochan, sleek, still, its dark surface sprinkled around the rim with water lilies of purest white. As fast as I could through the deep heather, I made my way to it, and threw myself down on my stomach, stretching out a greedy hand for the nearest of the exquisite flowers. I secured one, but it had a long rubbery stem which seemed endless as it came up out of the water. I broke off the flower head. But so far from feeling satisfied,

turn her peats, peats are stacked to dry before they are used for fuel. They have to be turned during the drying process.
lochan, small loch.

I felt greedier than ever and reached out further for another
flower. It was beyond my reach. I called to Oonagh, who had
come back but made no effort to assist me, begging her to see if
her longer arm could secure it.

I remember she came slowly, as if weighted down by her long
heavy skirt and heavy boots, then got down awkwardly beside
me. The wind had dropped for a moment. It was so still that
reflections appeared in the water as if in a glass; the dark shape
of the hillock; the clouds patterning the blue of the sky; a wild
duck flying up to meet its counterpart flying down. Close to the
brink our two reflections appeared. Then a small breeze came,
and wrinkled the surface. The images were gone. Oonagh put
out her arm. Her brown fingers closed below a flower and she
pulled at it, dragging the stem like a discovered thing up and out.
Another and another she procured, six or seven, cheerful and
humming, her pipe laid down by her side.

I was about to say I had enough, and restrain Oonagh from
further effort, when I found there was no need. The wind had
dropped once more. The surface of the lochan was smooth, with
images appearing on it again. Now Oonagh was bending so low
her face almost met the water, shading her eyes with a hand
spread on either side.

'What is it, Oonagh?' I asked. 'What are you looking at? Are
there fish?'

'Aye are there fish!' She turned her head over her shoulder to
address me. Her wrinkled sunburnt face wore a radiant smile.
'Put you your head down low and keep looking, *m'eudail*, and
you will be seeing them. Grey like silver they are, leaping this
way and that. Then suddenly they will leave the water and fly
through the air.'

'How can fish leave the water? They would die.'

She said 'Tst!' impatiently, and turned from me to gaze into
the water again. I felt I was missing something and followed her
example, bending down so low I smelt the heavy smell of water
thick with weeds.

She was staring in, rapt, like a clairvoyant.

'What are you seeing now?' I pestered her.

She pointed. 'See, see! See the palm trees moving.' I could see the stems of the water lilies swaying to some little depth, the currents moving them.

'That's not –' Something stopped the words on my tongue, the realization of the absurdity of it: how could palm trees grow in this cold windy place? I looked closely at Oonagh to see if she were joking at my expense. I took it upon myself to say, 'See will you fall in!'

She cried sharply, '*Bith sochd*!' – Be quiet! Her pointing finger moved like a magician's over the still water. 'Look now, what bonnie! A lily pool, it is lined with white stone, and a fountain in the middle of it, and the fishes are golden – look at them jinking this way and that between the flowers. White the flowers are, as sheets laid –' If I had a question, I could not ask it, for something froze the words upon my lips. 'See yon! There it is, the house itself. It's coming. Look at that now!' She turned her face towards me, smiling but with eyes unfocused, then turned to the water again. Her voice was so low it was all I could do to catch what she said.

What house? What house? I had heard – who has not? – of houses, villages overwhelmed by water, but away up here on the moor who had at any time built houses? And how could a little lochan cover them?

She put a hand on my back and pressed me down. 'Here, look down here. Can you not see the house? It's down there, deep, deep in. The white pillars and the steps and the roof with a shine on it. That's the stars, *m'eudail*, bonnie stars they have there.'

I would have liked to ask her to let us leave the lochan and be going home. Indeed, I rose up on my knees, but she was talking still, chuckling to herself. 'Aye there's them! There's the dark men, it's coming this time, the dark men with the bright clothes on them.'

I felt a longing for home keener than my past longing for water lilies. The game, if game it was, was over for me. I should never be able to see more in the lochan than lily stems and the reflections of hill and cloud and our own faces. There, clear in the water, I saw Oonagh's face, and was startled out of my senses; for the

jinking, dodging, ducking.

face in the water was young, the curve of cheek and chin like a girl's. I looked in astonishment from the reflected to the real face and found it was indeed bright, youthful, transfigured with joy.

She was chanting to herself in an ecstasy, 'When it is quiet he will come, himself will come. Out from between the pillars of his house, into my arms.' Here ecstasy melted into tears, and she cried with both smiles and tears, '*Tha m'ulaidh ort! Tha m'ulaidh!*' – I love you! I love you!

I cried out to her in fear, 'Oonagh!' And just as I spoke, a stiff breeze came. It ruffled the water from middle to brink. The still mirror was gone.

She jumped up and looked round at me in intense anger. Her face, old and brown, menaced me. Then, as if passing through a double enchantment, she was quiet and serene again, familiar, friendly, my companion of the summer.

She said, sighing, 'Aye, aye, just so. It is always the way. He willna stay for long. There's aye a something. But when it is his time, he will come and stay.' She looked down at her knees where the damp peaty earth had stained her dark skirt, and stooped and picked up her clay pipe and stuck it between her lips. She took it out once to ask me, 'What were we doing at the lochan?' But I was the silent one. I left my lilies behind, and walked with dragging steps after the cart and pony.

I was late home that evening. My mother was helping my grandmother at her churning. She called to me. Where had I been? My grandfather had come home without me.

I said I had been talking to Oonagh. Then, in a sudden longing to be reassured, I told the whole of it; about the lochan and how she had stared down into its depths and spoken of things she could see. My mother cried out, then stopped short with a hand at her mouth. It was left to my grandmother to speak. 'You must not go far from the place with Oonagh. It is not safe. Your grandfather should have warned you.'

'Why?' I cried, angry at the hint of blame.

My mother had regained control over herself. 'There is nothing against her, Ellen. Nothing at all. She is a good woman. For all they do not like her in their houses at such times as churning, she is respected. She has never done harm to a living. She is even mindful of the means of grace' – by which she meant she was a churchgoer – 'All the same, you will do well to keep away from her when she goes near water.' She made a signal to my grand-mother.

But my grandmother did not see it or did not heed. 'She fell in love with the lochan itself, they say.' She paused maddeningly, took off the wooden lid and pulled the plunger up, a weird mass of horsehair and cream, and tested for butter forming. 'Some say the *eachd uisge* has put a spell upon her.'

My mother cried out along with me in remonstrance. My grandmother at last saw what was required of her and said nothing more, but began to churn mightily, singing a Psalm to swallow up any inauspicious influence and make the butter come firm and sweet.

My mother came to me when I was in bed. 'About the *eachd uisge*; you must not be afraid. There is no such thing. Your father, at any rate, would not approve of it. And about her being in love with the lochan; that is all nonsense, for she had a human lover. That is to say, there was a man she loved.' Her blue eyes grew thoughtful. The story hid within them. I lay still in my bed, listening with an eagerness near to apprehension. Yet it was like a story told already, I needed only the details.

It was some childish disappointment – my mother thought that Oonagh's new dress, such a rare possession, had been usurped by a sister – which made her run away over the moors to the lochan to hide her tears there. By its brink she should have been alone, but she began to hear the small clatter of oars in rowlocks. Curiosity drew her. It was not Jock from Corrie, nor Lachlan from Reneudin: it was a stranger. When he saw that she was weeping, however, he pulled in to the shore. 'Why are you weep-ing?' he asked in Gaelic, that tender language; and in the same tongue she answered him, 'For nothing at all.' For suddenly it seemed as nothing. When he put a kindly hand to her head,

---

eachd uisge, water horse (Gaelic). This was a beast with magic powers, a sprite or kelpie. Given the chance, kelpies were said to drag their victims under the water and drown them.

straightening the snood ribbon, a feeling she had never known swept all through her, swept over him too.

Often after that, so ran my mother's whispered tale in the darkening room, they met at the lochan. He had come for a holiday to Glen Urquhart, for the fishing. He would take his boat out and sit with dipped oars, while she knelt at the boat's rim trying to see his image in the water, too shy still to look directly at him. Later they would lie by the brink. What passed between them my mother did not say, nor would I have known.

Summer was nearly over when he told her what surely she must have known all the time. He was going away, and not to the town, not even to Aberdeen or to Glasgow; over the unimaginable seas to a foreign land. Seeing her face, he avowed, 'I will not forget you. One day when I have got rich I will come back and we will be always together.' She saw his image there in the water as he said it; saw it plainly in the still water, for all time, forever. Then a breeze came and it was gone.

I could picture Oonagh as winter set in, snow on the far mountains, a bitter wind searing the nearer hills. In the cold of the morning she would crouch at the hearth, relighting the fire, clinging to her dreams, unwilling to leave them for the long vacuous day. But she was not forgotten, my mother said. Letters, a great novelty, came from foreign parts. Many people would have liked to examine them, but she would snatch them and run away with them over the moor to the lochan. It was in her light step and her singing that the contents of the letters could be guessed at. But sometimes she talked of the marvels of life abroad. So fantastic it seemed that people laughed as if at a jest.

Then after a while – did I not know? – the letters stopped coming. Months went by, seasons went by, and years. I pictured them in the mutations of the rowan tree: its young leaves; its pale blossom; its berries going from green to orange to red; then the tree bare again. But the reality was toil, long toil, hard toil, many reverses, little to eat. Years went by; father and mother dying; sisters marrying and settling in other homes; Oonagh left where

snood ribbon, worn by young, unmarried women, bound around the brow and tied at the back under the hair.

she was. Even if she had had the inclination to look into the small dim mirror in the house she had little time. Only in the coming of young men about the place might she have known she was comely to look at. They had brought gifts, as wooers; but never could she give answering love, and by and by they had grown discouraged – who could blame them? – and had found other girls as beautiful and not so strange. For she had strange ways. She would leave tasks in the midst and run off over the moors to the lochan. She began to say she had a lover, a husband, a home in its depths.

At last only one brother remained, and a hard life he had of it trying to keep the croft with her fitful aid. He took a dislike to the place. He had a sweetheart whose family moved to the east, where farming was more rewarding. He could go there, and take his sister with him.

But when he told her of the plan, Oonagh would not hear of leaving. How could she leave her home, the trysting place, where alone she had hope of being with her lover? And perhaps in his heart her brother was not sorry to escape.

'She has lived ever since, as you see, alone.' My mother rose to go, but I held her back.

'He never came again then, her lover?'

She paused, as if reluctant to continue the story, but at last she said, 'Yes, he did come. That was the funny thing, he did come back to her.' One day a carriage and pair was observed coming up the Brae, along the main road past Druim, to Loch Laide. It stopped where some men were working at the side of the road. A gentleman got out, dressed I suppose in old-world style, twin gold chains reposing on his stomach, one for his watch, one for his sovereign case. To the surprise of the men he put his question in Gaelic. 'Was there a family living yet in the moorland croft behind the Leitir? And a girl called Oonagh, was she married yet?' The older among them knew who he was then, and I have no doubt they left the ditch uncleared to go and spread the news. The time was come at last. That poor solitary woman, whom some shunned as unlucky because lovelorn, would get her due

carriage and pair, carriage driven by two horses.

reward at last. There was no mistaking the eagerness on the stranger's face.

I cried out, 'Then why – ?'

My mother seemed to shiver. He returned in less than an hour. This time he did not speak, but went away as fast as he could. The account of their meeting came from a child who, curious, ran over the heather and got near enough to witness the manner of it. Oonagh came to the door to receive her caller, then stopped short at seeing a stranger. He held his hands out. 'Do you not remember me? I have come back as I said I would.' She stared at him bewildered, making no move towards him, no sign of recognition. 'I have never loved anyone as I could have loved you. I am home now. I will make up to you for all the years I have left you forsaken.'

'Then why? Did he not live long after coming?'

'He lived all right. He is still alive, alive and prospering. He is in business in the town. It was Oonagh who would not . . . It was as if she had never seen him before. She would not let him touch her. She said the only man she loved was in the lochan. I tell you only what you know.

'From that the story has grown that she is in love with the spirit of the lochan, or even that the *eachd uisge*, about which your father will tell you there is no such thing, has put a spell upon her. It is only now and again the idea takes hold of her. She is quiet and has done no one any harm. All the same, Ellen, if you go to her place you must not go out on the moors with her.'

I needed no forbidding. I was a timid child. I doubt if I went to the tiny croft ever again. And she never asked me. Whenever we met, at school-house service or on the Druim road, she would smile from her wrinkled sunburnt face, if she were not contentedly puffing at her clay pipe. That was all.

But sometimes, when I heard the creaking sound of a cart upon a rocky road, I would be visited by a perverse longing to go with her again to her lochan and see that ecstasy I might not share.

PART SIX

ENVOY

WHY EVERYONE SHOULD BE ABLE TO TELL A STORY

John Lorne Campbell

Once there was an Uistman who was travelling home, at the time when the passage wasn't as easy as it is today. In those days travellers used to come by the Isle of Skye, crossing the sea from Dunvegan to Lochmaddy. This man had been away working at the harvest on the mainland. He was walking through Skye on his way home, and at nightfall he came to a house, and thought he would stay there till morning, as he had a long way to go. He went in, and I'm sure he was made welcome by the man of the house, who asked him if he had any tales or stories. The Uistman replied that he had never known any.

'It's very strange you can't tell a story,' said his host. 'I'm sure you've heard plenty.'

'I can't remember one,' said the Uistman.

His host himself was telling stories all night, to pass the night, until it was time to go to bed. When they went to bed, the Uistman was given the closet inside the front door to sleep in. What was there hanging in the closet but the carcass of a sheep! The Uistman hadn't been long in bed when he heard the door being opened, and two men came in and took away the sheep.

The Uistman said to himself that it would be very unfortunate for him to let those fellows take the sheep away, for the people of the house would think that he had taken it himself. He went after the thieves, and he had gone some way after them when one of them noticed him, and said to the other: 'Look at that fellow coming after us to betray us; let's go back and catch him and do away with him.'

They turned back, and the Uistman made off as fast as he could to try to get back to the house. But they got between him and the house. The Uistman kept going, until he heard the sound of a big river; then he made for the river. In his panic he went into the river, and the stream took him away. He was likely to be drowned. But he got ahold of a branch of a tree that was growing on the bank of the river, and clung on to it. He was too frightened to move; he heard the two men going back and forth along the banks of the river, throwing stones wherever the trees cast their shade; and the stones were going past him.

He remained there until dawn. It was a frosty night, and when he tried to get out of the river, he couldn't do it. He tried to shout, but he couldn't shout either. At last he managed to utter one shout, and made a leap; and he woke up, and found himself on the floor beside the bed, holding on to the bedclothes with both hands. His host had been casting spells on him during the night! In the morning when they were at breakfast, his host said:

'Well, I'm sure that wherever you are tonight, you'll have a story to tell, though you hadn't one last night.'

That's what happened to the man who couldn't tell a story; everyone should be able to tell a tale or a story to help pass the night!

THE TAIL

John Francis Campbell

There was a shepherd once who went out to the hill to look after his sheep. It was misty and cold, and he had much trouble to find them. At last he had them all but one; and after much searching he found that one too in a peat-hag, half drowned; so he took off his plaid, and bent down and took hold of the sheep's tail, and he pulled! The sheep was heavy with water, and he could not lift her, so he took off his coat and he *pulled*! But it was too much for him, so he spit on his hands, and took a good hold of the tail and he PULLED! And the tail broke! And if it had not been for that this tale would have been a great deal longer.

peat-hag, ledge of peat, cut for fuel (often from a bog).

NOTES ON THE AUTHORS

Anon.

As stated in the note on story attributions (at the end of the Introduction), many of the stories listed on the Contents page are ultimately anonymous. But with the exception of only two texts, all show the name of an author under the title. The two listed as being anonymous are two Border ballads, 'Thomas the Rhymer' and 'Tam Lin'. The version of 'Thomas the Rhymer' used in this book is taken from Sir Walter Scott's *Minstrelsy of the Scottish Border* (1802) and 'Tam Lin' is from *The Scots Musical Museum* (1797), as communicated by Robert Burns. Both texts, even in those days, were of considerable antiquity. And having several points in common, it is possible that both of these ballads derive from the same source.

Many versions of these stories were collected in the nineteenth century. Although the ballad details are unique to Scotland, the motif of capturing a person by the use of supernatural powers is found throughout European folklore. The main distinction of Thomas the Rhymer is his gift of prophecy (from the Queen of the Fairies), evident also in the twentieth-century version collected in South Uist by Margaret Fay Shaw. He was also unable to tell a lie. One theory traces the story back to the thirteenth century, and to the life of Thomas of Ercildoune (c. ?1220–?1297, also called Thomas Learmount and 'True Thomas'). The village of Ercildoune is today called Earlston, a small market town in Berwickshire. The historical personage called Thomas of Ercildoune is said to have had the gift of prophecy, and to have predicted the death of King Alexander III (in 1286) and the battle of Bannockburn (in 1314). A romance of 'True Thomas' and his 'ladye gaye' dates to the fifteenth century.

John Buchan (1875–1940)

A son of the manse, John Buchan was a Borderer by extraction and inclination: most of his childhood summer holidays were spent there. He attended Hutcheson's Grammar School in Glasgow, followed by Glasgow and Oxford Universities. It was at Oxford that he first became acquainted with the public school set, whose ethos is depicted in so much of his fiction. Thereafter he pursued a public career as barrister, publisher, journalist, civil servant (as an intelligence officer he was a Director of Information during and after the First World War), Conservative Member of Parliament for the Scottish universities (1927–35), and Governor-General of Canada (1935–40).

As a writer, Buchan was influenced by the craft and style of Robert Louis Stevenson. His adventure novels, especially *The Thirty-Nine Steps* (1915), *Greenmantle* (1916) and *Mr Standfast* (1919), are in the mould of Stevenson's *Kidnapped*, and achieved similar wide popular acclaim. Buchan called them his 'shockers', regarding them as the product of the private imaginative or fantasy world into which he liked to escape. But he also – and simultaneously – wrote history, the major project being *Nelson's History of the War* (1915–19), in twenty-four volumes. There were also books of poetry (*Poems Scots and English*, 1917), biography (of Montrose, Cromwell and Sir Walter Scott), and several books of short stories. His fairy tale 'The Magic Walking-stick' appeared in an anthology for younger readers, edited by Lady Asquith, entitled *Sails of Gold* (1927).

Robert Burns (1759–96)

The poet's father was William Burnes (1721–84), a tenant farmer and gardener at Alloway, just south of the town of Ayr, in Ayrshire. William had been reasonably well educated in general knowledge and scripture, and he tried to ensure that his children also had this advantage. So, although we still tend to remember his son Robert Burns as 'the ploughman poet', Robert grew up to be a keen reader, cultivated and literate not just in English-language book culture but also in the vernacular culture of the Scots language. He probably owed his interest in the latter to Betty Davidson, a widowed relative who lived with the Burns family and was fond of entertaining the children with 'the largest collection in the county of tales and songs concerning devils, brownies, witches, warlocks, spunkies, kelpies, elf-candles, deadlights, wraiths, apparitions, cantraips, giants, inchanted towers, dragons and other trumpery . . .' (*The Letters of Robert Burns*, 2nd edn, edited by J. De Lancey Ferguson and G. Ross Roy, Oxford: Clarendon Press, 1985, p. 135).

Thus it is not surprising that the adult poet wanted to give something back, and took a more than amateur interest in the collection of oral texts, especially songs and popular poetry, making large contributions to the early volumes of James Johnson's six-volume *Scots Musical Museum* (1787–1803), George Thomson's six-volume *Select Collection of Original Scotish Airs* (1793–1841), and volume 2 of Charles Grose's illustrated *Antiquities of Scotland* (1791). 'Tam o' Shanter: A Tale' appeared in this last volume, alongside an account and picture of the half-ruined Alloway Kirk, where the poet's father lies buried in the churchyard. The poem had first appeared in print a few months earlier, in the *Edinburgh Magazine*.

Burns is known the world over as Scotland's greatest poet; and 'Tam o' Shanter', his only narrative poem, is widely regarded as one of Scotland's greatest folk tales. The story is based on a local Ayrshire tale. In it, Farmer Tam is riding home after a night's heavy drinking in Ayr, and accidentally disturbs a witches' ceilidh in Alloway Kirk, just outside the town and near the cottage where Burns had grown up. A coven of witches then chase him for his life, as he flees their wrath on his good mare Meg towards the brig o' Doon. Tam knew (as everyone did in those days) that he had to put a running stream between himself and the witches in order to escape their clutches safely. Alloway Kirk had only ceased to be used for public worship in 1756 – less than forty years before the poem was written – but it was soon in a ruinous state and offered an ideally spooky background for a supernatural tale.

John Francis Campbell, of Islay (1822–85)

J. F. Campbell was born and raised on the Hebridean island of Islay and, as the eldest son of the laird, he would normally have succeeded his father in the lairdship. But the family had incurred such large debts in the course of undertaking substantial land improvements across the island that they had to sell it. However, even though Islay had passed out of his family's possession, John Francis was always to be known as Campbell of Islay. Educated at Eton and Edinburgh University, Campbell became a lawyer and secretary to his cousin George, 8th Duke of Argyll, as well as to the Lighthouse Commission and the Coal

Commission in Scotland. He had all of the natural scientific curiosity of a Victorian polymath, and was a keen inventor, geologist and naturalist; one of his inventions was an instrument for measuring the power of the sun's rays.

A fluent Gaelic speaker, Campbell devoted much time to collecting Gaelic folklore throughout the Highlands and Western Isles, and it is for this work that he is mainly remembered. His *Popular Tales of the West Highlands Orally Collected, with a Translation* (4 vols, 1860–62) was a magisterial landmark publication, a ready quarry for later folklorists. He also published the *Leabhar na Feinne* (1872), a celebrated collection of Ossianic ballads in Gaelic.

John Lorne Campbell, of Canna (1906–96)

John Lorne Campbell was born in Argyll, and trained at Oxford University as a rural economist, but he is best remembered as a scholar of Gaelic folklore. He went to Barra in 1933, and it was while working there in partnership with Compton Mackenzie that he met his future wife, Margaret Fay Shaw (see p. 226). He worked on Barra on a practical campaign to protect the livelihood of local inshore fishermen in the Outer Hebrides (he was secretary of the Barra Sea League) and, again in partnership with Compton Mackenzie, wrote *The Book of Barra* (1936). Margaret and John married in 1935, and lived on Barra until 1938 when Campbell bought the island of Canna and took on the lairdship. Conservation issues, environmental and community challenges were then to occupy much of his time. With Margaret, he built up a significant Gaelic library at Canna House over the years. John first visited the Gaels of Nova Scotia in 1932, and with Margaret he was to revisit the Canadian maritime provinces in 1937.

His main books on folklore include *Stories from South Uist* (1961, with Angus MacLellan), which contains 'Why Everyone Should Be Able to Tell a Story'; *Canna: The Story of a Hebridean Island* (1984); the three-volume *Hebridean Folksongs* (1969, 1977, 1981, with Francis Collinson); and *Songs Remembered in Exile* (1990), being a repertoire of traditional Gaelic songs from Nova Scotia.

Arthur Conan Doyle (1859–1930)

Many people express surprise at this writer's Scottish antecedents, but he was born in Edinburgh and studied medicine at Edinburgh University. One of his medical teachers in Edinburgh was Dr Joseph Bell (1837–1911), a rather coldly scientific professor, but whose deductive skills later provided Conan Doyle with one of the models for Sherlock Holmes, his popular and bestselling detective. Another was Sir Patrick Heron Watson, whose warmth and humanity is echoed in 'my dear Watson'. A different bestselling creation was Professor Challenger, the scientist hero of *The Lost World* (1912) and *The Poison Belt* (1913). But long before these creations, several of Conan Doyle's early stories are set in and around the city of his birth, and made their first appearance in *Chambers's Journal*, then an important Edinburgh literary periodical.

Conan Doyle entered the Edinburgh Medical School in 1876. He was something of an adventurer in his youth, and in 1880 he served as a ship's doctor in the Arctic in order to raise sufficient funds to complete his medical studies in 1881: a practical and useful Victorian 'gap year'. Later, his writing skills took him as a war correspondent to South Africa to cover the Boer War, about which he was to publish the two books for which he was knighted: *The Great Boer War* (1900) and *The War in South Africa: Its Causes and Conclusion* (1902). Conan Doyle's easy, flowing narrative style resembles that of his near-contemporary Edinburgh fellow writer, Robert Louis Stevenson.

Like so many good supernatural tales, 'Through the Veil' is well grounded in the realistic detail of an archaeological dig at the Roman remains at Newstead, near Melrose, in the Scottish Borders. The story's three characters, Mr and Mrs Brown and Farmer Cunningham, are all ordinary country folk naturalistically depicted. But this is also a story of second sight and – unusually – of a vision of the past shared by a husband and his wife. In this context, it is perhaps relevant to note that Conan Doyle had lost a son at a young age in the First World War, and that in later life (like others similarly bereaved) he became engrossed by spiritualism in his efforts to communicate 'through the veil' with the young son who had 'passed over to the other side'.

Elizabeth W. Grierson (1869–1943)

There is very little in the public domain about the life of Elizabeth Wilson Grierson. Miss Grierson was 'privately educated' and apparently spent some time in Germany. She published about thirty books between 1906 and 1935, with some reprints as late as 1950. She was born, grew up and lived at Whitchesters, a farm near Hawick, in the Scottish Borders. One of her best-known books was an illustrated collection called *The Scottish Fairy Book*, printed in 1910 and reprinted in 1935. She cites Campbell's *Popular Tales of the West Highlands*, Leyden's poems, Hogg's poems, Scott's *Border Minstrelsy*, Chambers's *The Popular Rhymes of Scotland* and *The Folklore Journal* as her sources for this publication. Her other books include *Children's Tales from the Scottish Ballads* (1906), *The Northumbrian Saints* (1913), *Early Light-Bearers of Scotland*, *The Book of Edinburgh for Young People* (1914), *The Book of Celtic Stories* (1927), and *Tales of Scottish Keeps and Castles* (1928). So one may hazard the notion that she was a writer who tried to provide young people with 'improving' literature in the fields of Scottish history, literature and the early church. Like many other female writers of the period, including her fellow workers in the field of Irish folklore (such as Eleanor Hull, Letitia McClintock and Maud Joynt), Miss Grierson appears to have been content to leave few traces.

The Popular Rhymes of Scotland (1820) by Robert Chambers is Miss Grierson's source for various folk tales, including 'The Milk-white Doo'. Her version of this story is fuller than the Chambers version, but perhaps easier to follow, losing little of the horror in Chambers. It is an old folk tale that (like 'Katherine Crackernuts') focuses on a wicked stepmother. The stepmother kills one of her stepchildren and – as if infanticide isn't enough – then cooks the infant and feeds his flesh to his father. Such a dastardly and unnatural act calls the supernatural powers into play. The agent of justice is a 'milk-white dove', magically constituted from the bones of the dead infant. Walt Disney may have more recently established the tale of Snow White and the Seven Dwarfs as the archetypal text about a wicked stepmother, but the theme is quite ancient in oral folk literature and has an international resonance.

Interestingly perhaps, the villain of the piece in Chambers is the infant's mother; Grierson changes this detail into a stepmother. (Did that make her crime slightly less unnatural?) Chambers points out that the story was 'familiar in every Scottish nursery fifty years ago' (i.e. around 1780) and that it was also prevalent in Germany, where the Plattdeutsch version of the bird's song is almost identical to the Scots.

Chambers also has a story, called 'The Pado' (or frog), which Grierson uses as the source for her 'The Well o' the World's End'. Both stories involve a supernatural talking frog, or puddock, which eventually turns into a handsome prince. In folklore, a frog is viewed as slightly 'unchancy' or 'fey', and looks almost human – albeit in a stomach-churning way. The moral? Be kind to animals, even if the sight of them repels you. This story too has a very similar German version, and Sir Walter Scott is said by Chambers to have traced a version to the Kalmuck Tartars.

James Hogg (1770–1835)

Born and raised in Ettrickdale, then as today a remote and rural part of Selkirkshire, in the Scottish Borders, James Hogg grew up in considerable poverty to become a shepherd, like his father. But through his mother, Margaret Laidlaw, he was also raised in a rich storehouse of oral tradition which she and then he carried on. He took pride in claiming to share the birthday of Robert Burns (25 January), and indeed saw himself as one of the latter's successors as a poet. And if Burns was known to his peers as 'the heaven-sent ploughman', Hogg was happy with the equally apposite cognomen of 'the Ettrick shepherd': for that is what he was.

Hogg was largely self-taught, and he was in his mid-thirties before he acquired much celebrity. *Scottish Pastorals*, his first collection of poems, was published in 1801. He was encouraged in his writing by Sir Walter Scott, with whom he shared an interest in oral literature and the Border ballads. In 1810 he moved to Edinburgh to try his hand as a professional writer, and enjoyed considerable success after publication of *The Queen's Wake* (1813), which contained two of Hogg's best-known supernatural poems, 'Kilmeny' and 'The Witch of Fife'. For a while his poetry was as popular as Scott's and Byron's, and his four-volume *Poetical Works* (1822) probably marked the apex of his success as a poet.

Hogg also wrote prose, which was also heavily influenced by the Border ballads and legends. His short stories appeared in *Blackwood's Magazine* and his brand of magic realism was popular, leaving his readers to choose between belief and scepticism. Sadly, his reputation in his own lifetime suffered as a result of two problems. First, much of his prose was published in bowdlerized 'genteel' editions, losing something of its impact as a result; and secondly, the upwardly mobile and socially genteel middle classes of Edinburgh took against this 'upstart' peasant, in a snobbish reaction they had not adopted with Robert Burns twenty years earlier. It was not until the second half of the twentieth century, when reliable texts of Hogg's work started to reappear and undergo rediscovery, that his reputation rose significantly, thanks to books like *The Brownie of Bodsbeck and Other Tales* (1818), *The Three Perils of Man* (1822) and his masterpiece *The Private Memoirs and Confessions of a Justified Sinner* (1824). As Douglas S. Mack points out in the *Oxford Dictionary of National Biography* (2004), it is now easier to see that 'Hogg ... created a space in which the allegedly "marginal" and "primitive" culture of the old Scottish peasantry could speak with eloquence and power'.

Violet Jacob (1863–1946)

Violet Jacob was from the landed gentry: she was a member of the Kennedy-Erskine family from the House of Dun, near Montrose (now in the care of the National Trust for Scotland). Her fluent mastery of the Scots tongue was gained in the company of her estate workers. In 1895 she married Arthur Otway Jacob, an army officer from an Anglo-Irish family. They spent some of their early married years in India, and Jacob's poetry from that period of exile expresses her longing for Scotland. Her only son was killed in 1916 at the battle of the Somme, aged twenty.

Jacob worked in a variety of genres. She wrote fiction and poetry for children in *The Golden Heart and Other Fairy Stories* (1904) and *Stories Told by the Miller* (1909). *Flemington* (1911) was a historical romance for adults, set in the period of the Jacobite rebellion, 'the best since *The Master of Ballantrae*', in the opinion of John Buchan, who later published some of her poetry in his *The Northern Muse* (1924). Hugh MacDiarmid also published some of her poetry in all three issues of his periodical *Northern Numbers* (1920, 1921, 1922).

The poems of Violet Jacob are very strong on atmosphere, and the two poems included in this book are no exception. They date from 1919–21, by which time Jacob was living back at the House of Dun. The *Times Literary Supplement* describes her poetry of the period as 'excursions into the eerie', and there is an element of the supernatural – of a world beyond the human – in both 'The Kelpie' and 'The

Rowan'. One reader (James O'Hagan) recalled 'sleepless childhood nights after reading the atmospheric Violet Jacob poem that finishes with the devastating "For the warlock's livin' yet – But the rowan's deid!"' Similarly with 'The Kelpie': the beast of the title isn't even there, but the mere *idea* of it in its spooky habitat is almost overwhelming to the poem's young narrator.

Some people regard the Loch Ness Monster as a giant form of kelpie. However that may be, the *Dictionary of Celtic Mythology* (Oxford University Press, 1998) defines a kelpie as

> ... a fairy water-creature of Scottish folklore, initially thought to inhabit lonely, fast-moving streams and later any body of water. Usually thought to be a horse, sometimes human, the kelpie is most often described as at least mischievous and more likely malevolent. The creature entices travellers on to its back and then rushes into deep pools to drown them. His tail strikes the water in thunder and he disappears in a flash of lightning. In human form, the kelpie is a rough, shaggy man who leaps behind a solitary rider, gripping and crushing him.

Joseph Jacobs (1854–1916)

Jacobs was born and raised in Sydney, Australia, travelling to Britain in 1873 to study at St John's College, Cambridge. He later spent a postgraduate year in Germany and then made a home with his wife Georgina Horne in north London, where he became prominent as a prolific writer, intellectual and polymath. He had three children, and it may have been their advent in his life that directed his scrupulous scholarly attention into the field of folklore and fairy tales. He became editor of *Folklore Magazine* and compiled and wrote popular editions of Aesop, as well as English and Indian fairy tales; while his illustrated and user-friendly annotated *Celtic Fairy Tales* (1892) and *More Celtic Fairy Tales* (1894) have been almost continuously in print since their first appearance. His skills as an editor of folklore, judiciously topping and tailing stories, and simplifying without altering their sense, were considerable.

The two stories included in this book are from *Celtic Fairy Tales*. Jacobs tells us that the Macdonald of Saddell Castle (who features in 'The Sprightly Tailor') was a very great man indeed. Once, when dining with the Lord-Lieutenant of Argyll, an apology was made to him for

placing him so far away from the head of the table. 'Where the Macdonald sits,' was the proud response, 'there is the head of the table.'

In 1900 Jacobs emigrated with his family to New York after making
a successful lecture tour in the USA four years earlier. In New York
he wrote a scholarly history of the Jewish people, became an editor of
the *Jewish Encyclopaedia*, and later was a professor at the city's Jewish
theological seminary.

Andrew Lang (1844–1912)

Son of the town's sheriff-clerk, Andrew Lang was born in Selkirk, in
the Scottish Borders, where he attended Selkirk Grammar School. He
went on to St Andrews University and Balliol College, Oxford. But
after his studies he decided he wasn't cut out for the academic life,
becoming instead a working journalist, historian, critic and poet in
London. He was happy there to be described as 'an elegant hack' and
is probably best remembered today for his interest in folklore, and for
his rainbow of twelve classic fairy-tale collections, colour-coded from
The Blue Fairy Book (1889) through red, crimson, green, grey, olive,
pink, violet, yellow, rose and orange to *The Lilac Fairy Book* (1910),
which all became bestsellers in their day. That some of Lang's sources
seemed a little unscholarly in no way detracted from their popularity.
He was a founding member of the Folklore Society in 1878.

Lang is said to have been the first British author to give serious
consideration to the fairy tale as an art form. But his interest in folklore
is clearly traceable to his own Border origins and to the earlier – but,
in his day, still recent – fieldwork of Sir Walter Scott (who had been
sheriff of Selkirk), James Hogg and others in this part of the world.
He is thought to have imbibed much of the lore of the Border ballads
and stories from his childhood nurse, Nancy. 'It was worth while to
be a boy then in the south of Scotland . . .' he wrote. 'Memory brings
vividly back the golden summer evenings by Tweedside, when trout
began to plash in the stillness – days so lovely that they sometimes in
the end begat a superstitious eeriness. One seemed forsaken in an
enchanted world; one might see the two white fairy deer flit by,
bringing to us, as to Thomas the Rhymer, the tidings that we must go
back to Fairyland.'

The Gold of Fairnilee (1888) is an original fairy tale carefully
grounded in a period of documented history (the Scottish defeat at the
battle of Flodden in 1513, and the years following this national disas-
ter). It also has a precise geographical location near the town of

Galashiels, less than fifty miles from the English border. But fairy markers run throughout this otherwise historical tale. In chapter 1 we learn that Fairnilee – still a real house – means 'the field of the fairies'. In chapter 2 we read of the 'bad omen': little Randal sees the ghost of his father Sir Hugh on the day of his death at Flodden, fifty miles away. The old nurse who looks after Randal fears he may be 'fey' – susceptible to fairies. In chapter 4 we learn that the nurse is herself more than a little fey, much given to stories about elves, fairies, bogles, kelpies and brownies; she is even compared to 'Whuppity Stoorie, the wicked old witch with the spinning wheel'. Throughout the story there is much discussion of the 'good folk' and of local legends pertaining to Fairnilee.

The story is thus steeped in fairy lore and legend, and later – via a wishing well on St John's Eve (the feast of Beltain) – the boy Randal is stolen away for seven years into Fairyland by the Queen of the Fairies, just as Tam Lin had been. The story is charmingly told and, like all the best fairy tales, has an entirely satisfactory and happy conclusion.

Lang wrote only four or five original fairy tales, and *The Gold of Fairnilee* is by far his best. The others (*The Princess Nobody* (1884), *Prince Prigio* (1889) and *Prince Ricardo of Pantouflia* (1893)) are more light-hearted, more fantastic and more suited for children. Only *Fairnilee* has something of the steely menace that probably derives from the Border fairy ballads.

Although he spent most of his very successful writing career in London, Lang returned to St Andrews, his Scottish alma mater, for a period in the 1890s during which he wrote a history of the town (1895).

> But dearer far the little town,
> The drifting surge, the wintry year,
> The college of the scarlet gown.
> St Andrews by the Northern Sea,
> That is a haunted town to me!
>   (from 'Almae Matres')

The best biography is Roger Lancelyn Green's *Andrew Lang: A Critical Biography* (1946). Among other things, this quotes Robert Louis Stevenson's genial send-up of Lang, written shortly after the pair first met in the south of France in 1874. Although they had much in common (sadly, even including poor health), Lang struck the forthright Stevenson as being languid and affected and he didn't initially take to the older man, as his sketch indicates:

My name is Andrew Lang,
Andrew Lang
That's my name,
And criticism and cricket is my game.
With my eyeglass in my eye,
Am not I,
Am I not
A la-dy da-dy Oxford kind of Scot,
Am I not?

George MacDonald (1824–1905)

MacDonald was the son of an Aberdeenshire farmer, born at Huntly. A graduate of Aberdeen University, he was hostile to Calvinism and in 1850 he became a Congregationalist minister at Arundel in Sussex after studies at Highbury Theological College in London. But he had to give up this work after doctrinal differences with his church, going on to make his living by lecturing and journalism.

MacDonald wrote poetry and much fantasy fiction, including the novels *Phantastes: A Faery Romance for Men and Women* (1858) and *Lilith* (1895); he also wrote the children's stories *At the Back of the North Wind* (1871) and *The Princess and the Goblin* (1872). Probably his best-known fairy tale is 'The Golden Key', a sort of Pilgrim's Progress allegory published in his *Dealings with the Fairies* (1867). 'The Grey Wolf' was published in his collected *Works of Fancy and Imagination*, vol. 10 (1871). MacDonald was friendly with Lewis Carroll, and his writings were to influence J. R. R. Tolkien and C. S. Lewis.

Non-specific as far as the period in which it is set and its precise location, 'The Grey Wolf' occurred once upon a time in stormy weather in an outlying fragment of the Shetland Isles – that is to say, on the very edge of the British Isles. There is no detail to suggest the author had ever been there, and the vagueness of the setting contributes to the spookiness of the tale. The protagonist is a young English student who has become lost. He is rescued from a sea cave and given shelter by a young woman 'with a smile that bewitched him, revealing the whitest of teeth . . .' This is an eerie version of the Red Riding Hood story, where the hungry wolf is female and the potential victim is male.

Alasdair MacLean (1926–94)

A crofting son of a crofting line in Ardnamurchan, the most westerly peninsula of the British mainland, Alasdair MacLean left school at fourteen. He worked for a period in the Clyde shipyards, did national service, served in the British and Indian armies, and worked as a lab technician in London and Canada. Later, he attended Edinburgh University as a mature student and worked as a librarian in Fife. Both his parents died in 1973, and after their death he returned to Ardnamurchan where for a while he attempted to continue their crofting tradition.

MacLean wrote several children's stories as well as 'The Lonely Giant', but perhaps first and foremost he was a poet. His poetry has a sure and unsentimental eye for natural detail, giving it an affinity with the work of Norman MacCaig and Ted Hughes. Like MacCaig, he wrote poetry in English not Scots, famously insisting on being dropped from the paperback edition of *The Faber Book of Twentieth Century Scottish Poetry* (1992): he didn't like to be labelled in this way, or to be seen as part of somebody else's canon. His poetry collections are *From the Wilderness* (1973) and *Waking the Dead* (1976), and they feed into his most famous book, the autobiographical memoir, *Night Falls on Ardnamurchan: Twilight of a Crofting Family* (1984), where he interweaves extracts from his father's diary with his own meditative journal. In it he says, 'If I have done nothing else in my life that will count when the time for counting comes, I have at least sat on a hillside in Ardnamurchan and looked down on a croft that I had harvested unaided and against considerable odds ... And if I felt sad at being the last in a long line I also felt for the first time, truly and confidently, that to be last in a line is still to be part of that line.'

Eona MacNicol (1910–2002)

Born Eona Fraser in Inverness, she was raised in the village of Abria-chan (just like Ellen, the narrator of 'The Man in the Lochan'), in the hills above Loch Ness – and we all know what is reputed to live there. So her childhood background was rural and had a Gaelic dimension. She attended Inverness Royal Academy and Edinburgh University, graduating with first-class honours in English. She taught in India for some years, returning to Britain with her husband Roy (also a teacher of English, later a minister) and their children in 1955. Her first novel was *Colum of Derry* (1954), about the early life of St Columba. There was a sequel, called *Lamp in the Night Wind* (1965). But it was as a short-story writer that she made her reputation, publishing her stories in *Blackwood's Magazine* and *The Scots Magazine*. Many of her best stories highlight the old vanished culture of the Highlands and some of the semi-mystical, supernatural qualities of life there. In retirement, she lived in Edinburgh.

Her three books of stories are *The Halloween Hero and Other Stories* (1969), a Highland collection; *The Jail Dancing* (1978), an Inverness collection; and *A Carver of Coal* (1979), set in a modern mining community.

Note that the start of 'The Man in the Lochan' is set in a carefully depicted if slightly idyllic landscape. That kind of realistic detail is often an effective 'trick' of a supernatural writer.

Margaret Fay Shaw (1903–2004)

Born in Pennsylvania, Margaret Fay Shaw was Scottish by blood and by culture, her great-great-grandfather having settled in Philadelphia in 1782. In her autobiography, *From the Alleghenies to the Hebrides* (1993), she recalls her happy and stable early childhood in the valley of Glenshaw, Pennsylvania, with its mountain laurel and crayfish, its scent of woodsmoke and apples, and the sleeping-cars rolling past on the railroad to Chicago and the great American West.

Her father ran an iron foundry, but both parents died when she was young and, already a good pianist, Margaret was sent to boarding school in Helensburgh, Scotland. Here she experienced – and accompanied – the 'art' songs of Marjory Kennedy-Fraser, derived as they were from Hebridean Gaelic song. Margaret wanted to hear the real thing, and soon did just that on a cycling visit to the Outer Hebrides. She was enchanted by this experience, and in due course went to live there, first of all on South Uist (from 1929 to 1935). Here she started her long, lifetime collection of Gaelic culture, soon moving to Barra, and then in 1938 to Canna.

On Barra she met John Lorne Campbell (1906–96, see p. 216), a kindred collector of Gaelic song and story. They married in 1935, and bought the Isle of Canna in the Inner Hebrides in 1938. Here they came to settle and, during the course of two very long and productive working lives, they built up a formidable library and archive of Gaelic culture – books, film and sound recordings from South Uist, Barra and Nova Scotia in particular. Margaret's *Folksongs and Folklore of South Uist* (1955) was a major field contribution to this archive.

The Campbells had no children, and in 1981 they gave Canna and their home, Canna House, into the custody of the National Trust for Scotland, though they continued to live there until their deaths. Along with the St Edward Centre, an old church converted to provide accommodation for visitors to the island, Canna House today is a lantern for Gaelic scholarship in the Hebrides.

Robert Louis Stevenson (1850–94)

'Black Andie's Tale of Tod Lapraik' is a gripping stand-alone story within a story; it occurs as an episode in chapter 15 of the novel *Catriona* (1893), a sequel to one of Stevenson's most successful and best-loved historical novels of adventure, *Kidnapped* (1886), set at the time of the 1745 Jacobite rebellion. One of the heroes of these novels is David Balfour, and in *Catriona* he finds himself imprisoned on the Bass Rock. Black Andie, a minor character in the novel, tells the story of his grandfather's time in charge of the fortress on the Rock. The fort had been used as a prison for Covenanters, persecuted by the authorities for their strong religious beliefs. But the Bass Rock, in the Firth of Forth just off North Berwick, was then and remains famous as a nesting place for gannets (*Sula bassanis* being their Latin name, or 'solans of the Bass'), the solans of the story; and gannet flesh and eggs once provided much of their diet for the soldiers on the Rock. Reading the story, it is hard to decide about Tod Lapraik: is he a supernatural being? The tale tells us a lot about him – what he looked like, where he lived, what he was like as a person, what he did for a living, what people thought of him, what made him different from others, and what happened to him. But readers are left to make up their own minds about what he *was* – man or sprite.

The dangers of collecting young gannets on the end of a rope on a sheer rockface, the dangers of the open sea in bad weather and of isolation from one's fellows, all contribute to creating the ideal atmosphere of excitement, suspense, anticipation and high tension in this well-crafted supernatural tale. The story's treatment of the supernatural shows the influence of Hogg, Scott and the ballads, and it stands well alongside some of Stevenson's other atmospheric masterpieces, such as 'Thrawn Janet', 'The Bottle Imp', 'The Body-Snatchers', *The Master of Ballantrae* and *Weir of Hermiston*.

Stevenson was brought up in Edinburgh, attending the city's

Academy and University. He suffered much from ill-health, and as a boy was regularly sent to recuperate at North Berwick; so he knew the shoreline of East Lothian and its offshore islands very well. Indeed, the nearby island of Fidra is said to have been the model for his first novel, *Treasure Island* (1881), and he almost certainly also visited the Bass. His father or grandfather had built many of the lighthouses around this coast.

Betsy Whyte (1919–88)

Betsy Whyte was born at Blairgowrie into a family of travelling folk, and her classic autobiography *The Yellow on the Broom* (1979) and its sequel, *Red Rowans and Wild Honey* (1990), tells with clarity and freshness the story of her childhood and growing up in this culture, moving around the farms of Perthshire. She gave up the travelling life when she married and had her own family to raise, but she continued to narrate her travellers' stories at readings and ceilidhs until the end of her life. She was also a regular contributor to *Tocher* magazine.

'The Man in the Boat' is a recording of an oral folk tale, as told by Betsy to students at the School of Scottish Studies, Edinburgh University, in 1981. The idea that everybody should be able to tell a story to help pass an idle hour may seem strange in an age of instant canned entertainment, but it is a very old one that crops up in many world literatures. An older and more traditional version of the same topic is 'Why Everyone Should Be Able to Tell a Story', by John Lorne Campbell of Canna, on pp. 209–10 of this collection.

PENGUIN CLASSICS

FAIRY TALES
HANS CHRISTIAN ANDERSEN

Blending Danish folklore with magical storytelling, Hans Christian Andersen's unique fairy tales describe a world of beautiful princesses and sinister queens, rewarded virtue and unresolved desire. Rich with popular tales such as *The Ugly Duckling*, *The Emperor's New Clothes* and the darkly enchanting *The Snow Queen*, this revelatory new collection also contains many lesser-known but intriguing stories, such as the sinister *The Shadow*, in which a shadow slyly takes over the life of the man to whom it is bound.

'Truly scrumptious, a proper treasury ... Read on with eyes as big as teacups' *Guardian*

'With J. K. Rowling and Lemony Snicket bringing black magic to the top of today's children's literature, the moment seems ripe for a return to the original' *Newsweek*

'Tiina Nunnally's wonderful new translations of Andersen are an invitation to open-ended, mind-engaging reading' Rachel Cusk

Translated by Tiina Nunnally

Edited by Jackie Wullschlager

PENGUIN CLASSICS

IVANHOE
WALTER SCOTT

'Fight on, brave knights! Man dies, but glory lives!'

Banished from England for seeking to marry against his father's wishes, Ivanhoe joins Richard the Lion Heart on a crusade in the Holy Land. On his return, his passionate desire is to be reunited with the beautiful but forbidden lady Rowena, but he soon finds himself playing a more dangerous game as he is drawn into a bitter power struggle between the noble King Richard and his evil and scheming brother John. The first of Scott's novels to address a purely English subject, *Ivanhoe* is set in a highly romanticized medieval world of tournaments and sieges, chivalry and adventure, where dispossessed Saxons are pitted against their Norman overlords, and where the historical and fictional seamlessly merge.

This volume is based on the acclaimed Edinburgh Edition of the Waverley Novels whose first edition was drawn from Scott's original texts. It contains an introduction that examines Scott's use of history in the light of contemporary ideas, a chronology, bibliography, glossary and extensive notes.

'It remains one of the most exciting stories in the language' A. N. Wilson

Edited with an introduction by Graham Tulloch

PENGUIN CLASSICS

THE NEW PENGUIN BOOK OF ROMANTIC POETRY

'And what if all of animated Nature
Be but organic harps, diversely framed'

The Romanticism that emerged after the American and French revolutions of 1776 and 1789 represented a new flowering of the imagination and the spirit, and a celebration of the soul of humanity with its capacity for love. This extraordinary collection sets the acknowledged genius of poems such as Blake's 'Tyger', Coleridge's 'Khubla Khan' and Shelley's 'Ozymandias' alongside verse from less familiar figures and women poets such as Charlotte Smith and Mary Robinson. We also see familiar poets in an unaccustomed light, as Blake, Wordsworth and Shelley demonstrate their comic skills, while Coleridge, Keats and Clare explore the Gothic and surreal.

This volume is arranged by theme and genre, revealing unexpected connections between the poets. In their introduction Jonathan and Jessica Wordsworth explore Romanticism as a way of responding to the world, and they begin each section with a helpful preface, notes and bibliography.

'An absolutely fascinating selection – notable for its women poets, its intriguing thematic categories and its helpful mini biographies' Richard Holmes

Edited with an introduction by Jonathan and Jessica Wordsworth

---

PENGUIN CLASSICS

KIDNAPPED
ROBERT LOUIS STEVENSON

'There was no doubt about my uncle's enmity ...
and he would leave no stone unturned that might compass my destruction'

Orphaned and left penniless, David Balfour sets out to find his last living relative, miserly and reclusive Uncle Ebenezer. But Ebenezer is far from welcoming, and David narrowly escapes being murdered before he is kidnapped and imprisoned on a ship bound for Carolina. When the ship is wrecked, David, along with fiery Alan Breck, makes his way back across the treacherous Highland terrain on a quest to see that justice is done. Through his powerful depiction of the contrasting personalities of his two central characters – the romantic Jacobite Breck and the rationalist Whig David – Stevenson dramatized a conflict that was at the heart of Scottish culture in the aftermath of the Jacobite rebellion, as well as creating an unforgettable adventure story.

This edition contains an introduction and historical note to illuminate the social and political background of the novel, and also includes notes and a glossary.

Edited with an introduction and notes by Donald McFarlan

PENGUIN CLASSICS

THE FAERIE QUEENE
EDMUND SPENSER

> 'Great Lady of the greatest Isle, whose light
> Like Phoebus lampe throughout the world doth shine'

The Faerie Queene was one of the most influential poems in the English language. Dedicating his work to Elizabeth I, Spenser brilliantly united Arthurian romance and Italian renaissance epic to celebrate the glory of the Virgin Queen. Each book of the poem recounts the quest of a knight to achieve a virtue: the Red Crosse Knight of Holinesse, who must slay a dragon and free himself from the witch Duessa; Sir Guyon, Knight of Temperance, who escapes the Cave of Mammon and destroys Acrasia's Bowre of Bliss; and the lady-knight Britomart's search for her Sir Artegall, revealed to her in an enchanted mirror. Although composed as a moral and political allegory, *The Faerie Queene's* magical atmosphere captivated the imaginations of later poets from Milton to the Victorians.

This edition includes the letter to Raleigh, in which Spenser declares his intentions for his poem, the commendatory verses by Spenser's contemporaries and his dedicatory sonnets to the Elizabethan court, and is supplemented by a table of dates and a glossary.

Edited by Thomas P. Roche, Jr, with C. Patrick O'Donnell, Jr

PENGUIN CLASSICS

THE THIRTY-NINE STEPS
JOHN BUCHAN

'My guest was lying sprawled on his back. There was a long knife through his heart which skewered him to the floor'

Adventurer Richard Hannay has just returned from South Africa and is thoroughly bored with his London life – until a murder is committed in his flat, just days after the victim had warned him of an assassination plot that could bring Britain to the brink of war. An obvious suspect for the police and an easy target for the killers, Hannay goes on the run in his native Scotland, where he must use all his wits to stay one step ahead of the game – and warn the government before it is too late. One of the most popular adventure stories ever written, *The Thirty-Nine Steps* established John Buchan as the original thriller writer and inspired many other novelists and filmmakers including Alfred Hitchcock.

In his introduction to this new edition, John Keegan compares Buchan's life – his experiences in South Africa, his love of Scotland and his moral integrity – with his fictional hero. This edition also includes notes, a chronology and further reading.

Edited with an introduction by John Keegan

PENGUIN CLASSICS

THE DEATH OF KING ARTHUR

'Lancelot has brought me such great shame as to dishonour me through my wife,
I shall never rest till they are caught together'

Recounting the final days of Arthur, this thirteenth-century French version of
the Camelot legend, written by an unknown author, is set in a world of fading
chivalric glory. It depicts the Round Table diminished in strength after the Quest
for the Holy Grail, and with its integrity threatened by the weakness of Arthur's
own knights. Whispers of Queen Guinevere's infidelity with his beloved comrade-
at-arms Sir Lancelot profoundly distress the trusting King, leaving him no match
for the machinations of the treacherous Sir Mordred. The human tragedy of
The Death of King Arthur so impressed Malory that he built his own Arthurian
legend on this view of the court – a view that profoundly influenced the English
conception of the 'great' King.

James Cable's translation brilliantly captures all the narrative urgency and spare
immediacy of style. In his introduction, he examines characterization, narrative
style, authorship and the work's place among the different versions of the Arthur
myth.

Translated by James Cable
